WYNN IN THE
WILLOWS

Robin Shope

WYNN IN THE WILLOWS

Contact Information: titleadmin@pelicanbookgroup.com

All scripture quotations, unless otherwise indicated, are taken from the Holy Bible, New International Version(R), NIV(R), Copyright 1973, 1978, 1984 by Biblica, Inc.™ Used by permission of Zondervan. All rights reserved worldwide. www.zondervan.com

Cover Art by *Nicola Martinez*

White Rose Publishing, a division of Pelican Ventures, LLC
www.pelicanbookgroup.com PO Box 1738 *Aztec, NM * 87410

White Rose Publishing Circle and Rosebud logo is a trademark of Pelican Ventures, LLC

Publishing History
First White Rose Edition, 2014
Paperback Edition ISBN 978-1-61116-334-6
Electronic Edition ISBN 978-1-61116-333-9
Published in the United States of America

Dedication

To my beloved children Kimberly and Matthew, and my beloved grandchildren Kingston and Karter. Also dedicated to You. It has always been You.

Praise

"Robin Shope continues to write captivating books. She is at her best with multi-layered characters." ~ Kyle Saylors, TV producer

"If I were doling out stars, I would give Robin Shope's books five stars!" ~ Loree Lough, author

"Robin writes the most poignant stories I have run across in years. The words sing in your heart and summon you to a deeper, nobler existence." ~ Kathi Macias, author

Prologue

Wynn Baxter considered life a series of birthday presents. Some she grew out of like a pair of jeans, or purple hair. Some presents came wrapped in paper, but once the paper was removed, she'd know in a glance if she loved it or hated it. The very worst gifts came unexpectedly and stuck around for a lifetime, such as the memory of her father lying in his casket on her sixth birthday, and her mother taking off.

Her mother, Ruth, suddenly developed an inexplicable burden for the Pygmies of the Ituri Forest in Central Africa.

Who knew? Certainly not Wynn. Not Grammy or Gramps, either. Not even her mother's twin sister, Roxie. But her mom was gone and quickly dubbed as the black sheep of the family.

After that, Wynn was referred to as the lost lamb.

That was twenty years ago.

1

"For whatever we lose (like a you or a me) it's always ourselves we find in the sea." ~ Frederic D. Oberland

Wynn smiled. It was early morning, plenty of time for birding. Her backpack was fully equipped, packed with binoculars, cameras, and the basics for fieldwork. She added a logbook and electronic tablet from the desk, cradling it between the soft pads in the pack, and then drew one of the arm straps over her left shoulder. Outside, she walked down the tree-shaded path to her Aunt Roxie's cottage.

A flicker of wings caught her attention. A Kirtland's warbler darted back into the island's foliage.

Wynn cupped hands over her eyes, but she didn't see the bird now. As soon as she could make an entry into her Life List she'd note its sighting.

Just ahead was her destination, a blue clapboard cottage trimmed with white shutters and heart cutouts. Wynn zigzagged across the yard to keep from bumping her head into all the birdhouses hanging from tree limbs.

People talking rolled from one end of the porch to the other. Through the wavy, old glass she saw that Aunt Roxie's Bible Club was in session. Wynn had assumed the club would meet later in the day. What should she do?

She'd simply go birding alone.

The sun stretched a welcoming pool of light across the front lawn. Twenty feet below the granite cliffs was Lake Michigan, turquoise blue and white capped today. The island ferry was moving down the shore to dock at the Yacht Club, blowing its horn in salutation, announcing its impending arrival.

Wynn paused at the sound of her aunt's angry voice through the open windows, "Stop it, stop it! Think about what you're saying for once, will you? Every time you bring up that subject, it does nothing but stir up trouble on the island for many of us old timers who've experienced similar situations. My niece sure can't find out about what I did. It's taken me years to get her back here and I won't let you, or anyone else, ruin my plan. Promise me, no more talk about it! Ladies? Promise me."

A flood of agreements followed.

Ruin her plan? What was Aunt Roxie talking about?

Wynn ducked her head. Too late.

"Wynn, is that you? Wynn! Come inside and meet my friends."

"I'm coming!" Wynn called.

The door opened with a whine of complaint.

Five female Bible club members got their good first look at the island's latest summer tenant.

Wynn's large eyes, the color of wet green leaves, stared back. With that, the day took a new direction.

"Ladies, I want you to meet my niece, Wynn Baxter." Roxie announced a bit too cheerfully. "She's staying in my garage apartment. Lemonade, dear?" Still clearly upset, she forced a wide smile while holding up a pitcher loaded with ice cubes and fat lemon wedges.

"Sure." Wynn answered as she slipped into one of the wicker chairs. She awkwardly pulled at the strap on her backpack. "Sorry, I forgot today was your Bible club. I came to ask you to go birding with me. But I can go alone."

"Nonsense, we'll go birding another day. We're glad you're here, aren't we, ladies?" Aunt Roxie asked, quickly obligating Wynn to stay by handing her a glass. "If you had come earlier, you could have joined our meeting. Now we're to the eating part. You must stay and get to know everyone."

"I don't know how to play bridge, but I sure know how to eat. I've come at the right time." Wynn took a long sip.

The women chuckled and nudged each other as though they shared some private joke; what had Roxie told them about her?

"What's so funny?"

"We don't actually play bridge, my dear. Our official name is Bridge Over Troubled Waters Ladies Club. Quite a mouthful, I know. You see, God is our bridge and the troubled waters are life. And here we are...the ladies!" Roxie curtseyed.

"Ahhh. I see." Wynn smiled at them.

"How are you enjoying your time here on the island, Wynn?" A blonde woman asked just as her cell phone played. "Sorry...I have to answer this call." Turning her back she flitted to the far end of the porch.

"I just had an idea!" a blue-jeaned lady said. "How about we all plan a girl's day together with Wynn to get to know her better?"

"Ladies, although I'm overjoyed to have my niece with me, Wynn's real purpose here is to study plant life. She has no time for socializing, at all. But before she leafs in the fall, I'm hoping she'll cure my rose's mold problem. Get it? Before she leafs in the fall?" Roxie chortled.

"Actually, I'm here on a grant from the University of Wisconsin to create a record of the island's rare plant species. I'm also interested in learning more about the aquatic life. They're all inter-related." Wynn threaded her fingers together. "And, as for your rose mold problem, Aunt Roxie, try mixing two tablespoons of fine horticultural oil with one tablespoon mild dish soap and a large tablespoon of baking soda. Mix with one gallon of water and stir until it's dissolved. A clean paint brush is ideal to apply the mixture."

"God blessed my twin sister with a smart child, didn't He?" Smiling broadly, Roxie kissed the top of her niece's head.

"And what a dark-haired Irish beauty she is, too."

"Ladies, why don't you go ahead and introduce yourselves to Wynn?"

"Me first! Hello Wynn, I'm…"

"Sheri," Wynn interrupted with a smile.

"How did you ever know? Did someone tell you my name? Don't tell me you are psychic? Not that I believe in those sort of things, oh no…I do not."

Wynn pointed at the nametag pinned to her blouse.

"Oh, you!" Sheri laughed.

"Sheri Mills runs one of the island's most popular tourist shops," Roxie said.

"Maybe you've seen it? We're right on the beach and its shrimpy pink."

"Hard to miss," Wynn said, remembering the building.

"Thank you. We sell souvenirs, postcards, straw

hats, and wild t-shirts, among other trinkets." Sheri wiggled her gray eyebrows. "If you drop by sometime, I'll give you a beach snow globe."

"Wynn, it's such a blessing to meet you. I'm Faith. Here, try one of my éclairs." The cell-phone lady had ended her call and now held out a platter.

"Sure. Thanks, Faith." Wynn slipped one onto a china plate circled in pink roses. "They look wonderful. Homemade?"

"Nothing but!"

"Faith Montgomery bakes heavenly desserts when she isn't selling real-estate," said a large woman in a flowered caftan.

"I give all the glory to God. And praise the Lord, these days, real-estate is sizzling on the island. Tourist money just keeps rolling in on the waves." Faith's cell rang again. "See what I mean? Pass these out for me, will you, Wynn?" Faith handed the platter to Wynn as she answered the cell. Her voice faded as she walked away.

Steadying the platter with one hand, Wynn set her éclair back on her plate and began serving the women.

"I better pass on those éclairs, Wynn. My clothes are starting to get a bit tight." A petite brunette tugged at the waist of her linen capris. "I'm Jackie Bennett. My husband is in the import business. We live in a mid-century house above the granite cliffs. Perhaps you've seen it. It's the best house on the island with the loveliest gardens, thanks to Owl's nephew, Doug Reed."

"It's nice to meet you." Wynn smiled.

"When is Boone due back from his business trip to…where did you say he was?" Sheri asked Jackie.

"Boone went to Nepal this time," Jackie answered.

"Right now, he's most likely trudging down the Himalayan slopes alongside Sherpas who are loaded down with rare Asian artifacts for his business, and for me—of course. Communication is nonexistent when he is out so far, but he managed to find a cyber café in Kathmandu, where he emailed me to say he would be home soon. I can't wait. It's hard sleeping without him right beside me."

Wynn handed the empty tray to Roxie and returned to finish her éclair, but it was gone.

"I think you've met everyone except for Wilda." Roxie referred to the woman in a flowing caftan, who was busily devouring both her dessert and Wynn's.

"Most people call me Owl."

"Isn't that my éclair?" Wynn pointed.

"Of course it is. Owl always finishes what we leave behind," Roxie whispered to Wynn in an informative tone.

Owl licked her fingers. "Yes, I do. I hate waste. Waste not, want not. And I also like to register my opinion, Wynn. People know this and come to me for advice. You might do well to remember that."

"Undoubtedly, I will."

"Since you're new to the island, let me tell you about its history and some of its mysteries. I'm known around these parts for shooting from the lips because I say things straight out. It's the only way to be."

Wynn rubbed her temples against a migraine. The unexpected calling of a nearby loon eased the pain. Now if she could just see the bird. Dare she go for the binoculars inside her backpack?

As if sensing her discontent, Roxie scooted her chair closer to Wynn, and patted her hand to get her attention.

"I bet this is a fascinating story. Tell me every detail," Wynn prodded, hoping to please Roxie.

"I will." Owl began, "In the late 1800's my ancestors, Joseph and Anna Reed, bought the string of Willow Islands and built a mansion on the south end of this one. It was real fancy, no doubt about it. Italian plasterers did the first floor walls. Not only were there European imported marble fireplaces, but also marble windowsills a foot wide. Anna wouldn't have any but the very best wallpaper for the second floor, and every piece of furniture was handmade to her specifications. It took four years to build the manor, and six months more just to ferry over all their furnishings from Egg Harbor.

"But then tragedy struck and what happened next has affected the island to this very day. Because of it, there are those who refuse to take a step onto the island for fear of..."

Nonchalantly, Roxie reached out and pinched a flap of skin on Owl's arm.

"Ouch!" Owl cried rubbing the red mark. "Roxie! Why did you do that?"

"There was a crumb on your arm I was trying to brush away. Sorry Owl." Roxie excused herself and left the room.

Wynn wondered what had just happened. Had Roxie warned Owl in some way to keep her from continuing the story?

Owl grew silent, as if in a trance, and then the words poured from her lips like a stream down a mountain. "On the Reed family's last trip to the island before winter set in, the boat capsized in a horrific storm. Anna was able to save her two little boys, James and Joel, but her husband drowned and his body was never found. Anna searched the shoreline for years hoping her husband's body would someday wash up so she could give him a good Christian burial. It never did." Owl leaned forward. "For many years this island was referred to as…Widow Island. There's been a curse on the island ever since. Like a summer cold, only some residents get it."

"A curse?" Wynn asked, intrigued.

Maybe this quiet island had some mystery, after all.

2

The air was fragrant with lilac. Bits of sky could be seen through the throng of summer leaves where a mosaic in blue and green shifted gently in the wind. A squirrel bounded across a limb, its thick tail raised.

Wynn hadn't told Aunt Roxie she'd come home to find out what really happened to her dad. She was brought back to the present by Owl's voice.

"I'll explain the circumstances." Owl took the last sip of her lemonade.

Roxie brought a new plate of éclairs out and held it in front of Owl. "All these are for you, Owl. Eat them while they're still fresh."

"Ohh-h, Rox-ie! Thank you!"

Wynn pulled on a tendril of hair.

Aunt Roxie was keeping Owl from talking about the tragedy.

After her grandparents moved Wynn off the island, she'd never had a chance to really get to know Aunt Roxie. On the day of Wynn's high school graduation, a letter arrived with a fat check inside. It was enough to pay for her entire college education and then some. And now, Roxie opened her home to Wynn for the summer.

Wynn jumped at the chance to know her family better.

Only now it seemed her aunt was hiding something. Could Roxie be trusted, or not?

"What were you saying, Owl?" Wynn prodded, leaning forward.

Much to her chagrin, Owl's mouth was filled with creamy éclair. She pointed at her sealed lips. But those éclairs wouldn't last forever.

Wynn could wait her out.

Faith returned, rewinding the conversation. "How long ago was the name changed from Widow Island to Willow Island, Owl?" she asked.

Owl swallowed hard. "It's been about fifty years now. I was in fifth grade at the time." She picked up her empty glass. "I'll need more lemonade, Roxie, if I'm going to finish telling the story properly."

Roxie poured lemonade to the rim, squeezed extra lemon into the glass, and then handed it back.

Owl slugged down a few inches of lemonade, puckered, and coughed. "That tastes a bit more sour than my last glass...I can hardly speak."

"Then I'll finish the story," Roxie happily cut in. "Where were you? Oh yes, the island officials felt the name change was better for tourism."

"And it certainly worked!" Faith agreed. "The prices of cottages on this island have skyrocketed in the last twenty years. See Jackie? You aren't the only wealthy woman here."

"Girls, girls, be nice," Roxie scolded. Her face flushed nearly the same color red as her hair. "This is Wynn's first club meeting with us, and you don't want her to hear us bickering already, do you?"

"Of course not." Jackie and Faith agreed in unison.

Wynn moved to a chair closer to Owl. "So what became of the Reed mansion? Does anyone live there now?"

"Oh yes, it's become an icon of Willow Island!

About thirty years ago Joel Reed's grandson sold it and the new owners made it into a bed and breakfast. The old Reed Mansion is once again a showplace. Wynn, you must visit it. They have a wonderful chef, who is none other than Faith's brother. Also, the vistas of Lake Michigan from the verandas are gorgeous. That alone is worth the price of a meal, although I must admit Roxie's view is almost as breathtaking."

"My vistas are even more breathtaking," Jackie interrupted.

"Instead of a girl's day out, let's hold our next Bible club meeting at the Willow Inn and afterwards have brunch," Sheri suggested.

"Good idea. I'll text my brother right now with the reservations." Faith went for her phone. "I'll also ask Frank to personally prepare our meal."

"I just remembered. Wynn has a birthday coming up. Let's celebrate it at our next Bible club," Roxie said. "I'd never forget your special day. We must celebrate it in high style to make up for all the birthdays we weren't together."

"No, no!" The last thing she wanted was birthday recognition. Celebrating would be pure torture. Wynn always spent it in her own way, and it usually involved exploring waterways.

"What a wonderful idea. I'll have Frank bake you a cake, too. Is chocolate OK?" Faith began texting.

"Roxie, please don't…" Wynn had terrible visions of someone walking in with a chocolate cake while the servers sang to her, holding balloons.

Maybe there'd even be a red-nosed, freakish clown in the vicinity. Everyone would turn and look at her. Nightmares were made of this. It was hard focusing on the conversation while trying to figure out a way to get out of attending her birthday bash. Suddenly she knew what she'd do. She'd call in sick.

"Pay attention, Wynn," Aunt Roxie nudged her. "Owl is asking you a question."

"Oh, sorry…what did you say?"

"I said, do you know that people still dig through the sand trying to uncover poor Joseph Reed?" Owl's eyes widened for emphasis.

"You're kidding."

"When you go to the beach Wynn, you'll see cute police signs that say, 'No digging for Joseph Reed'," Sheri said.

"That's actually a problem?" Wynn asked.

"Oh, yes indeed, we've lost shoreline because of it. Digging used to be one of the island's tourist draws, but now it garnishes a hefty fine."

"That's right. Thanks to my nephew's complaints to the town board," Owl pointed out. "He is concerned about the damage to the island."

"I see him out in his sailboat quite often," Jackie commented. "Last summer he took Boone, his mother, sister, and me out on it for the day."

"Isn't it a sloop?" Faith asked.

"No, a schooner." Owl corrected and continued with her story. "Anna grew to be an old woman on this island and never remarried. Poor thing."

"Her two sons went to boarding school on the mainland." Roxie said impatiently. "End of story."

"One of them remained there and lost his inheritance as a result. The other child, Joel, came back and never left," Owl said.

"True and he built a lovely home just down the road from here. But have you noticed the newest residents painted it an awful shade of ochre? It's the only house on Zoha Lane. It's much smaller than the grand mansion, of course, but still quite nice." Faith stated.

"Zoha Lane? Isn't that the house where my parents and I once lived, Aunt Roxie?" Wynn asked as a long ago memory floated to the surface.

"Oh," said Roxie. "Yes, I believe it was."

"Your family once lived in the Reed house?" Faith nearly came up off her chair with curiosity.

Wynn opened her mouth to answer, but Roxie took over. "Yes, but they decided to move away. We're fresh out of éclairs, but there's more lemonade. Anyone?"

"We moved after my dad died." *Instead of my sixth birthday party, there was a funeral.* But Wynn didn't say that out loud.

"Your dad?" Owl asked.

"Yes, he ran a greeting card shop on the beach. My mother sold it. We left the island." Wynn wanted to know more about the mystery. "Earlier, you said something about a curse."

"Don't pay any attention to that kind of talk, Wynn. The Bible speaks against it. There's no such thing as curses, and it'll just upset you, and drive down the real-estate prices." Faith's phone rang again. "OK, that's it ladies, I really have to be getting back to the office now." She picked up her briefcase, tucking the cell against her chin. "Hello? I'm on my way to the office this moment." Faith closed her call. "Wynn, I enjoyed meeting you. If you ever decide to make Willow Island your residence, I have a listing you might be interested in seeing...just don't wait too long."

"Thanks, but I'm quite content staying in Aunt Roxie's tree house."

"You're staying in a tree house?" Faith's hand fluttered.

"It's actually Aunt Roxie's efficiency apartment over the garage, but its tree top level. It's my tree house."

"You and I are going to be great friends, I can tell." Faith hurried out the porch door.

Faith's departure created a domino effect. They hugged Wynn one by one, calling her a blessing.

Wynn felt their sincerity. She now belonged to the Bridge Over Troubled Waters Ladies Club.

3

By the time everyone left, the best part of the day had passed. Wynn pitched in with the clean-up.

Above the sink were jalousie windows that overlooked the back garden, now filled with late afternoon shadows. A warm breeze shifted through the screens, ruffling the hems of lace curtains.

Water thundered down into the sink as Wynn squeezed the belly of the plastic dish soap bottle.

"There's something I've wanted to ask since you moved in, but have hesitated. I don't want to hurt your feelings by dredging up what might be best left alone."

Hurt. Such an ambiguous word. By what degree did one gauge pain? Physically she was strong, but inside she was shredded. Wynn looked into her aunt's indigo eyes trying to recall her own mother's eyes.

"Go ahead, ask me anything," Wynn said.

Sentences never opened well when prefaced by 'I don't want to hurt your feelings, but…'

"Have you heard from your mother recently?"

Not too far down the lake, a lawn was being mowed. A dog barked just beyond the fence. Life moved on, even when she was sure time had stopped for a few seconds.

"Not for months, but that's not unusual. Eventually another one of her greeting cards will arrive with only her signature."

"Perhaps another card will arrive in time for your

birthday."

"I doubt it. I never mentioned I was coming here." Wynn touched her aunt's arm, leaving an unintended cloud of suds. "You've heard from her?"

"Me? No! I haven't heard from her in years." Roxie dried the glasses and set them neatly by rows on the open shelves.

"But you're her sister. She should have written to you."

What secret was Roxie keeping about her parents? She was quite positive the women of Willow Island knew.

"And you're her daughter; I thought she'd at least keep in touch with long letters."

Tears stung Wynn's eyes as she pulled the plug in the sink and watched the water twirl down into the hole, leaving behind a skirt of bubbles. "What's wrong? Talk to me."

"Nothing is wrong. It's just that I miss your mom so much. You remind me of her."

Unsure she liked the comparison, a worm of sadness wiggled through Wynn. "If that's true, it's purely through genetics."

"Spoken as a true scientist!" Roxie kissed Wynn's forehead, and then took a deep breath. "But I must admit, genetics is all your mom and I ever had in common, too. There was always something between us."

"Like what?"

"Our parents' affection. Ruth thought I was the preferred twin."

"Were you?"

"Not as far as I was concerned. There was also competition between us."

"Sports competition?"

"No, it was all about the opposite sex. We seemed to always compete for the same man. Whenever I liked someone she enjoyed trying to get him. It's silly. Never mind that." Roxie waved the towel in the air as though she was wiping away such pettiness. "What matters is you. For a short time I had the privilege of being an indulgent auntie to you, but that was cut short when your father…passed. Ruth and I were never close. And once she left the island, a curtain of silence seemed to drop between us. I would have given anything to have had you here with me."

"I never knew that. After Grammy and Gramps died, my uncles came for me. Why didn't you?"

Roxie set her lips into a firm line while her hands clasped the dishrag. "Your mother wouldn't hear of it."

"But she was in Central Africa. Still is. She couldn't have stopped you."

"Well, she did. Even from there."

"But why would she do that? I mean, the island was my home and I knew you. My uncles were strangers to me at the time."

"I hope they were good to you."

"Yes, they were very good to me. I grew to love them very much. They loved me, too, from the very first moment." One of her sharpest memories was the day her uncles decided to share their home with her. The memory of the following years was a beautiful, happy note.

The sound of a lawn mower stopped. A silence fell between them.

Should she talk about her life with Uncle Dill and Matt? Two bachelors, who had plenty of time on their hands, which they gave unselfishly to her. They made sure her homework was always done and they kept track of her whereabouts—especially during those tumultuous teenage years. But Wynn couldn't think of a way of telling Roxie this without making it sound as though she was better off with them.

"Now that you're older, there's a new chance for me to know you. I hope we become good friends."

"Me, too."

"The last time you and I were together was at your dad's funeral. We took a long walk together afterwards."

"I'm sorry, but I don't remember that."

"It's OK. You were so little and it was a very long time ago."

Wynn felt suspended, waiting for something to happen; the air to be stirred by a voice. The wall of secrecy between them seemed to be crumbling. Wynn decided to take advantage of the closeness. "My turn. Now I have a question for you."

"Oh?" Roxie's eyebrows arched. "Ask away."

"How did my dad die?" Wynn clenched her teeth so tight it made her jaw ache. Over the years, knowing what became of her dad had become an obsession, a fierce, fiery need gnawing away at her gut.

Roxie's eyes widened with surprise as her hand slowly trailed up to her mouth. "Oh, my. You don't know? Your mother never told you?"

"And my grandparents refused to talk about it. So now, I am coming to you. What happened?"

Roxie gave a big sigh. "I'll have to dig through old information to be sure. My memory doesn't serve me so well these days."

"I don't understand. How can you possibly forget something like that? It seems amnesia runs rampant in our family," Wynn said.

Roxie was a clever woman who easily memorized Bible verses and knew everyone's name on the island. A failed memory was only an excuse. And a poor one, at that. It was obvious her aunt was holding out on her.

"It's been a lot of years and I never dwell in the past. If you would be so kind as to allow me to get my facts straight first, I'd appreciate it," Roxie said, dodging Wynn's gaze.

"Uncle Dill recently said it was in the island newspapers for weeks at the time of his death. I want to see the clippings. Do you happen to have them?" Wynn couldn't wait another moment.

"I don't think I saved them. As I told you, I never dwell in the past."

Wynn was suspicious and even more determined to find the truth. "Never mind, I'll take the ferry across to Egg Harbor. The library should have it on microfiche."

"Oh, Wynn, some things are better left alone. The past should be left there." Roxie struggled with her words. "Let the past remain buried. Don't dig it up."

"You mean like Joseph Reed?"

"What?"

"The island residents don't want tourists to dig up the sandy beaches looking for Joseph Reed, and you don't want me digging up information about my dad. Why is everyone afraid of the past?" Tears burned at the back of her eyes.

"Oh, all right. If you're really bent on knowing, I'll go to Egg Harbor with you. Meanwhile, your priority is that research project. Don't bother with family trivia for now. Live in the present. Do not look backwards, that is not where your future is." Roxie spotted a truck pulling into her drive. "Would you check my house plants to see if they need watering, dear? I'll be back in a moment."

Her aunt went outside to greet the young man getting out of the truck with the words, Reed's Landscaping, printed on the side. So that was Doug Reed, the man Roxie claimed not to like. What was he doing here?

His face was shaded by the brim of his cap.

Roxie spoke for a few minutes, and then walked to the front of the house.

Wynn snatched the watering can, filled it with water, and then moved to another window for a better view.

Roxie pointed to a tree as he chewed on something that appeared to be a red drinking straw.

By the time Roxie returned to the cottage, Wynn had watered the plants and the last of the plates had been put away.

"Thanks for finishing up. Come on, I'll walk you back to the Tree House. You can help me refill the feeders along the way." Roxie snatched a straw hat and plopped it on her head. She picked up a small bucket of mixed birdseed. "And your name for the apartment on top of the garage is quite clever. I like it. 'My Tree House.' Makes it more homey, more woodsy."

Wynn held the tops of bird feeders as Roxie emptied a scoop of seed into each one. At the last one, Wynn spotted a small yellow bird with a black underbelly. "Look!" she pointed. "OK, time for a quiz. What kind is that?"

"Let me think," Roxie said. "My mind is crammed so full of interesting things I can't remember them all. I will look it up in the bird book later."

"That's cheating," Wynn sweetly chided. "By the way, I like your friends a lot."

"Which ones; my feathered garden visitors, or the ladies?"

"Both." Wynn looked up. "But I was referring to your friends."

"The ladies like you, too, I can tell." Roxie smiled slightly. "There's a reason we call her Owl."

"Because she's a plain talker, doesn't let food go to waste and shoots from the lips?"

"No. Most nights Owl walks the island, like Anna Reed walked the beach looking for her husband. It's been happening for as long as anyone can remember."

"Insomnia runs in the family?"

"I love Owl—but how can I put this nicely?" Roxie lowered her voice. "She's got a screw loose. She married an old hippie who runs in the post office and reads all the postcards before they are delivered. That family tends to stray from the norm, and none more than Owl's nephew, Doug Reed."

"The man who was just here? The landscaper?"

"He runs the island's only landscape business, and he's quite good. I have a half dead tree that needs taking out before it falls on the house. His prices are reasonable, especially with no competition. But that's business. That is non-negotiable. He likes pretty women, too. He has island charm and silver tongue sweet talk, so watch out." Aunt Roxie set the bucket down on the ground, spilling some of the seeds on the grass. "I'll leave those for the squirrels. Now follow me; we're going to take a detour. I have something for you."

4

They stopped in front of an old wooden carriage house almost hidden by Virginia creeper vines.

"I like driving my golf cart on the roads and pathways around the island during the summer months." She reached up over her head and felt around for a key. She pulled on the handle and the large door swung wide flooding the place with sunlight.

A canvas covered a vehicle.

"For a long while now I've had my eye on a car over in Egg Harbor. When I heard you were coming for the summer it gave me a good reason to buy it. As soon as it comes in, the dealer will bring it to the island. In the meantime, this is for you." Roxie tugged at the cover

The blue and white 1970's Jeep had plenty of room for all her equipment. "You're letting me use this?" Wynn ran her fingers over the pristine original finish.

"You may have it! It's just been serviced and I'll transfer the title to you sometime this week." Roxie pointed to the key waiting in the ignition. "Go on and try it."

Wynn got into the front seat, and turned the key. "I'll never be able to thank you for everything you've done for me."

"Oh, Wynn," Roxie sighed, "it does my heart good to see you so happy."

"Come on, let's go for a drive!" Wynn beeped the horn.

"I think I left my sunglasses in here somewhere." Roxie popped opened the glove box and stared at the mass of papers jammed inside. "Oh dear, I forgot to clean this out."

"No problem, I'll clean it out for you." Wynn hopped out.

"I thought we were going for a drive?"

"We are! I need my driver's license. Wait here; I'll be a sec." Wynn dashed to the Tree House.

It was a comfortable two-story dwelling with the garage on the first floor, now converted into her work space. The second floor was one large, open room, with a kitchenette on one side. The other three sides were encapsulated by floor to ceiling windows that looked out into woods, with breaks in the trees to see the lake. Not only was the space roomy, with a large closet, and adequate bathroom, but it was an attractive arena for being part of nature.

The recently added ten-foot wide deck put her right into the tree top branches, which would have been problematic if holes in the decking hadn't been cut. The branches served as the perfect sitting place for reading.

Wynn grabbed her purse and left. She got into the Jeep, rolled down the windows and tucked her hair behind her ears. "Do you want to lock your cottage first?"

"No need."

"Well then, are you ready, Aunt Roxie?"

"Ready, Niece Wynn!"

Wynn backed out of the garage. Within minutes they were wheeling down the lake road. A cold wind came off the water.

Wynn needed to trust Roxie. If only she'd open up. She glanced over at her aunt.

Roxie was watching the scenery float past.

For a while the women fell into a companionable silence. They headed towards the forest preserve, a thirty-acre piece of land in the center of the island that dipped into a valley. The granite cliffs that were too sharp and steep to climb hemmed in one side, with a residential area on the other side.

"Aunt Roxie?"

"Yes, dear."

"Why did Mom sell the house and leave the island with me?"

Roxie turned towards her.

"I mean, why didn't we just stay here?"

"I wanted you both to remain here. I thought it was a golden opportunity to be close to my sister again."

"Again? So, you once were close?"

"Yes, closer than one could imagine. Our dad called us ying and yang."

"What happened?"

The start of storm clouds rolled across the sky. The sunny day had crumbled and was now becoming overcast.

"Life. Jealousy. Disagreements." She sighed. "Just normal sisterly stuff. Being the only child, you don't know how things can get between siblings."

Wynn tested the windshield wipers as she pulled into the reserve.

Campers were allowed to stake tents in the forest but trailers, ATVs, and three wheelers weren't allowed on the island.

"Why don't I park and we take a trail?"

Roxie glanced at the clouds and shook her head. "Rain is close; I smell it in the air. Besides, I don't have on good walking shoes and my ankles tend to twist on uneven ground. Let's plan on another day."

"OK, but you now owe me two days, one for birding and one for hiking." Wynn turned and headed back towards the cottage. She wanted to press her aunt more, but decided against it. She needed her aunt's full cooperation to learn the depths of the past.

"Drop me at the Tree House and I'll walk back down to the cottage."

Wynn pulled up to the front of her summer residence. "This car is so perfect. It fits me. Thank you, so much."

"Well, it thrills me to give you something you can use, Wynn." Roxie got out.

Wynn got out, too.

"Why don't you come down for dinner in a little while?"

"Great. Then you can explain to me this curse Owl was talking about."

"Forget about the curse. It is nothing but nonsense. As a scientist you must know that."

"Well, something sure keeps Owl up at night, walking." Wynn turned to go inside. "I'll see you later."

"Wait." Roxie froze.

"What?"

"Listen. Don't you hear it, too?"

"Hear what?" Wynn listened, thinking she'd catch the trill of a songbird. "No, I don't...wait, I do think I hear something...someone's...calling our names?"

"Roxie! Wynn!"

Wynn felt a ripple of fear.

"Where are you?" Owl stumbled out of the woods and faltered down the path. Her skin ran with perspiration. "It happened again! The island curse struck, there's another widow!"

"Whose husband is it this time?" Roxie asked, concern etched on her features.

"Jackie's husband is dead!"

5

A week later, Wynn drove along the coast with Verdi's Rigoletto music soaring. She planned to explore the sandy beach near the cliffs where fish were known to be in small pools of water during low tide. She'd take samples of the plankton and check the nitrogen levels at her lab.

She pondered her aunt's circle of friends, the flurry of activity as they circled around Jackie, who was waiting for her husband's body to come home and be prepared for the funeral. They received visitors who dropped by with condolences and food.

Wynn had never really been part of a community who loved and helped each other so much. She found it mesmerizing and something inside her heart longed for the same sense of belonging. She'd only been able to help out a little, because her research project was using up the better part of her days.

The sugar-white sand had patches of crushed gray shells of zebra mussels and mats of rotting algae. She navigated across it to reach the base of the rock face and stood in the shallows of a small basin. It was nice shelter and the current was nonexistent; the perfect place for catching minnows in her hand or skipping stones; skills she learned from her dad.

Climbing back out of the shallows, she dug through her backpack for a sample jar. As Wynn dipped the glass into the water she nearly lost her balance. A flash of orange from another pool caught her attention. She crossed the rocks to investigate and discovered male pumpkinseed fish busy building nests. She took dozens of camera shots of the colony using their caudal fins to sweep out the bottom into saucer shaped depressions.

She lowered to a sitting position and sat cross-legged; observing, scribbling notes, and sketching rudimentary illustrations. By the time she finished, the sky had turned a bitter blue. Sand was in her shoes and pants and under her nails.

Wynn gathered her logbook, camera and instruments and returned them to the backpack, musing how happy she was here. Most women fell in love with a man, Wynn felt blessed because she had lost her heart to the sea. She hopped in the Jeep and took off for home. Her stomach growled, reminding her it had been hours since breakfast. She worked the wrapper off a protein bar just as a truck glided past.

Reed's Landscaping.

With a fast approaching curve up ahead, the truck cut back in front of her, making her brake hard. A tin container shot out from under the seat and hit the heel of her shoe.

Wynn blasted the horn.

Doug Reed took a sideways glance at her before disappearing over the hill.

A few minutes later, Wynn was home.

Roxie waited for her, dressed in black.

Wynn reached for her backpack, and slipped a hand down to pick up the container that had hit her foot. The old world painted gold swirl design was remarkable. The small lock at the top wouldn't open. Wynn shook it and heard a clunk from something inside. As her aunt approached, Wynn slid the tin into her bag. She had no idea why she needed to hide her find, but she'd examine that feeling later.

"There you are! I thought we'd attend Boone's funeral together."

"Oh, sorry, I'd forgotten it was today. It'll only take me ten minutes to shower and get ready." The sense of community wrapped around Wynn's heart again.

Wynn and Roxie tiptoed into the chapel of the funeral home. They took seats at the back.

Jackie's head was bowed in prayer,

The organist played melancholy music. Wynn hoped she'd switch gears to something inspirational and lighten the mood. Mourners needed hope.

"What exactly happened to Boone?" Wynn whispered, realizing she didn't know, despite being in and out of Jackie's home throughout the week. She imagined him losing his footing, making him cartwheel off the side of a mountain as the Sherpas watched in gape-mouthed terror.

"Boone arrived back in the States earlier than planned, just as he told Jackie he would. On his way to catching the island ferry, a truck hit him and killed him instantly," Roxie said.

Wynn sat in silence, the somber music wafting sadness.

Jackie now stood up front near the casket, touching a flower here and there. She moved to look at Boone, forever stilled.

Memories of her dad's funeral flooded Wynn's emotions, tightening inside her heart.

Wynn's thoughts turned back to that time.

Her dad had never been so still. Even in his sleep he was full movement, but there he had been, laid out in a coffin with make-up smeared all over his face.

Who would eat asparagus the long way without chopping it up first? Who would explain the difference between a mean solar day and the sidereal day? Who would wipe honey from her chin with his fingertips? Who would teach her how to navigate a boat? Who would teach her how to fall in love? How could she survive?

Six-year-old Wynn looked down at her shiny patent leather shoes, crisscrossing her legs over one another, back and forth; back and forth.

Then a woman began singing a sad song.

Everyone was crying. Even the men were wiping their eyes.

Relatives hung over the coffin and leaned ghoulishly close to the corpse.

Wynn looked up into her mother's face for reassurance, but she was crying hardest of all, shoulders shaking. Wynn looked again at the singer of sad songs. It was that lady's fault; the player of sad tunes Wynn patted her mom. "It'll be OK. I still have you and you still have me."

Mom smiled for the first time that day.

Encouraged, Wynn got on her knees to hum her mother's favorite tune into her ear. Something was wrong with the words and the sentiment. Who would be true to death? It was a song her mother always sang, but today it wasn't working its magical powers. As time passed, Wynn would sing this same song when she needed comforting.

The next day, Wynn was certain the funeral had been a terrible mistake. Her dad would be awake and in the house someplace. She looked at his chair on the porch. She opened the bathroom door slowly to see a squeezed toothpaste tube lying on the sink edge, a comb next to it, the hamper, and his shoes on the floor.

In her parents' bedroom, her mother took her dad's underwear from the top drawer, still folded, and placed them into a box. Socks from the next drawer followed. Silently, Mother moved to the closet, removing his belts and shoes. Then she pulled his shirts and trousers from hangers, making them clink together in a concerto of goodbye.

Wynn smelled wisps of dark earth on some clothing and parts of the sea on others. There on the bureau was the model sailboat they had assembled with hopes of sailing it. If her dad was really gone, how could she ever get to sail the boat?

Her dad's cardigan was hanging at the back of the desk chair. It had been his favorite…made his eyes more pronounced. He had such wonderful eyes, affectionate and laughing. Wynn hoped her mom would leave the blue sweater as a beacon for his return. It was his treasure. Ruth pulled it off the chair, held it to her nose, hugging it. Then she placed the sweater with the rest of his clothing. It would never be worn by her Dad again.

He wasn't coming back.

❧

Wynn willed herself to ignore the depression that was trying to attach itself to her like a leech, sucking her dry. She had so many good things going for her right now; she had a grant which put her back on the island. She was reunited with Aunt Roxie. The ladies of the Bible club would refer to these as 'blessings'.

Wynn shut her eyes, envisioning water. The rise and fall of the sea comforted. She could almost hear the whoosh of waves rushing on shore and the call of gulls overhead. She longed to get up and walk. "We're way early or we're the only ones showing up for the service."

"I promised Jackie we'd be here early and stay late, for support." Roxie remained stoic, but her jaw quivered.

Jackie turned, revealing exquisite studded diamonds in her ears. Her one-of-a-kind satin dress with an overlay of Italian lace had probably cost enough to keep an endangered species alive for an entire year. Tears and grief were etched on her face.

"His mother and sister should be arriving from Egg Harbor any time, now. They're renting a boat over to the island. Be sure to stay close to me when Marilyn and Agatha arrive will you?"

"How are you doing? Are you all right?" Roxie opened her arms wide as she moved towards Jackie.

"It's too soon, I can't tell yet. Thank the Lord I have Him to lean on."

"Amen to that."

"I'm sorry about your husband," Wynn said. "Let me know if there's anything I can do to help."

"Thanks. Sweet, sweet Wynn, you never even met Boone. You hardly know me and yet here you are, lending your support right along with Roxie's, my long time, dear friend. It means a lot to have you both here. She leaned towards the casket. "You can meet him right now."

Wynn's heart somersaulted

Mr. Lansing, the funeral director, hurried into the room. "Ms. Bennett, allow me to once again offer my condolences."

Jackie nodded and fumbled for a hankie as her eyes leaked tears again.

Roxie and Wynn waited.

Jackie returned the hankie to her purse, rummaged, and then held up a vintage box covered in old velvet. She handed it to Roxie. "I need to place this ring on Boone's finger."

"Of course." Roxie looked down at the box.

"It's a family heirloom."

"Why would he want to be buried with an heirloom? Wouldn't you rather keep it?"

"When we were first married, he showed the ring to me and said it carried the island curse. He left instructions that if he died before me, I was to bury it with him to make the curse leave the island," Jackie explained.

"Nonsense. The curse is nothing but nonsense."

"I am following through with Boone's wish by placing the ring on his finger."

They looked at the large ruby ring encrusted with diamonds around the entire band.

"Wynn this is my husband." Jackie stepped up to the coffin and lifted the lid, locking it in place, and then stepped away.

Taking even steps and breaths, Wynn walked to the casket and looked down at the stranger.

Jackie gazed into the coffin, and then released a long, agonizing scream, right before she fainted.

6

Wynn dropped to her knees and checked Jackie's vitals.

"That's not Boone." Roxie said. "Could we be at the wrong funeral?"

Minutes later, Wynn sat on a coffee table next to Jackie, who had been laid on a couch in a private parlor. Wynn waved smelling salts under Jackie's nose. "Can you hear me? Wake up, Jackie."

A tall, elegant woman walked into the room, followed by a younger woman with hunched shoulders, who nervously fingered a cameo brooch worn tightly at her neck

"Hello Marilyn, Agatha," Roxie greeted.

"Forgive me for fainting," Jackie groaned, and then struggled to her feet. "I think I'm all right now."

"Oh, stop with your theatrics," Marilyn told her daughter-in-law. "You're not the one who died, so stop trying to make this all about you. You had your wedding day, now let my Boone have his day."

"Don't look in the casket."

"Casket? Why would I look in a casket? Boone's been cremated," Marilyn stated.

"Why would you think that?" Jackie stared. "Mr. Lansing, where is my husband's body?"

"Ms. Bennett, you must remember that people always look different in death. Your husband is here, this is the body my assistant was instructed to pick up days ago. Let me get the paperwork to prove it to you."

"Forget the paperwork. Come with me. We're looking in that coffin together." Jackie hooked Mr. Lansing's arm and took Wynn by the elbow, guiding them both into the chapel. "You all stay here." Her look at Roxie signaled she wanted Wynn's aunt to stay and keep an eye on the other two women.

Roxie nodded.

The three of them returned to the casket.

"Good heavens!" Mr. Lansing exclaimed. "That's not Boone! I didn't work on him personally, my new assistant did, as I was out of town."

"I told you." Jackie sniffed.

"There certainly must be some kind of mix-up."

"Did you say, 'mix-up'? A mix-up is when you order chicken and get turkey. What we have here is a catastrophe! There are people coming to the funeral soon and they expect Boone to be here."

"Perhaps we should look at those papers?" Wynn suggested.

"We'll sort all this out, privately." Mr. Lansing led them to his office and closed the door.

Jackie sat down in the armchair directly in front of his desk, while Wynn remained by the door.

Mr. Lansing began shuffling files. He read the information before passing it across the desk to Jackie.

Wynn read over Jackie's shoulder. "There's Boone's name, but who identified his body?"

Mr. Lansing pulled the papers from Jackie's fingertips and turned to the second page. His blue eyes focused under heavy graying brows, and he read aloud. "It says here you did, 'Jacqueline Bennett'."

"Impossible!" Jackie fumed. "The last time I saw Boone, he was boarding a corporate jet for Chicago, next stop Katmandu. Then I got a call from the coroner with the news that Boone was dead. No one invited me to view the body, they just informed me he'd…he'd died. Whoever called me told me I didn't need to identify the body there as it was an accident and Boone had his ID on him. I assumed when I asked for it to be sent to Willow Island and to this funeral home, all was as it should be. I want his body. Find it."

Mr. Lansing's face tightened as he picked up the phone. Carefully reading the phone number of the coroner's office at the top of the invoice, he dialed. "Hello? This is Curtis Lansing of Willow Island Funeral Home. We have papers here concerning a Boone Bennett, but the man in the coffin is not…" His chin dropped and his eyes rolled as he listened, making tsking sounds.

Wynn tuned out, as Jackie fluttered, seeming on the verge of hysteria. She rubbed the woman's shoulder, trying to soothe.

"What's he saying?" Jackie asked.

"Just let him finish his conversation."

"OK, I understand. Yes, thank you." Then he cupped his hand around the receiver and spoke into it in a whisper. "I may have to call you back later." Mr. Lansing hung up and turned to Jackie, red-faced. "Your mother-in-law is correct, Boone was cremated."

"But I never authorized that. I didn't, I didn't. I spoke with them and told them exactly what to do. I told whoever called me to send the body here, we planned a full funeral." Jackie looked between Mr. Lansing and Wynn, as her voice seemed to fade. "Where are his ashes?"

"They've been picked up."

"By whom?"

"You. He said you picked them up yesterday and he knows nothing about sending over a body. He says papers were signed by you to authorize cremation, and he sent the body to the crematorium. And you picked up the ashes yesterday."

"Then how did we acquire this body that professes to be Boone's?" Jackie's voice rose.

"I am not sure. My assistant informed me via cell phone that he would be picking up Boone's body, based on a phone call from the coroner. Everything went smoothly, until just this moment."

"Did the coroner mention they were missing a body?" Wynn asked, concerned that some other grieving family must be wondering where their beloved might be.

"No, they have no queries from any family, nor do they think anything is amiss. That's why I mentioned I'd have to call them back. Somehow, we have a body that doesn't belong here."

Jackie began to dig around inside of her purse; She jerked out her cell phone. "Maybe Boone isn't dead after all, and this is some horrid mistaken identity. He's probably having a drink somewhere this very moment." Jackie sat with the phone pressed against her ear. "No answer. It goes to voicemail." Jackie dropped the cell and began to cry again. "Oh God please help me. My trust is in You."

Wynn hugged her, letting her cry.

"I also have the police department's report of Boone's accident." Mr. Lansing laid it on the desk. "He's deceased, Ms. Bennett. At this point in time, we aren't sure where his body is. This isn't our fault. But, I will get this resolved shortly, if you would be kind enough to give me some time."

Wynn read the report. It was direct and to the point. After handing it back to the jittery funeral director, Wynn turned to her friend. "Let me take you home, Jackie."

For several long minutes Jackie didn't move, and then she rose to her feet, and squared her shoulders. She took Wynn by an elbow.

The room was now filled with mourners. Some were crying, a few were quietly talking.

Wynn shushed the organist's hands from playing another depressing note.

Jackie took the microphone and stood on the podium. "Hello everyone, may I have your attention please? I have some very sad news. My husband's body is missing, so that concludes our funeral for this morning. We will reschedule. Your attendance is noted and means so much to me. In the meantime, we invite you all to congregate at our house where you will find superb food, prepared by Chef Frank."

The abrupt ending resulted in an immediate conversation hum. Several people walked forward with questions, but Jackie successfully waved them away and hurried back to the parlor, closely followed by Wynn.

Marilyn asked for the family ring.

"Isn't this a little premature?" Jackie asked.

"That ring has been in our family since the late 1800's. With Boone dead, I want the ring back," Marilyn snapped. "It should be returned to his blood family."

"This isn't the time for that, Marilyn," Roxie interceded.

"Boone told me he wanted that ring buried with him, and as soon as I find Boone that is exactly what will happen."

"Are you saying you've lost the ring, Jackie?" Marilyn seemed on the verge of hysterics.

"I know exactly where it is—with a trusted friend."

"Are you hiding it from me?" Marilyn accused.

"I have the ring." Roxie held it out.

Marilyn snatched it away and just as quickly shoved it back at her. "Paste! No, this isn't the ring."

"That is the ring I got out of our safe this morning." Jackie took the ring from Roxie. "I was just getting ready to put it on Boone's hand..." Her voice trailed off as she slid it on and curled her fingers.

"Who is that man in the coffin, anyway?" Roxie asked Mr. Lansing, averting the catfight that appeared to be brewing between Boone's mother and his wife.

"I will find out and alert the family. Ms. Bennett, I have no idea how this mix-up, er, situation occurred, or who's to blame—although I can assure you that the Willow Island Funeral Home is not at fault here in any way. I assure you that I will make every effort to find Boone's body, or ashes."

"Mr. Lansing, your reputation is at stake. If this matter is not cleared up immediately no one in this small community will ever trust you again to take care of their dearly departed." Marilyn huffed.

"God bless you Mr. Lansing. I for one, have full confidence in you." Jackie turned towards her mother-in-law, her voice an accusation, "Marilyn, what was that you said a bit ago, concerning Boone's body being cremated?"

"Oh? Did I? Boone always said he wanted to be cremated just as his father had been. I just assumed it was done. That's why I became confused over all the talk about the coffin and putting the ring on Boone's finger. Let me make this perfectly clear, I want the real heirloom ring in my possession by the end of today. You may keep the paste ring. I will see you at Boone's home with the other mourners. Come Agatha." She grabbed the young woman by the arm and steered her towards the door.

7

Emotionally drained, Wynn drove along the coastal cliffs—windows down, hoping the surf might work its calming effect on her nerves, and restore the logic she had come to count on seeing her through any tragedy.

Maintaining faith like the Bible study women was nice for them, but for her, reality was best. It harbored no false illusions. She'd drive to the Bennetts', express her condolences, and go home.

Aunt Roxie went ahead in Jackie's car, and would probably stay for a little while with the widow. If not, Wynn would bring her home, too.

She huffed out a breath to get her blowing hair out of her line of vision, and noticed the tide was down. The water was way too choppy for sailing, which also explained the absence of smaller boats in the water. Wynn rolled up the windows as she turned inland and headed down the shady two-lane road towards the forest preserve. Deer-crossing signs blazed in yellow around each turn.

The passing sight of a rare Calypso Orchid nearly landed her in a ditch. The road was way too narrow to do a turn around. Up ahead, there was a private driveway. She pulled the nose of the vehicle in just enough to crank the steering wheel around and back out.

And there it was again, the Reed's Landscaping

truck.

Wynn was curious, despite Roxie's warning, becoming more intrigued with every sighting. She pulled the car behind common shrubs and hardwood trees. Wanting to get a good look at the infamous Doug Reed, she opened her backpack and fished for her birding glasses. Lowering the driver's window, she raised the binoculars and searched up one end of the yard, down the other end.

The binoculars zoomed in and framed the man; he was covered in dirt, wrestling with brambles. Tightly muscled and wearing heavy gloves, Doug cut back a coagulated collection of brutal looking vines with his razor-sharp garden shears. Shrubs and foliage had grown so thickly over the frame of a decaying cottage that it had nearly kicked it off its foundation. He dispatched the mesh of vines, as dirt and sweat ran down along the outline of his body, plastering his shirt to him.

She sneezed. By the time she blew her nose and was ready to refocus her sights, Doug was gone. Where? Wynn looked up the road and as far into the garden as her gaze could see.

His wheelbarrow was still there and so were his garden tools. The heaps of debris were left chaotically where he had dropped them.

Wynn's binoculars were heavy so she took the strap from her neck just as someone banged on the window on the passenger side. With a jolt, she turned around.

His hair was the color of wheat and his eyes, very willful, were like the sky right before a tornado—sea gray with a shadow of black.

Against her better judgment she rolled down the

window. "Hello."

"Who are you and why are you spying on me?" Doug nodded towards her binoculars. He removed the straw he had been chewing on and slid it into his back pocket.

Wynn reflexively set them in her lap and covered them with her purse, as her throat went dry. Embarrassed, she considered subterfuge, but thought better of it. "Aren't you Owl's niece, Doug?"

His gaze told her he thought her a lunatic.

"...I-I mean nephew, Doug. Right? You're Owl's nephew?" Wynn felt her face warm. "I was on my way to the reserve when I thought I caught a glimpse of an atypical orchid."

"You must be Roxie's nephew, oops, I mean niece from Madison." He chuckled, draping his arms over the window frame. "Owl told me about you, too."

"As I was saying, I thought I caught sight of a rare orchid," Wynn cleared her throat again. "I was using this driveway to turn around and go back for a closer look."

"Oh? Were you practicing this closer look on me? And does this orchid have a name?"

"Its common name is Calypso, but its scientific name is…"

"Calypso Bulbosa, also referred to as the fairy slipper or Venus's slipper," he finished her sentence. "Sure, they're nearly extinct on the island because of deer and rodents."

"That's too bad."

"Do you always dress gothic?" Doug looked at her from head to toe.

Wynn looked down – she was in black shoes, black itchy pantyhose, black dress, and a black hat which she immediately snatched off her head and tossed over her shoulder into the backseat. "No. I've just come from a funeral."

"Oh, that's right. Jackie Bennett's husband died." Doug pushed away from the car.

"Yes. Well, no funeral after all, his body is missing."

"His body is missing?" Doug's face twisted into a disbelieving frown. "How odd."

"Well, nice meeting you." Wynn shifted into gear. "I am back to scouring the island for vegetation which I'm required to keep a record." She snatched up her logbook and waved it out the window.

"Do you like sailing?" he asked.

Wynn wondered if he was asking her out on a date. "I can't go. I'm busy tomorrow," she answered bluntly.

"Who said anything about tomorrow?"

"I'm busy then, too, but nice meeting you!" Rattled, Wynn backed out, nearly colliding with a car coming around the corner. How embarrassing to have Doug catch her red-handed staring through binoculars. She drove down the road searching for the flower. But stray thoughts kept interrupting her concentration.

And then, there it was—the rare orchid, but now a rabbit was nibbling on it.

Wynn blasted the horn, causing the rabbit to leap away into the underbrush. She grabbed her camera and tape measure. Ten steps later she knelt by her prize nestled amongst the sorrel. How easy it was to miss this little orchid growing in the shade of the cedar trees. Only the wild life that searched these out to munch on knew it was there. But it wouldn't be here for much longer.

Although the orchid was known to display red or purple flowers, this one was pale pink with a white lower lip. How she'd love to relocate it, but since it was a protected species, she'd risk a hefty fine for moving it. A photo was all she could take. She scribbled the sighting into her book. Reluctantly, she left the orchid behind for the rabbit to finish off. Hopefully, he'd leave the bulb untouched and it would return to bloom again next summer.

At the Bennetts', Wynn walked between large planters of ivy that dangled like dead men, and straight into another argument between Marilyn and Jackie. Wynn had the impression it really wasn't about the missing ring, but more about the woman who took Marilyn's precious son away. Hating drama, Wynn wheeled away and strolled through the garden to enjoy the sprawling view of Lake Michigan. Finally, she decided to get a bite to eat; hoping by then, Roxie would be ready to leave.

On the patio, Jackie was seated like a queen, surrounded by mourners offering condolences as she wept into her lace hankie. Among the bereaved were the women from the Bible study. They were ready to come to Jackie's aid anytime she signaled. Neither Roxie nor Sheri took their eyes from the new widow for very long. Owl eyed the food, but her gaze darted to Jackie and the mourners, assessing even as she piled a plate high.

Wynn's heart skipped a beat when she spotted a tray of red caviar on beds of butter lettuce.

"How can you meet new people if you insist on isolating yourself? Mingle." Roxie demanded. Then she handed Wynn a plate.

Wynn promptly filled it with fresh vegetables,

canapés, and crackers heaped with caviar. She gobbled it down, and then returned for seconds and thirds, washing it all down with sparkling water, feeling a bit like Owl must have felt upon seeing the food.

Scanning the crowd for Roxie, she spotted Faith offering guests a platter filled with little cups of fruit salsa with a cinnamon chip sticking out. Wynn worked her way towards the woman she wanted to know better. "Hello Faith. I see Jackie is keeping you busy today."

"You remember me."

"It was hard to recognize you without a platter of éclairs in your hands, but yes, I believe you're Faith Montgomery." Wynn reached for a salsa cup.

"Wasn't that a mess this morning at the funeral home?" Faith shook her head as she rearranged the serving table. "Who has ever lost a corpse?"

"At least the mourners turned out." Wynn noticed Faith was missing a pearl earring. "Wow, this food spectacular. Did you and your brother make all this?"

"Today it's all Frank, but I like to help serve. Come on and I'll introduce you to him. He's in the kitchen grilling chicken with a mango glaze that's to die for. Oo-ops, very bad choice of words to use today." Faith led her through the traffic of mourners and hired servers, up the limestone patio steps, through the great room, towards the gourmet kitchen.

Photos adorned the hallway walls. No one could go from the patio to the front door without getting a pictorial view of the Bennett's life together. Jackie looked stylishly thin in every shot, whereas Boone appeared well-muscled. The photos made them appear to be the ideal contented couple.

"Frank!" Faith called.

Her brother was carefully placing the last chocolate covered strawberry on the three-tier silver serving tray. His thick fingers worked nimbly, placing his delicate touches on the food—his art.

Chef Frank's large features fit his frame. Even his belly told the story of all the good meals he had devoured over the years, sacrificing his health for the sake of his profession. Under the tall mushroom hat, Frank's face lit at the sight of his sister. "Good, you're just in time. I have two more platters for you to take out, Faith. Where are the rest of the servers we hired? I need them in here now."

"I'll round them up as soon as I introduce you to my new best friend. Wynn, what is your last name again?" Faith asked.

The words, 'best friend', short-circuited her brain for a split second. "Hello Frank, I'm Wynn Baxter, Roxie O'Malley's niece."

"Hi there Wynn, nice to meet you!" He wiped his pancake-sized right hand on his apron and shook hers. "Roxie is my favorite Irish redhead. Welcome to the island. Everyone who crashes my kitchen has to help with something. Do you know how to make canapés?" Frank asked without taking a breath between sentences.

"No, but I'm a fast learner." Wynn rolled up the sleeves on her dress.

"Tell me, what seems to be going the quickest out there?"

"Everything, but my personal favorite is the caviar canapés. Yum."

"The caviar is the hors d' oeuvre, whereas canapés have at least four ingredients."

"And each one of them delicious," Wynn fully

agreed.

Frank told her what to mix into the bowl. She began by coarsely chopping the olives, as Frank got to work on artichoke hearts.

Faith returned to swap empty trays for newly filled platters in order to satisfy the ever-growing crowd of mourners.

Frank pulled the chicken from the fire and put his final glaze on it. Soon it was sliced and placed onto warming trays that Frank personally took around to all the guests.

Wynn pondered on the ways of dealing with major passages of life and how they involved food. Someone died—bring the green bean casserole, seven layer salad, bake a roast, baste a chicken. Make a rich cake. Bring sugar cookies and a couple of peach cobblers. Sugar meant solace.

But here on Willow Island, when the death was someone of importance, the food turned out to be gourmet.

8

Marilyn spoke outside the door of the kitchen, followed by Jackie's and Agatha's voices.

Wynn, who'd been helping with dishes, watched through the narrow space between the door and the wall as she mused about her hiding place in plain sight.

"I'm not going back with you, Mama," Agatha said. "I would rather live under a bridge than live under your roof again. Jackie said I could stay here with her, and that is exactly what I plan on doing."

"Jackie only wants you here to get back at me."

"That's not true," Jackie sweetly insisted. She stepped towards Agatha, and passed out of Wynn's view. "Can't Agatha stay for a bit, so I won't be rattling around this place without…without Boone?"

"What about your medicine?" Marilyn asked her daughter.

"I'll be sure Agatha takes her mood stabilizers. Marilyn, at least let her stay for a few weeks," Jackie pleaded.

"How dare you betray me like this, Agatha. If it weren't for me and my money paying for your doctors you'd already be living under bridges along the freeway. It's only my soft heart that has kept me from institutionalizing you."

"You mean Boone's money," Jackie said.

"What?" Marilyn countered.

"You said if it weren't for your money. Actually, it's Boone's money. Boone has been more than happy to help. Marilyn, let me take Agatha. It sounds like you need a break." Jackie remained composed.

"I see your top priority isn't finding Boone's body, and It makes me wonder why."

"What a cruel thing to say, Marilyn, and it's certainly not true. Down deep, I believe Boone is still with us. I can feel him inside of me, calling to me."

"Face reality, Jackie."

"If I am wrong, then I have no fear that Boone's body, or ashes, will turn up at any moment now. Curtis Lansing will see to that. If not, then we'll contact the police, but I suspect this is nothing more than a huge mistake, or a cruel hoax."

"Police? The police will be contacted? Are you referring to the two brothers who drive golf carts around the island in lieu of patrol cars?"

"They only drive the golf carts in the summer." As Jackie defended them she moved back into Wynn's view, but now she blocked the view of Marilyn.

The front door was open. The breeze off the lake ruffled Jackie's dark hair and picked at the hem of her dress. Jackie kept clenching and opening her hands. "There are patrol cars for them to use during the winter months."

"Somehow I have no more confidence in your funeral director—who lost my son—than I have in Officers Tom and Jerry."

"Their names are Don and Berry."

"Whatever. When I get back to the mainland, I'm hiring a private detective."

"You do that, Marilyn. I welcome the added help."

"Mother, I am of age and I am going to stay with

Jackie," Agatha insisted, backing further away as she touched her cameo brooch. "I don't care if I ever see you again."

How could Agatha not want a relationship with her mother? All her life Wynn had yearned for her mother. Did one always want what they didn't have? Ever since returning to the island, Wynn felt her mother's presence everywhere; she couldn't rid her from her senses. Small pieces of memories erupted, and then blew away like morning fog on the lake. Other times it was as if her real spirit was buried in the graveyard alongside her dad. Wynn felt tears deep inside her throat. Or was it something that the women would refer to as faith?

If there truly was a God, then there had to be a day of reckoning, or punishment for Ruth, for abandoning her daughter to her grandparents. Wynn forced the thoughts out of her mind.

Marilyn looked even more furious. "OK, Agatha, you can stay, but after two weeks with Jackie, you'll be begging me to let you come home. I've had a lifetime of your problems. Let Jackie handle you from now on. I'll have my life back." Marilyn capitulated. "By the way, Jackie, I'll need my share of Boone's life insurance money as soon as possible. When can I expect it?"

Jackie's face bloomed with genuine surprise. "I-I haven't even contacted the insurance company, yet, and now with Boone's body missing, I'm sure they'll launch an investigation of their own. There is no telling how long it will take."

"Then I'll need some funds to tide me over." Marilyn demanded help. "Boone would want it this way."

"You've spent all of Boone's last check?"

"Of course. I have expenses, too!"

"There's not much left in our personal account right now, and I don't have access to his business account. I'll talk to our accountant by the end of the week to see what can be done."

"End of the week? Make it Monday, first thing."

"Are you sure you don't have any money to use until this is all settled?" Jackie's voice cracked.

"There's not old money in our family, only old people." Agatha laughed.

"All right. I can write a check for a few thousand. It's the best I can do for you right now. Just make sure it lasts. I still have my cleaning lady, and the gardener, and then there are the…"

"I'll take it!"

"Good, then I'll get my purse." Jackie headed towards the kitchen.

Not wanting to be discovered, Wynn dashed across the room to the sink. The women breezed through the room without a glance in her direction.

Marilyn walked out alone, struggling down the steps with a large suitcase, and a check pursed between her lips. The cabbie jumped out, took hold of the luggage and crammed it into the trunk. Within seconds, they pulled out of the drive. Immediately the air seemed cooler; the sunshine a bit brighter.

The guests began to leave. The hired servers were cleaning up the rest of the kitchen allowing Wynn to resign her post.

She walked out onto the patio to, hoping there was still plenty of lobster bisque and fresh fruit for the guests. Sparkling water would go down so nice, too – after being in the hot kitchen.

It was disappointing to see the tables being folded

and loaded back into the catering trucks. On the other side of the patio Jackie sat on the lounger. An envelope was crushed tightly in her hand.

Roxie hovered protectively.

"What's wrong?" Wynn asked.

Jackie twisted the paper in her hands. "Someone is holding Boone's body hostage."

"Hostage! This is a joke, right?"

"Here! Read for yourself!" Jackie held out the letter.

Now that we have your attention, we want you to know that we have Boone's body in our possession and are willing to trade it for the ruby ring. Details will follow.

"Where did you get this?" Wynn asked.

"It was in the stack of sympathy cards on the table. The author didn't sign it—but I suspect Marilyn." Jackie was wringing her hands.

"We need to let the police and Mr. Lansing know and wait for developments." Roxie said with an air of practicality, as if discussing who to have for tea.

"I will take care of that." Jackie's tone was wobbly, but she straightened her shoulders and said goodbye to the last of her guests. "Roxie, you should go home and rest, Wynn, take her with you. I have Agatha here and I plan to notify the police of everything."

Roxie stared hard at Jackie and something passed between them, unspoken.

Wynn marveled at their silent communication, a testament, once again, to old friends who knew each other well.

Wynn and Roxie said their goodbyes to one another at the Tree House.

Thoroughly exhausted from the long and emotionally charged day, Wynn got ready for bed. Coming out of the bathroom, her gaze caught sight of the backpack on the table. She unzipped it and took out the old container she found in the car.

The subtle gold swirls against the dark navy color were delicate, as though hand painted with a small brush held by patient hands. Mysterious.

Wynn tried snapping the lock open, but the metal was too thick and sharp. Maybe a knife would pry it open, but she held back; concerned it would scrape the lovely design. Perhaps old photos or love notes? It was fun to think about.

She brought the box into her room, and then set it on her night stand, staring at it as she climbed into bed.

At midnight, just as Wynn drifted off, the sound from a motor traveling past woke her. She lay there looking up at the moon thinking about a little toy she and her dad built.

It was a model engine powered boat, painted blue and white. They tested it the bathtub where it worked just fine. Why didn't they try it out on the lake? Whatever happened to that boat, anyway? Why was she thinking about this now? And why did the word 'twirling' suddenly come to mind?

Wynn flipped her pillow to the cool side. She'd always loved boats and the sea. Maybe she should have become a sailor instead of a scientist. She had been scratched on rocks and thorns, she had gotten poison ivy so often that she began to regard the rash as freckles, and she had gotten stung by ground bees more than she cared to remember. Something was bubbling up inside of her.

Roxie would probably refer to it as a spiritual

awakening, but Wynn thought she might be getting closer to the truth. Never before had she felt close to other women. Was it because of her mother being so remote? In school, she found most girls dull because they obsessed about boys, and dates, and twirling in their new dresses bought from high end department stores. *So that's why she thought of twirling.*

Wynn turned over in bed holding the old container like a beloved teddy bear and went back to sleep.

9

Wynn's hair flew wildly as she rode atop a large leaf from the Scalesia forest above the Galapagos Islands, relishing the reverberation of life forms. If only she had remembered to bring along her binoculars. A sound of pellets smashed against her leaf, nearly thumping her from the sky.

"Wynn! Wynn! Are you up there?" The voice popped the wind, sending her careening towards the earth. She landed with a thud.

Wynn opened her eyes to look around; stunned that she was inside of a room and not knocking around in the sky. Sometime between sleep and waking, she had wrapped up in her feather comforter and rolled clear off the bed. Disoriented, she blinked against the sunlight streaming into the open window. She stared bleary-eyed at the clock on the wall. "It's seven in the morning!"

"I know it! I need your help!" the voice from below called again.

It had been a week since Boone's not-funeral. Roxie had gone every day to support Jackie in her time of need.

Wynn had continued to do her research, content in the knowledge that if Jackie or Roxie needed her, they'd say so.

Wynn shook loose the sheet that ensnared her right ankle. She stumbled over the tattered shoebox containing fifteen years worth of cards that she reread as part of her nightly ritual. Just as she reached the window a handful of pebbles hit again.

"Finally! There you are!" Jackie breathlessly called.

"Jackie? What are you doing here?" A pebble had lodged itself between the screen and the window frame. Wynn popped the screen until she was able to grab hold of it. "Hey, this is a Petoskey stone! Where did you find this?"

"They're all over the place down here." Jackie snapped. "Roxie's not at home. Do you know where she is?"

"No, I haven't any idea. What's up?"

"I have an appointment with my accountant in twenty minutes and I don't want to go alone. I have a feeling he has bad financial news for me," Jackie explained.

Wynn looked around at the island plant life she had started to collect and chart. As soon as it was photographed, pressed and logged, it would join the rest of her research on the first floor of the garage. With a deadline looming, she really needed to stay here and work, but Jackie sounded pathetic. "Want me to come? I'm not Roxie, but I might be able to offer…"

"Wonderful! Just hurry!" Jackie called.

"OK, just give me a minute to throw on some clothes. I'm coming." Wynn pulled on her blue jeans and a sleeveless white cotton top. After brushing her teeth, she put blush on her suntanned cheeks, and then added a touch of gloss to her lips. Her hair was gathered into an unforgiving ponytail. Before rushing down the steps, she caught sight of the container that had slipped from bed. She needed to tuck it away someplace, but where?

Jackie called again.

"I'm coming!" Wynn hid the container behind the pots and pans in the bottom cupboard. She hurried down the steps and slammed the door. "OK. Ready!"

"That was fast. It took you less than five minutes. It takes me at least an hour to get ready."

"Yea, but you look so much better than I do," Wynn said getting into her vehicle. "Come on. I'll drive. What street am I looking for?"

"Main Street." Jackie wore black slacks with a silk top.

"Why are we going to see your accountant? Will the office be open?"

"Yes, I was told to come in before business hours."

"Have you heard anything more from...?"

"Boone's body snatcher? No. I'm not sure the island police are doing much about it, either. As much as I hate to admit it, Marilyn might be right about them." Jackie pulled down the visor to check herself in the mirror, but there wasn't one. She scowled and shoved it back up.

"Are you doing all right?" Wynn asked as the Jeep slid nose first into a parking spot.

"I'm about to find out. Come in with me?" Jackie nodded towards the door that read Peter Shamus, C.P.A.

"Ah, I can give moral support from out here, but what goes on in there is really your private business."

"I suppose you're right." Jackie disappeared inside the office.

Wynn's stomach growled. She contemplated going into the diner across the street for scrambled eggs and toast, but decided to wait. She leaned back, looking up.

The ceiling of the Jeep had a small brown stain on

it. Wynn touched the spot. It left a gooey residue on her fingertips. She detected an oil like odor. Maybe the mechanic had gotten something on the inside of the car while he was checking it out. Had someone been in her Jeep? If so, why?

She pressed the button on the glove compartment and pushed through the contents, hoping to find a napkin. There were fistfuls of old papers and receipts, some dating back years. Deciding a ten-year-old dry cleaners receipt was of no value, Wynn wiped her fingers. The compartment wouldn't close. Wynn looked around for a bag. Not finding anything, she noticed a bakery next door to the C.P.A's. She returned to the car with two empty plastic bags, and a jelly donut.

She took everything out; went through every receipt, every scrap of paper, reading notations jotted on the back of napkins. In one bag, she put things Roxie might need or want, like car insurance and recent receipts. In the other bag went papers of no use anymore. The compartment was finally organized with only car maintenance information.

Wynn tried closing it again, but something jammed. She pulled and the compartment door came off. The edge of a paper stuck in the plastic molding. She yanked it out. She turned the yellowed envelope over. There was no name or address on the front. No stamp or markings. Intrigued, she pulled out the letter.

My darling,

I tried to talk to you, in person, but you would have none of it. I don't blame you. Not after your sister's news. Loving you has become impossible. I betrayed you. Both of you. One by secrecy, the other by love. You've heard my surprising news. I'm going to be a dad. Imagine—me a dad. There's no role I would rather have. Our relationship has to stop. It's not right that I should love you this much when these feelings should belong to someone else.

Forgive me, Steve.

Paralyzed, she could only stare down at the note. "Steve?"

Her heart tumbled in her chest. Her dad's name. She laid her head against the steering wheel and inadvertently beeped the horn.

An elderly lady walking in front of the car jumped and dropped her sack.

"Sorry!" Wynn waved apologetically.

There was no date. Was this Steve her dad? Had there been a love triangle between her dad, her mom, and her aunt? Was she holding the root of the reason she and her mom left the island? Steve was a common name.

Her parent's marriage was thirteen months before she was born. Could they have adjusted the year so Wynn wouldn't know they had to get married? Maybe he had written notes to her aunt. If she could find a sample…guilt flooded her at the thought of snooping through Roxie's correspondence.

Guilt. Perhaps that was what her college money and this vehicle was really all about. Roxie's gift of generosity was about culpability; recompense. It wasn't about reconnecting and love as she hoped. Tears pooled in Wynn's eyes.

The passenger door opened and Jackie got back into the Jeep. "My life is over!" she wailed.

Wynn clutched the note, blinking tears, trying to recover.

"Didn't you hear me? I said, 'My life is over.' Say something comforting. Quote a scripture."

Wynn struggled to answer unemotionally. She was certain if there was a God, he wasn't a God of convenience, but one of commitment. Reciting a Bible verse wasn't about to happen.

"You look positively ill." Jackie said, tears in her eyes and her voice.

"I'm OK really. Just ate a donut."

"Carbs and sugar. Transfats."

"Right. It isn't setting so well. Tell me what happened, if you don't mind sharing."

"It seems Boone's business is bankrupt." Jackie set her jaw. "I'm going to have to find a job. Can you believe it?"

"Things could be worse."

"I don't know how." Jackie sniffled.

"Work can be quite self-fulfilling and rewarding." Wynn slid the letter into her purse.

Jackie was too upset to notice. "That's easy for you to say. You have an education. Me, I just have a pretty face, oh all right, a beautiful face, but it's not getting any younger."

"What about Boone's insurance money?"

"Boone's body hasn't been found. And someone masquerading as me made the identification. It reeks of fraud to the insurance company."

"I'm sorry, but if the coroner verified Boone's death that should be enough for the insurance company."

"There'll be an investigation."

"I know you're going through a rough time. I hate speculating, but do you have any idea who has Boone's body?"

"That's the three million-dollar-question, which happens to be the amount of Boone's insurance policy. If I could only find that stupid ruby ring, I'd gladly trade it." She paused. "That sounded harsh. I'd give anything to have Boone back again, safe and sound. I've only loved him. I still cannot believe he's gone. I wake up at night expecting him to be beside me in bed. Other times I think I hear his voice calling my name. You probably think I'm crazy. Maybe I am."

"Shouldn't you be praying, or something?" Wynn drew a calming breath.

"I have been praying, it's what keeps me sane. God is there for me, but I don't see how He's going to help me out of this mess."

"I'm the last one who knows about faith, but if you don't see how God can help you, then what good is He?" Wynn murmured. If faith was a gift from God, then she wanted that present. But she had to be sure.

"You don't believe in the existence of God?"

"I believe in what I can touch, smell, and dig out of the earth and water."

"Oh Wynn, you do miss so much. Even if God doesn't help me, or never answers yes to a prayer of mine, He has already done everything for me."

Wynn started to ask what she meant, but Jackie's cell rang.

"It's Roxie." Jackie told Wynn. "Hello…where were you?…I'm with Wynn now. She came with me to my accountant's…OK, I'll ask." Jackie turned. "Roxie wants us to meet somewhere for breakfast."

"Sure, where?"

"We're both game, how about The Cafe? See you soon." Jackie hung up. "OK, Wynn turn right here and it's just up a block on the right."

Wynn parked under the dappled shadow of an oak. The note in her purse kept her on edge. She had so many questions to ask. And she was fairly sure Roxie would side-step each one. Both she and Jackie needed answers about their loved ones.

With Roxie out of her cottage, this was the perfect opportunity to snoop for a note or a card. Guilt overcame her, but the need to know ate at her heart.

"I need to get going." Wynn glanced around anxiously.

"Oh?" Jackie looked puzzled.

"A deadline looms. I need more samples of the island's rare plant life." It wasn't a lie.

"What about breakfast?"

"The jelly donut is still hurting my stomach. You can go on in and get a table for Roxie. Do you mind? Give her my apologies and tell her I'll see her later. I'm sure she'll understand."

"She will understand, and so do I." Jackie leaned over and gave Wynn a hug. "Thanks again for coming with me. I'll pick up my car at your place after lunch."

"See you then."

10

Wynn decided to go the long way around the island to avoid a run in with her aunt. She drove on the coastal road without noticing the water.

She shot right past the Tree House and through the winding road between the trees. Seconds later, she pulled to a stop at the rear of Roxie's cottage. She had at least thirty minutes, but she'd look for twenty minutes.

Riddled with guilt for snooping, but driven by that lifelong desire to find the truth, Wynn reached for the doorknob. She went into the hallway. Each piece of furniture was in its place. An afghan had been folded over the back of the sofa. The wooden floors were freshly swept. Wynn became acutely aware of the ticking of the wall clock.

Where should she look? Where would Roxie keep information about the past?

There were bookshelves that lined one wall floor to ceiling. Family photo albums were on one shelf.

Wynn paged through, checking the clock every couple of minutes. There were pages and pages of Wynn, first as a baby, and then as a little girl. Most of them were of her in a crib or high chair; others were taken with her parents. The photographs were something Roxie would let her see.

Wynn had to find what Roxie didn't want her to see.

The antique pencil desk caught her attention. Wynn opened the top drawer. Pens were lined up side-by-side. Envelopes were stacked on top of stationary. A checkbook lay parallel to the monthly budget along with house bills. Stamps, tape measure, paper clips.

Wynn went upstairs and pushed open Roxie's bedroom door. She wiped clammy hands on her jeans, and stepped into the room of pink painted walls. The neatly made bed looked perfect; the table had a lamp and a Bible was centered on the shelf beneath it. The tidy dresser held a comb and brush set, and a silver framed picture of Roxie and Ruth as teens. The smell of furniture polish was strong.

Across the room there was a picture of Jesus holding a lamb. A heavy burden of guilt crept over Wynn, but if she knew the truth, then she could finally be close to her mother's sister and perhaps even forgive her mother. Maybe then, there would be closure and she'd be able to find peace.

Wynn opened the closet door. It was like the rest of the house, fanatically in order. Roxie's clothes were sorted by color. Wynn took down shoeboxes and old hat boxes from the shelves, but found nothing in them other than sensible shoes and silly hats.

She moved to the tallboy dresser. Perfectly centered on the top was a small cherry wooden music box. She lifted the hinged lid expecting to hear the delicate tinkling sounds of its song, but it was silent. Wynn began to wind it up when she heard a noise. She set the box down and went to investigate. A bird on the windowsill was flapping its wings against the windowpane.

She returned to the tallboy and pulled out the top drawer. It held socks and cotton underwear; the next two drawers were filled with cotton nightgowns. The next drawer contained jeans folded in half. It was the bottom drawer that yielded secrets. A metal box was at the very back. It was unlocked. Of course. The woman lived alone. There was no one to keep out of it until today.

Wynn sat cross-legged on the floor. Guilt flooded her heart. She looked at the picture of Jesus and cringed. But how else would she find what she sought? How else could she reconnect with her mother, if everyone kept secrets?

She opened the box and found old silver dollars. Next was a five by seven faded picture of her mother and dad sitting together on a couch, holding a baby. Roxie was in it too, looming over them all. Wynn flipped the picture over and read the names written in ink; Ruth, Steve, Roxie, Baby Wynn. It even had the date. Nothing in the box had her dad's handwriting.

Roxie had changed. The color of her hair had deepened and her face was filled with laugh lines. Only her eyes remained the same. Wynn wondered how her mother looked today. Perhaps a bit like Roxie. Was her need to find the truth partially rooted in reconnecting with her mom through her aunt?

"There is a little piece of me that is lost. A bit of my spirit anchored itself to the past. I have to come to my own rescue and find out what happened," she whispered.

The island was a keeper of secrets; it also kept hers. Wynn held onto a germ of hope that she'd be able to untangle them.

Wynn slid the photo into her shirt pocket. Next she found her birth certificate…Mother Ruth O'Malley Baxter and Father Steven Wallace Baxter. Roxie's elementary teaching certificate and her diploma from the University of Minnesota. There was a passport. Wynn turned the pages to see it had expired without a single stamp. Last, she took out a small brown envelope. A piece of paper had the name and address of an Egg Harbor Bank along with a safe deposit box key. There was also a password: TheCove. The contents of the envelope were pocketed.

She checked her wristwatch. More than twenty minutes had passed. Quickly, she put the birth certificate, the diploma, teaching certificate, and passport back into the box in the reverse order of how they had been removed, scattering the silver dollars on top; just as she had found them. At last, the box was placed back in the drawer which she softly closed.

It was past time to go. As she passed the basement, she stopped. Her heart hammered against her ribs. She swallowed hard.

It was too soon for Roxie to get home yet. They were just finishing up with lunch. It would take fifteen minutes to make the drive. There was a bit of time left—if she hurried.

Wynn heard a vehicle pull into the drive. Panicking, she slammed the basement door and went for her purse. Where was it? Where had she left it? Wynn darted from room to room searching, but it was nowhere to be found. Out of time, Wynn scrambled down the outside steps. Just as she rounded the corner of the house near the hollyhocks, she came face-to-face with Doug Reed.

"Whoa!" He took a step backwards.

"Pay attention where you are walking and driving. You nearly ran me off the road the other day."

"I know—I'm sorry about that. I was looking

down at my phone when it happened." He pulled the red straw from his mouth.

"Do you know how dangerous something like that is?" She tried to steady herself with a deep breath. "If you're looking for my aunt, she isn't home."

"It doesn't matter. Roxie has a dead tree. She hired me to take it out when I had the time."

"Well, then I won't keep you from your work." Wynn hoped Doug didn't sense her guilt. To her relief, the purse was on the floor of her car. She drove around to the Tree House.

Racing up the stairs, Wynn gathered up the cards she'd scattered this morning in her rush. She gazed at the greeting cards, remembering how, after her dad's death, she used to hover around her mother. Wynn squashed the cards against her heart in a big hug.

She had thinking to do. She carried the cards outside and sat in the shade of an oak. A dragonfly with translucent wings buzzed over the red wheelbarrow glassy with rain water. Bees hummed at the edge of the woods.

Meticulously she arranged the cards in order of receipt. This was the only contact she had from her mother in nearly two decades. Other than the sympathy card for her dog, there was one card for each birthday and one card for every Christmas. In between there was nothing but loud silence.

The feeling of rejection by someone she needed never went away. Wynn wiped at her eyes. She still loved her mom and missed her. The cards could not replace the longing. The letters mattered.

Wynn slipped the first card from its envelope. Inside she stared at the birthday cake scene: A group of giggling girls in party hats holding brightly wrapped packages. Inside the card was the blue ink scroll of her mother's words;

Happy Seventh Birthday, my darling. I am thinking of you all day today. When you hear the sound of laughter, think of me. All my love, Mom.

Could one of the cards hold a clue as to why Ruth left?

Although Wynn had read them many times, she might have missed something. It just might have something to do with Aunt Roxie. Had her college tuition been about guilt?

It was then she remembered the tin container.

The rumble of a truck made her look up.

"Are you all right?" Doug pulled a bandanna from his back pocket and handed it to her.

She stared into his handsome face.

"Are you all right?" he asked again as moisture dripped out of his hair.

"Yes." Wynn blinked the tears away, dabbed at her eyes and handed his bandanna back.

Doug sat too close and stretched his legs out, making her slide down a few inches. He made eye contact and smiled. "It's just that back there," he said pointing over his shoulder, "you seemed upset and after cutting apart a few logs, I thought I should check on you. And here you are saying you are all right, but not acting it."

Wynn tried to find the words to tell him that she was just having a moment.

"Pretty cards," Doug said, looking in her shoebox.

"Thank you. It's been an emotional morning for me."

"Are they from your boyfriend?"

"They're from my mom. I miss her." Wynn hated that her voice cracked.

"You two are close, then?"

"Not really. That's the problem."

"Maybe she will send you another card and everything will be better."

"That would be nice. But…she doesn't know I'm here on the island, and you see, there's no mailbox." She pointed to the top of the drive.

"Huh, no mailbox. Imagine that." He pulled a red straw from his back pocket and began gnawing on it.

"Roxie picks up her mail from a post office box in town."

"Oh."

"Why do you chew on those things? I don't think I've seen you without a straw in your mouth."

He pulled it from his mouth with a sheepish grin. "Oh, this. I gave up smoking a few months ago. Was up to a pack a day. Now I'm on straws. Down to two a day of these things."

Wynn laughed. "I'm sorry about earlier. I was pretty angry and took it out on you."

"No problem. Hope it made you feel better." He gave an adorable smile.

She fiddled with the cards and stole a look at him.

Doug smiled as if inviting her to say more.

"A week after my dad died, my mother and I left the island—the only home I had ever known. We moved across the lake to the outskirts of Egg Harbor where we lived together with my grammy and gramps. Mom met missionaries at church and soon her life was consumed by their overseas stories. She flirted with the idea of going herself—wanting to test the waters—and I could see it bringing her back to life. Just when I thought she was coming out of her grief, I woke up one morning to find her gone."

"And your only link to her is through the cards." His voice had a consciously meaningful tone.

She felt her world was made of quicksand and she was sinking down, down, down.

He took her hand in his own calloused ones. "It's not hopeless. It's important to keep hope tucked away right here." He touched his chest.

"Hope, huh?" Wynn drew a shaky breath but managed to keep her voice steady. "Mine ran out a long time ago. I need a fresh supply. Where would I get that?"

"I get mine in prayer."

"Now you're sounding like my aunt's Bible study women."

"I suppose it's because we all have the same source." He watched her steadily with big gray eyes.

"I never expected you to be the kind to read a Bible. But it's kinda nice to learn that about you."

"Well, thank you, I think."

"These cards are all I have of my mom. I still don't know why she left me."

"Maybe you answered your own question about why she left."

"I don't know what you mean."

He sat silently with her for a few more minutes before getting to his feet. "I am in the middle of cutting up Roxie's dead tree."

"And I should let you get to it," she remarked. She decided Roxie was wrong about Doug—she found him totally likeable.

Doug walked towards the truck, and then turned

around. "There's a coniferous bog on the north side of the forest preserve that you may find interesting."

"I'll check it out. Thanks."

"Take the last road into the Preserve."

"I will do just that."

Something had taken place between them.

As though sensing it too, a satisfied smile lifted his lips at the corners. Doug stepped up into the truck and backed down the drive.

11

Wynn decided to drive by her childhood home before starting her day in the woods. She turned down the narrow road and drove beneath the canopy of shade offered by the aged sumac trees. At the crest of the driveway, a perpendicular road intersected, generating a cross. A shaft of light spiraled from the sky culminating center to where Wynn now sat. A divine center? Was it a sign? She closed her eyes.

"God, are You really there? Because if You are, I could use You right about now in my life. Talk to me." She leaned her head back on the seat and held up her hands. Nothing. "I thought not." Disappointed, she drove onward. The lake shimmered below—blue and dazzling—the surf spilling onto the sand, and then chasing itself back. "Ah, this is where I connect with my own spirituality."

At the dip of the hill, there was an ocean of parrot tulips right next to a frost of trillium—which she remembered planting alongside her parents, so many years ago. Then Wynn caught sight of the roof of the ochre-colored house. Home. The all-consuming feeling of being here at last was intense.

She had forgotten the smell of honeysuckle that grew along the line of the woods, and the sound of waves echoing off the cliffs in the cove. The joy was overwhelming. The pull to get out of the car and walk around was all-consuming.

The driveway was empty of vehicles. She longed to saunter around the property, peek into the windows and pick a flower from the garden. Trembling, she was torn between embracing the memories of the past, or running from them. Her bedroom was at the front of the house, just at the top of the widow's peak which faced the sea. Were the curtains still lace? The ache inside her grew.

ॐ

Dad helped Wynn paddle through the mid-sized waves and they floated in the vast sea. She heard the water shushing and she stiffened with fear. Her dad caught her, allowing the waves to carry them back to shore.

Her mother had been watching them through binoculars. When she and her dad arrived home later, Mom was waiting for them in the yard, hands on her hips. Her hair was auburn and generous with thick curls circling her face, a face with sharp features—not rounded features like her redheaded twin sister, Roxie.

Wynn was sent inside while her parents talked in the yard. Side-tracked by the amazing colors of the shells they had collected that morning; it was a while before she walked outside with a Popsicle in each hand, a cherry and a lime. Her dad was at the far end, digging at the foot of an oak. Seeing Wynn, he walked towards her, crossing from shade to sunlight. The corners of his mouth turned downward. His eyes had a blank look.

"Is everything OK, Daddy?" Wynn held up both popsicles for him to choose.

He took the lime. "I'm fine."

"What were you doing over there?"

She cupped her hands above them and saw sorrow.

"I wasn't doing anything."

"Yes, you were. I saw you, right over there." Wynn pointed. "And, look, your pants are all dirty."

"You caught me. Remember when we planted the bulbs last year?"

Wynn nodded as a glob of red ice fell onto her shirt.

"This time I was planting something different. It was hope. I planted hope."

Right before the sunset had completely evaporated for the night, Wynn snuck out of the house with a trowel to unearth her dad's hope, wondering what it looked like. Wynn lifted the dark earth until deep red appeared. It was so pretty. She touched it with her hand. Hope was red and fluffy. She picked it up. It was a cardinal with a broken neck,

She screamed and dropped the bird and the trowel. Wiping tears with muddy hands, she wondered how a dead bird meant hope.

As the sun continued with its descent, streams of gold reflected off the cove. In the distance, a great egret broke from the trees and elegantly skimmed the waters, scattering the light. Then she knew. Those were her jewels.

When she climbed into bed that night, her dad asked her about the bird she dug up in the yard.

"How did you know?"

"You are never far from my sight. I watched you from the kitchen window."

"It's sad. But you said you buried hope. There was no hope."

"Ah, you are wrong. There was plenty of hope. You just didn't know it."

"I don't understand."

"You know what a sparrow is?"

"A plain bird."

"Right. It's very small. All brown. Just a little of white on it. It's not rare or endangered. But if just one sparrow falls from the sky…"

"and dies…"

"And dies, God knows."

"And that is hope?"

"Yes, that is hope. God is concerned with even a small sparrow. He is much more interested in you, and me, and your mom, and Aunt Roxie."

☙❧

What made her remember after all these years?

The wind whispered and carried a long ago message. A face came into focus. There was desperation in her dad's eyes. Fear made her afraid to listen, afraid to look, afraid to know the truth. Wynn pressed the bridge of her nose to hold back the tears.

No, she couldn't walk around the house to look for the lace curtains in her bedroom window. It would be wrong to snatch a flower for pressing. Her time had passed. It was someone else's turn to make memories here.

A tune began to play in her head. Once she knew the words by heart, but now they eluded her. The last few words came; "true to death, true to death, true to death." Why would she know this song?

Wynn put the car in gear and turned north. She'd go where the woods and bog were thick enough to hold her together. There was work to do. Look ahead, not back. Maybe Roxie's words were right after all; her life was in her future not her past.

The bog was peaceful among the black spruce, which grew on the carpet of sphagnum moss, a selfless spot on the island; a place for regeneration and biodiversity of sometimes misunderstood life forms— like her.

There was a healthy plant community of bog, cranberry, rosemary, and leather leaf. She cut and bagged them. Later, in her lab, she'd measure their nitrogen levels to compare with the lake samples. Perhaps this would help prove her thesis of water/plant balance.

It was peaceful among the black spruce which grew on the sphagnum moss mat. There were sedges, pitcher plants, and common orchids in the mix, but not a single Calypso. A bullfrog gulped his throaty call, and then became quiet, leaving only stillness.

The setting reminded Wynn of the time her uncles dropped her off at Bible camp as a young teen. Instead of falling in love with Jesus like everyone else, she fell in love with His creation. The first few days were so overwhelmingly wonderful that it made her cry her eyes out. Everyone thought she was homesick, but Wynn had found her calling.

Wynn sat on a decomposing moss-covered log. The air was damp. She leaned back. Creation was not designed by man, but by a Master artist, having carefully chosen the right palate of colors; fair-haired yellow, cinnamon brown, deep pumpkin, lobster red, kale green. Diverse creatures found this place utterly enchanting—a place that man would term as their 'habitat'. This was the fabric of her life; nature designed and executed by a Supreme Being Who cared about details. But was He the God whom Roxie and the other women worshiped? Was He the Supreme Being she learned about at Bible camp?

At times Wynn thought believing in God would make things easier. Things could be explained away by saying, "It's in God's hands."

Wynn wanted to talk to God, but didn't want to fold her hands. Folding hands meant one was serene and content. She was neither. She didn't want to pray. She wanted to talk. "As You know, I am not religious, so please excuse me, God, for speaking to You twice in one day when You haven't ever really heard from me, but You should know that I find You culpable in the dissolution of my family. You could have put a stop to it. All of it! But You stood idly by and watched my dad die, and did not one thing to keep my mom from running off. Just as I was healing and starting over for the third time, You decided to shake things up again and take Grammy and Gramps. What were You thinking? I was just a kid! You are as remote to me as my own mom. Strangers! How can I believe in You when I have been deserted!"

The central secret of her existence was that she despised God, Hated Him, even.

Wait...

That meant she did believe in Him. It became a revelation.

She believed in God!

In fact, she believed in Him just as much as the Bible study ladies. Only she didn't love Him like they did. Conflict and guilt set in as she considered the abundance of splendor that surrounded her. The One she hated, had created a beautiful, intricate biological system which only a unique, loving and creative Mind could. The dichotomy was unsettling.

Wynn grabbed her backpack and headed back. She had fooled herself into thinking she needed a mother—her mother, who had so willingly dismissed the child she bore. Well, she didn't need her, not at all. Not anymore.

She wasn't sure what she was going to do about God.

It was getting dark now and soon the bog would be impossible to navigate without a flashlight. Wynn returned to the Jeep and propped her feet up on the dash. Thunder sounded from miles away. She looked out the windshield at a clear, but darkening sky.

By the time she reached home, a storm cut a swath eastward across Lake Michigan. Clouds soaked up twilight like a sponge. The rain arrived full of electricity and wind.

Wynn looked at the sea of papers. She sat on a stool in her lab with a cup of tea, a plate of fruit, and a microscope. She studied nitrogen fixation caused by symbiotic bacteria and compared it to the plant life samplings. Her shoulders carried knots the size of rocks. Every time she shifted to get more comfortable, the rickety table threatened to collapse, taking her test tubes with it. Just as she started logging her findings, another crack of thunder split overheard, rattling the condenser lens. The lights dimmed, and then flickered for a few moments, before returning to normal.

Wynn muttered under her breath and raised the shade to look out at Roxie's beautiful flowers being lashed to the ground by the driving rain.

Tree limbs shook and the wind hurled sheets of heavy rain against the window. The ground was turning to mud. A narrow pond was forming on the other side of the driveway. The lights flickered again, and then went out completely.

Wynn waited for several minutes, hoping to complete this segment of her research tonight. When the power wasn't restored, Wynn rubbed the back of her neck and ran fingers through her rumpled hair, before going up the steps to her apartment. The sky was dark. Her thoughts turned to her box of cards, and her Grandparents.

Passed over. That was the term everyone used when Gramps died. He'd had a heart attack after a particularly pleasing meal.

Grammy was not only a splendid cook, but was also an overtly religious woman, which at times served as a stumbling block for Wynn's spirited individuality. The household was cold, regimented.

Every day, Grammy made Wynn practice hymns on the piano, as Grammy added her singing voice. Twice a week they mailed fat letters to Ruth in Central Africa, once they found out where she was. They drew close when they went to town to pick up mail, expecting a response from Wynn's mother.

"I guess she's too busy folding her hands in prayer," Grammy said, doing her best to put a happy spin on the loneliness they both felt. "She doesn't have time to write. God is keeping her too busy."

❧❧

It was the second winter after her mother had left. Grammy's clothes dryer broke and a new one simply wasn't in the budget. Grammy carried a basket of sheets outside to hang in the frosty sunshine.

Wynn watched a TV program about baby girls who got switched at birth. The thought occurred to Wynn that it could have happened to her. Her real parents could have discovered that and be coming to claim her as their rightful daughter. Wynn went to the window and checked the drive for cars.

All she saw was a single sheet pinned to the line. A dark figure lay motionless on the hoary ground as tufts of snow blew over it. Curious, Wynn put on her hat, boots, gloves and coat. She walked towards the shape, puffing out breaths of air. The wind pushed her coat against her legs and made strands of her hair fly.

Stiff, old snow crunched under her boots. Spots on the ground opened through the broken places showing earth. The air smelled sweet. And there was Grammy. Silent eyes starred right through her and focused above on a cloud. In the grip of her right hand was a clothes pin. There on her lips, was a frozen smile. Grammy had passed—the body vacant.

Perhaps Gramps came to visit with Grammy while she was pinning laundry to the clothes line—just like he used to do when his spirit was still housed in his body. Grammy must have smiled when he returned. And that smile prompted him to take her by the hand. Off they went; Grammy forgetting all about her earthly duty of taking care of Wynn.

Eight-year-old Wynn walked back to the house. Tears escaped from beneath her lashes, angry that God had His favorites and she wasn't one. She turned to the door. It was time to call someone to come.

The paternal Milwaukee relatives arrived and cleaned out Grammy's and Gramps's house; keeping a few things to take home, and selling off the rest. Among the things they kept was Wynn. She went to

live with her dad's older brothers, Dill and Matt—
confirmed bachelors who worked for the railroad. The
day Wynn left for her new home, she took Grammy's
angora knitted gloves from the hall closet and stuck
them into her coat pocket. She needed something soft
because she had a feeling life was going to be harder.
Wynn was wrong. Life with her carefree, rule-breaking
uncles suited her just fine.

Wynn realized she'd forgotten to eat and went to
the kitchen. Though the sky was dark, some light
penetrated the kitchen windows. Despite the power
being out, she could cook on the gas stove. She opened
the cabinet to grab a can of soup. As she reached for a
pot, she spotted the container. She really needed to
find out what was hidden inside. She took it out and
set it on the counter. The private guessing game of its
contents became entertaining. Once opened there'd be
no more speculation. She decided to wait a bit longer.

At dawn, the storm collapsed.

12

The Ladies Bridge Over Troubled Waters Bible Study was called to order at ten in the morning, on the south veranda of The Willow Inn. All the women were in attendance, plus Agatha.

The sunshine was bright and touched every piece of silverware on the table, but lunch was still another hour away.

Wynn noticed everyone hiding gift bags under the table when she walked out and, to her amazement, she felt a zing of excitement. Her face flushed with pleasure.

"With my husband still missing, maybe I shouldn't have come today." Jackie stood. "I wanted to get out of the house, but I feel I should be at home waiting."

"Nonsense, you need to be here more than anyone," Roxie said. "At times of trouble we bind together for comfort."

"You're right, Roxie. You women and the Lord keep me together." Jackie sat down. "I need everyone's prayers."

"And the Bible study to give you hope," added Sheri.

"All of us lift you up in prayer many times a day," Roxie said.

"I'm feeling a bit creeped out, because another letter about Boone arrived this morning."

"Another one?" Wynn asked.

"How terrible!" Faith gasped. "Have you considered perhaps Boone is still alive?"

"Yes, I have. But why wouldn't the person holding him tell me that?"

"Good point." Sheri straightened her name tag.

Jackie opened her Bible to Psalms, removed the paper, and passed it around the table. "I found it sticking out from under a flower pot on my front patio."

"That reminds me Jackie, I forgot to tell you how lovely your potted geraniums were on the day of the funeral."

"Why, thank you, Faith."

"Were you able to get a glimpse of the person who left this?" Wynn asked.

"No. It was there when we walked outside to get the morning newspaper," Agatha said.

"Excuse me, but should everyone be touching that paper?" Wynn was alarmed.

"I'm way ahead of you, Wynn," Jackie explained. "The letter came in a sealed envelope and I put on my Playtex gloves before picking it up, but I must say they were pretty bulky to get anything open, so I had to use chop sticks."

"I got them out of the drawer for her," Agatha interjected.

"That's evidence. Shouldn't you have called the police to have them check it for fingerprints?" Wynn asked again.

"I read it first, and then called the police. Officer Berry drove his golf cart out to see me. He has the original, what you're reading is a copy. They are having the envelope checked for DNA; saliva. I'm keeping a running log of everything," Jackie reached for her lemon water. "See Wynn, I can be a scientist, too."

Wynn read the letter aloud. "In forty-eight hours you will receive instructions on where to drop the ring. Within hours Boone's body will then be left at a pre-determined location."

"Who could be behind this?" Owl wondered.

"I have an idea, but not saying right now," Jackie answered.

"Oh, please tell them to drop Boone off at my shop!" Sheri begged. "Things have been slow lately and I could sure use the publicity."

"What is so special about this particular ring?" Owl asked.

"It's supposed to be an expensive heirloom, but now I can't find it, thank you, Marilyn. Sorry, Agatha."

"But didn't I hear Marilyn say it wasn't the right ring?" Roxie reminded her.

"Paste was the word she used." Owl cut in.

"Why would Marilyn want a worthless ring?" Roxie asked.

"It'd be just like Marilyn to say something wasn't valuable when it really was. Oh, sorry again, Agatha. As for the ring, Boone showed it to me one time and since I couldn't wear it, I didn't really get a good look at it. He said he wanted it buried with him, and then he put it back in the wall safe." Jackie dabbed her eyes with the linen napkin, smearing her black eyeliner. "I took it out when I went to the funeral home. But now both the ring and the box are gone from my purse."

"We need the Lord's peace in this matter. Maybe we need to refocus on why we have come together today," Roxie said.

"Please do," Agatha murmured as she played with the cameo brooch on her blouse.

"We have come to take our eyes from life's rumbling waters and to cross the bridge to where peace and joy awaits in the arms of the Lord. Our scripture for today is Romans 8:26-27. God's help in our weakness, which is very appropriate under the most recent circumstances."

All the ladies turned to the verse in their Bibles.

"Brand new one! Still in the wrapper!" Wynn held up her Bible, bought on the way to the meeting, and then tore off the protective wrapping. "OK, I'm ready. What page did you say we were on, Aunt Roxie?"

"We're in the book of Romans, dear. Chapter 8."

"And where is that?"

"Towards the end," Sheri told her, reaching for the Bible. "Let me help you."

"Wow, you're all way ahead of me. I'll never catch up. Maybe I need to find a group that is on page one. Look, just like it says right here in Genesis 1:1 'In the beginning God created the heavens and the earth'."

Agatha laughed. "You're joking right? About catching up to Romans?"

"No. Why would I joke?"

"You can start reading anywhere in the Bible. It's not like a novel where you have to start at the beginning. Just open it and read. Even I know that." Her voice turned frosty. "It's obvious you have never been to church."

"I have too been to church." Wynn held Agatha's gaze. "But not in a while."

"That explains a lot."

The ladies squirmed and remained silent.

"OK, let's just start with Matthew13: 31-32 instead

of where we left off the last time, shall we?" Roxie spoke up. "Wynn, follow along. You'll get the hang of it."

"The kingdom of heaven is like a mustard seed, which a man took and planted in his field. Though it is the smallest of all your seeds, yet when it grows, it is the largest of garden plants and becomes a tree, so that the birds of the air come and perch on its branches." Owl read.

"I have no idea what this means," Wynn confessed.

"There are many elements. First we have the sower," Roxie said.

"Who is Jesus," added Faith. "He atones for our sins."

"Then there is the mustard seed and the great tree which grows from it."

"Which symbolizes the Gospel and the tree is rooted in Jesus." Faith nodded at Roxie to continue.

"And lastly the birds perched on its branches."

"The birds mean to hear and understand the Gospel while the tree offers a refuge for His faithful to rest in Him."

"Thank you Aunt Roxie and Faith. Very nice image."

A pretty waitress walked up to the table. "Hello, I'm Paris and I'll be your server today. What drinks may I get for you?" She paused. "By the way, I have to ask, is there a Wilda Reed here?"

"That's me, Paris!" Owl answered.

"Owl, I didn't know your real name was Wilda. You have a call holding at the front desk from Paul Reed," Paris told her.

"Please tell my husband I'll call him back later."

The women all chose different specialty drinks.

"Chef Frank will be out soon to personally tell you about his epicure dishes." Paris gave a bright smile.

"The new owners of the Inn will be smart to keep Chef Frank," Owl said.

"Keep him and give him a raise." Faith added.

"Oh? Has the Inn been sold?" Wynn asked.

"Not yet, but it's up for sale," Sheri answered. "Are you handling the property, Faith?"

"I am."

"And here Chef Frank is now!" Owl announced.

Frank arrived at the table wearing his kitchen uniform; all white and starched. He was all belly and boastful as he greeted them. "I am personally preparing your dishes and will be ready for presentation in about twenty minutes. You are my guests. What appetizer may I bring you to enjoy as you wait?"

"How very thoughtful of you,"Roxie said.

"You know a plate of calamari to share might be a nice appetizer while we wait," Faith suggested.

"Yes, and I hear your caramelized onion focaccia is wonderful." Owl suggested. "Oh my—we're like lambs being lead to the slaughter aren't we?"

"Thank you, I take that as a high compliment. I hear we have a birthday girl lunching with us today." Frank winked at Wynn.

"Yes, we do," Wynn said, smiling.

"Wynn, I do believe my brother has his eye on you," Faith murmured.

Faith's words made Wynn's stomach twist into a knot. She had come to the island on assignment, certainly not to be the fodder of the latest gossip.

"Well, Chef Frank must wait in line. Wynn has a

date with my nephew, Doug." Owl informed them.

"What? I do not have a date with Doug Reed!" Wynn protested. "Who told you that?"

"He did. Doug told me you were checking him out with a pair of binoculars, right after Boone's funeral." Owl answered.

"Technically there really wasn't a funeral, remember?" Jackie pointed out. "So Wynn, tell us, did you like what you saw through your binoculars?"

"What else did he tell you?" Wynn ignored Jackie's questions.

"Nothing. "

"Is there more to tell?" Sheri asked Wynn.

"Of course not!" Wynn tried to smile. "Owl, when did your nephew tell you about the binocular incident?"

"The day after 'the incident' occurred," Owl answered. "He said you agreed to go sailing with him."

"Doug did mention sailing, but I told him I was too busy."

"That's the truth. You are too busy." Roxie insisted.

"Since you don't have a phone, Doug told me he was coming by your place tomorrow morning at six and to let you know." Owl grinned.

"Doug is a really nice guy. Go, have a good time, Wynn," Jackie encouraged.

"And tell us all about it at the next club meeting during refreshments," Sheri begged.

"Wynn is new on the island and Doug knows it like the back of his hand. He can help her with research," Faith said.

Doug was the only person Wynn had met who

listened without offering platitudes or Bible scriptures.

A Monarch butterfly with delicate patterned wings landed on the white linen tablecloth in front of Wynn, immediately causing her blood pressure to drop by ten points. Then the insect moved its wings together before it took to the air again. Wynn's gaze followed as it flittered across the veranda before heading to the purple butterfly bush, soon disappearing from sight.

The sound of a cart on squeaky wheels broke Wynn's concentration as Frank placed the appetizers on small plates in front of everyone.

Just as Owl filled her bowl with the soup, Paris handed her a phone message. Her eyes widened and she fell back, dropping the note into the onion bouillabaisse right on top of the rouille toast. Her right hand flickered to her chest as she tried to catch her breath.

Immediately Jackie leaned over the table waving a napkin. "Stand back everyone! Owl needs air!"

"Oh, no. It's Mae!" Roxie grabbed the note and read it.

The women gasped.

"Mae's had a heart attack. I must leave right away and go be with her," Owl spoke through tears, hoisting herself up.

"Owl, you're too upset to drive. Let me take you." Wynn reached for her purse.

"No, no—I'll just go by myself. Paul will meet me. I'm all worried up. Remember to pray for Mae?"

"We will," Sheri promised.

Owl left in a flurry of goodbyes.

13

Paris returned with the entrees; Red snapper sautéed to perfection, served with pine nuts and fresh asparagus, and arborio rice cake salad with a parmesan caper dressing.

"How sad Owl is missing such wonderful food," Sheri said.

"I'll take a to-go box to her later." Faith promised.

"Poor Owl, poor Mae. Is Mae Owl's mother?" Wynn asked.

"Oh no, dear, Mae is Owl's pet pig," Aunt Roxie explained.

"Pig!" Wynn exclaimed.

"When Owl was young, she was quite beautiful. I've seen pictures."

"I bet it was the reason that man kidnapped her and took her off the island," Faith murmured.

"Rumors. That never happened," Sheri said.

"Folks on the island seem to think it did happen, Sheri. Besides, wasn't she gone for a while? Reeds aren't known to be gone from the island for more than a few days at a time," Jackie insisted. "It's bad for them. Brings on bad weather, they say. Even though weather is in God's hands."

"The reason Owl left the island was to learn a trade." Sheri continued.

"Oh? What trade was that?" Wynn wanted to know.

"Belly dancing."

"No, no, no. That's wrong, too," Roxie insisted.

"It's the truth!" Sheri said.

"Wouldn't it be simpler to just ask Owl?" Wynn inquired.

"No, that is downright impolite," Faith told Wynn.

"We don't ever pry into anyone's life," Sheri said.

"No, never," Jackie agreed.

A chorus of Happy Birthday wafted over the restaurant, sang by servers waving sparklers. Chef Frank carried a cake in the shape of a flower. Candles burning, he placed it in front of Wynn. "Go ahead and make a wish."

Twenty-six year old Wynn closed her eyes and blew out the candles. "Do you know what just chemically happened here?"

"Yes, you're going to get your wish. Now open your presents!" Jackie urged.

Wynn looked around the table at the women, grateful for their acceptance. The gifts were thoughtful, too. Natural soaps made from goats milk, a book about Willow Island, a personal invitation to go walking with Owl, and a beach snow globe with a backscratcher attached.

"When you scratch, you make it snow!" Sheri illustrated her gift.

"A two-in-one gift. Thanks!"

Last was Jackie's, a gift certificate for a day at a spa for a massage and full facial.

After lunch, only Faith, Roxie and Wynn remained to drink tall glasses of cranberry juice while watching the sailboats in the harbor.

Frank returned with an invitation to show Wynn around the Inn. They started the tour in the gardens.

"Doug Reed designed the gardens and picked out every plant."

"It's beautiful."

Each garden was like a separate outdoor room with a different theme, but somehow it all tied into one another and flowed beautifully without obstructing the remarkable view of the lake.

"It only took one season for the completion. The owners were thrilled to snag him when he moved back from Chicago. It sure jump started his business here."

"Doug lived in Chicago?"

"He had a successful architectural business, but something pulled him back this way, and he started creating gardens."

"Not a bad choice."

"Next stop is the kitchen," Frank held open the side door. The short corridor opened up into a large kitchen filled with activity. Cooking pans and fat boiling pots sizzled on top of burners alive with open flames. Loud voices shouted at one another about a customer's order being late.

"Some people say the kitchen is the heart of the home, but I call this my command center. It's the heart of the Inn."

They reached the meat locker. Hesitantly, she slid into the over-sized jacket Frank handed her, and stepped into the freezer to have a look at the dead animals hanging on meat hooks.

"We get our beef, pork and mutton locally from farms on the mainland."

Wynn stopped in front of one carcass that wasn't farm raised. She scrunched her nose, looked closer, and then drew back. "Bear?" Wynn read the tag on one hunk of meat.

"Very good. Bet you don't know what kind of bear."

"Tell me."

"The carcass you behold is polar bear," he admitted proudly.

"But polar bears are listed as a threatened species." Wynn was aghast. She looked at him, struggling to associate the image of a well respected chef with a man who would serve up an exotic for the price of a meal.

"Threatened or not, they are not under federal protection in Canada and can still be legally hunted there. Each winter a select group of hunters provides the inn with a single carcass to be served to a specified elite clientele. We don't have it on the menu, but members know to order it when they arrive. By the way, I have a wonderful recipe. It would be my pleasure to serve polar bear to you in the private dining room some night soon."

"By no means!" Her estimation of his character took a nose-dive.

"You say that now, but once you taste it, you'll change your mind completely; threatened, or not." Lifting his fingers to his lips, he kissed them.

"It'll never happen."

They came out of the freezer in uncomfortable silence.

A pastry chef was filling a tray of small tarts. The men tipped their mushroom hats in greeting. It was obvious there was rivalry between the two. When introduced to Mario Barilla, Wynn was greeted cordially, but coolly.

"What was that about?" Wynn asked as they walked away.

"Competition. Mario wanted to be Head Chef, the position I now hold. To hold a spot like mine, you need to be able to create a wider spectrum of foods. He is only a pastry chef. You'll have to excuse his discourtesy; he may have mistaken you for a perspective buyer of the Inn, and wasn't happy that it was me, not the present owners, showing you around. Come Wynn; I want to show you the Inn's front entrance."

The foyer was splendid. As large as the reception area, it was surprisingly warm and cozy. A twenty-foot, one-hundred-year-old, hand carved oak counter greeted guests. The rest was divided up into smaller areas defined by couches and chairs. Palms and other exotic plants were thriving in huge pots artfully placed around the room. The windowsills were made of exquisite, foot wide, Italian marble that matched the fireplace in the grand entrance. Every window framed an exquisite view of the sea.

This used to be someone's private residence. Wynn marveled. She went to the grand piano at the far end of the room, sat on the bench and stroked the ivories.

"You play?"

Her answer came with her fingers dancing across the keys. Wynn played a popular song. When she finished everyone clapped. She looked up, gazing around the room, still dreamy with song. A particular painting caught her eye.

"Captivating, don't you agree? That is how the Inn looked when it was built in the 1800's as a home."

On top of the tallest peak of the cliffs which overlooked the western coast of Willow Island was the Willow Mansion, perched like a crown on a king's head. The stained glass windows glowed like rubies, diamonds and emeralds.

"It's breath-taking." Wynn ran her fingers over the gilded gesso edge. "This frame looks to be original."

"I wouldn't know about that. Antiques aren't my specialty."

The house was a deep purple whereas now it had white siding. The color was more practical, but not as charming. Although the mansion had several verandas, they had been enlarged since the time of the original design. Oversized parking lots for patrons had eaten into the landscape, as well as a newly minted golf course. The painting portrayed twilight and one of the windows on the top floor glowed. A female figure stood in the lighted room. In the bottom right corner there was a signature, Anna Reed.

Wynn felt a sudden chill.

"Wynn!" Roxie came up. "I'm going home with Jackie for the rest of the day."

"Is everything all right?"

Roxie and Jackie exchanged anxious expressions.

"Fine. Everything is fine."

"I'll see you for dinner, then?"

"Go ahead and eat without me tonight."

They headed to the parking lot.

"I'm free this evening," Frank offered light-heartedly, rocking back on his heels. "Seems to me you are as well."

"I really should be leaving, too. Thank you for the lovely meal, and the chocolate cake was beyond scrumptious."

"But, I thought we'd get together later."

"Oh, no, not today."

"Another time?"

"Perhaps." Wynn offered a token of hope, which

seemed to satisfy Frank.

When Wynn arrived at theTree House, she peered over the steering wheel.

A four foot tall black mailbox had mysteriously bloomed while she was gone. Silver brushed letters spelled out Wynn Baxter. She pulled the box open and found a common fossil. Wynn ran her hand over the smooth stone. "Doug, thank you," she whispered.

Climbing the steps, she considered the book of Matthew's mustard seed parable. Others found their refuge in God, whereas she found this place her refuge from the past.

Maybe her mother would realize just how much she needed Wynn, too, and promise never to leave again. Between her mother's absence, Roxie's mysteriousness, and going sailing with Doug, she couldn't stand being alone with her thoughts anymore.

What she needed was a good, long run.

14

The sun made the morning shadows vanish and took the chill off the air. The marina at Willow Island was already bustling with activity. A catamaran flying a brightly colored flag was loaded with tourists. The regular ferry that ran back and forth between Egg Harbor and Willow Island at three hour intervals was just arriving. Morning day-trippers, anxious to stake their claim to a front row spot in the sand with their umbrellas, held folding chairs and coolers.

"You aren't taking me someplace to hurt me, are you?" She joked as a lightness buoyed between them. "By the way, this is my first time on a schooner."

"That's not exactly what I had planned for the day." Doug laughed. "Besides, I'm probably one of the safest guys on earth."

"OK, can you tell me where you are taking me, then?"

"You will know when we get there. Until then, it's a mystery. It's how things work around here."

Taking Doug's hand, Wynn stepped off the dock into the stern of the eighty-foot schooner. Her attention was swallowed up by the style of the unique craft. "Just look at her lines! Not many boats are made entirely of wood anymore. What a beaut!"

"She was made in the nineteen thirties, during the FDR presidency," he explained. "We're cheating today. My vessel is motor powered, so we aren't pulling her sails this morning." Doug turned the key and the engines rumbled.

Water churned, yet the schooner remained docked until the cleats were slipped off the bollard. The throttle shifted into forward. The pier slipped away and they picked up speed. The bow pointed northeast.

Backpack filled with enough provisions for two days, Wynn was ready for her one-day excursion. Her skin warmed; she tugged off her light jacket and tossed it aside. She lounged back on a weathered deck chair, studying Doug, trying to figure him out, while still feeling the embarrassing aftershocks of the stupid words she'd uttered when he caught her with birding glasses. The unfortunate banter had turned words to cotton in her mouth.

Roxie had warned her about Doug.

Wynn suspected he was the one who built her a mailbox and left a small token inside of it.

Taking the fossil from the backpack, she rolled it over in her hand. Was her hypothesis correct?

"It's a good day for sailing, but you look far too serious. What are you thinking about?" he asked.

"I am thinking about thanking you."

"Good. You're having fun."

"I am having fun, but that's not what I meant." Wynn sat straighter. "I want to thank you for my mailbox."

"Mailbox? I have no idea what you are talking about."

"Really?" Wynn opened her hand. Holding the fossil between her thumb and finger, she displayed it and walked over to him.

A smile spread across his features.

"And now I have something for you." She pulled

out a red straw.

"Thanks." Doug stuck the end in his mouth.

There was an inside flutter, like a breeze across her heart that she couldn't ever remember having. "It's beautiful here," she said, and looked away.

The schooner rounded Willow Island.

Passing boats blew their horns as skippers waved.

Wynn left the bow and leaned over the railing, briskly waving right back.

"It's camaraderie of the high seas!" Doug laughed, and then turned his attention to the teens hot-dogging on jet skis. There was no choice but to give them right of way. Soon, the schooner left the hodgepodge of water traffic far behind. The coast disappeared.

Only miles and miles of total blue remained. The achingly beautiful view of the sea charmed her as much as the rich, dark handmade stained wood deck of the schooner cutting through the water.

The man who stood at the helm looked at home in that spot.

Wynn returned to her deck chair and listened to the sea's voice as it sang the serene melody of all the ships that had sailed this way before them. Inhaling, she experienced an enormous sense of joy because the air was ripe with adventure and the sun shone cheerfully on the water.

Twenty minutes later, she spotted it. The twisted spit of land rose from the water like an arthritic fist coming out of the morning sun. Waves broke against the rocky shore. The wind smelled fresh, like springtime. The coast looked rugged.

They cruised all the way around to the west side.

Doug opened the rubber craft, helped Wynn climb in, and then tossed in their backpacks. He leapt into the smaller boat, grasped the pair of oars and began rowing.

"This island is part of the Willow Islands. There's a string of three. The one we live on is the only one allowed to be inhabited. The one we are headed towards is a reserve and you have to have a special pass to land here." His light hair was soaked from the unseasonably humid air and intermittent showers of spray the wind threw over them.

"Do we have this special pass?" Wynn asked, braiding her hair back from her face.

"I have a permanent lifetime pass." His smile was charmingly cocky.

"And how did you rate this honor?"

"All three of these islands used to belong to our family, but they were sold off in parcels, except for this one. My grandfather left it to me as its sole owner and developers were thinking of every which way to use laws and government to snatch it away."

"I've seen that happen on the mainland, too."

"The last thing I wanted was condos going up, so I donated the entire island to the National Wildlife and Habitats Commission."

"Smart move. You don't like people much, do you?" Wynn asked uncritically, dipping her fingers in the water.

"I like people fine. What I don't like is how they take care of nature. You're about to see unusual migratory birds and colonial nesting birds, but that's not why we are here."

"Then why are you taking me here?"

"Patience, my dear."

They pulled the craft aground where the tide was negligible and there were breaks in the rocky shoals.

Wynn followed Doug up the one-man gravel trail along the side of the cliff. He pointed out another trail, into dense vegetation. The foliage muffled the sounds of the waves, and Wynn could hear the call of birds.

Doug patiently waited each time she stopped to take a cutting and bag it.

The path narrowed as they descended into a valley. Perspiration dripped from their foreheads as their clothes became sticky with humidity. Cinnamon ferns grew in great abundance alongside maidenhair, and hammock fern. Further along were huge bouquets of common striped native plants with long plumes of pink flowers. Sunny spots interrupted pools of breezy shade. The scent of wildflowers wafted. There were streams and hidden strawberries tucked among gnarly wild vines.

Doug stopped to point to the Dwarf Lake Iris and Pitcher's Thistle, both federally protected.

Wynn took pictures and noted it all in her logbook. When she finished cutting, and then bagging her last specimen, she looked up.

He held her gaze.

Only the sea had ever had this effect on her, this fluttery, adventurous spell, holding her captive. A blush bloomed on her cheeks.

"You do have the most mysterious expressions. I would love to know what you're thinking about now," he said. A faded white rope of a scar ran from his temple through his eyebrow.

Wynn stared at him, finding something both intriguing and incongruous about Doug's personality. He was slightly introverted, an observer—but totally charming once he let one in. And next to her dad, he had to be the most interesting person she had ever met.

He appreciated the wild—the sea, the growing things, the wonders of nature, just like she did.

"Hello?" He waved his hand in front of her face.

"This is the best day I've ever had. And I cannot help but compare what I see here with how I was raised on city streets. I can never be happy living with a postage stamp of a garden that is toxic with pesticides."

"I like you!" Doug turned and led the way again.

And I like you.

The terrain was uneven as they reached the top of a hillside, where the view was the best she had ever seen.

But Doug moved downward again, forged ahead with some secret destination in mind. When he stopped to drink from his canteen, he first offered it to her.

Although she had her own, she gratefully accepted his. They took a break and had granola bars. She sliced her apple in half sharing it with him. His sea gray eyes flashed from the apple to her face. "Thanks." The sound of his voice was thick and tender; making a lump form in her stomach that wasn't from the granola.

Wynn heard a songbird and looked up to see the flicker of feathers from a Kirtland's warbler. She grabbed the binoculars. A single male without any identification leg bands. These birds liked to live under the boughs of young jack pine trees, and there were plenty of them here.

"We're just about there." Doug grabbed his backpack and pressed on.

The stream they waded through was knee deep and felt refreshing. Wynn stopped halfway through and looked at the minnows swimming about her ankles in the clear water.

"Want to stop here for a few minutes?" he asked her.

"You bet I do!" Wynn slid her backpack off, gave it a hard push and sent it to shore. She pulled her hair out of the pony tail and plopped down into the stream, lying on her back, grateful to let the water flow over her body. Her hair floated out like tentacles. She kicked her feet and arms, trying to float on her back, but she sagged to the stream's bottom. "It's not deep enough!" she complained good-naturedly.

"You're not hard to be with." Dough laughed as he followed her example.

"Thanks. As you can see, I like nature." A minnow swam into her shirt tickling her. She sat up and jiggled it out. She let the water flow over her legs.

"You don't talk and scare away the wildlife. And you're not afraid of the heat." He sat up, too, bracing elbows on his wet knees.

"I consider those high praises."

"That's how I meant them."

"Thanks for sharing this place with me." Wynn locked gazes with him.

"How did you get so interested in biology and the ecosystem?"

"It happened long before college." Wynn leaned back on her elbows. "It's part of my DNA. It's a strand called imustknowthat."

"Oh?"

"Yep, I grew up going from one family member to another as if I was a project someone had to do. Since I didn't seem to attach to people well, I began to attach to whatever I found in the environment. I cleared out a dresser drawer to arrange my finds in alphabetical order. I'm not kidding."

"And what would I see in that drawer?"

"Glittery rocks, leaves, petrified geckos, a hornet's nest...I see my hobby as a refined talent." She wanted to run her hand through his thick curly hair.

15

"I was in the carriage house garage not long ago and got a good look at your lab. You've upgraded your collections since your drawer days."

"Really? You saw my collections?"

"As you would say 'yep'."

Wynn tried to cover her annoyance. Someone had dared to walk right into her lab that was filled with expensive equipment and endless hours of research. She needed to put a lock on that door. A curious person who meant no harm could easily ruin it, making her lose her grant.

"I didn't touch anything, Wynn. I was there to flip a switch in the breaker box. I know enough about research to know the smallest contamination could ruin months of work." Doug had read her consternation easily. "I can put a lock on the door, and next time, I'll make sure it's OK with you. At the time, I didn't realize that's where you'd set up."

"OK," Wynn was mollified. "I'm sorry, I tend to be protective."

"Rightfully so." Doug got out of the stream.

Five minutes later, they had arrived.

The sight took her breath away.

The valley was filled with colonies of the Calypso orchid.

It brought tears to Wynn's eyes to see it thriving prolifically. "This orchid seed is the tiniest in the world and they can travel for miles with a good wind."

"Take another look. We are enclosed on all sides by thirty-foot hills. It serves as a bowl effect which keeps most of the seeds germinating right here. And this is the perfect time of the year to see them like this." Doug dropped his pack and sat down, leaning one shoulder blade against it.

Wynn dug for her camera and began snapping shots. "These orchids bloom for just one month and then they'll be gone for another year."

They sat under the shade of a striped maple—and to Wynn's knowledge it was the first one to be seen on a Wisconsin island. She considered not logging this find into her record book. The fewer people who knew of it, the safer it would always be.

"You have emeralds hanging from strands of your hair," Doug smiled, pulled them out and opened his palm where little caterpillars squirmed. He gently placed them into the treasure box of ferns.

They sat still for the better part of an hour, just listening to the sounds of the valley, breathing in the fragrance of orchids.

"It's time we head back to the coast." Doug put on his backpack and picked up hers.

"I can take that," she told him as she slid the straps onto her shoulders. "What kind of wildlife is supported by the island?"

"The island has gray wolves that feed off small game. They thrive here."

"I thrive here, too, so I can understand that."

"I once planned on building a cabin to retire right here. As you know it's good hiking and the fishing is pretty good, too. But when my engagement fell to pieces, I couldn't see living here alone for the rest of my life."

"It seems to me that this island would be your healing," Wynn said.

"Finding the Lord was my healing balm. And this is a good place to pray."

"Pray, huh? My aunt hasn't said it in so many words, but she wants me to pray in front of her Bridge Club to accept the Lord."

"You're not up for that display of emotions?" His smiled was cockeyed and a bit bothersome.

"No, I'm more private. If I was to do something, I would do it alone in a place like this and look up at the sky and talk right out loud to God, not be all scrunched up with five sets of eyes watching and listening...analyzing." Wynn didn't tell him about her first and only session with God.

"What would you say to Him?" His gaze was far off where distant flora met the blue horizon.

"I'm not sure—it depends on the moment and what I feel. But at the right time it'll bubble from my heart right up to the surface and out my mouth."

"This island sure worked for me at the time of my break-up. I was searching for a way to let go of my pain." Doug winced, and held out his arm where a paper wasp had just stung him. He shook his arm and it flew off. He scraped his skin with a small folding knife and applied ointment from his pack, as if he did that sort of thing every day.

Which, as a landscaper, she supposed he did.

"With my business I can't get away too often during the summer, and in the winter it's nearly impossible to make it over here. But I come more frequently since spotting a family of feral cats roaming around. I don't want them to get at the federally protected birds that make their nests here, and I don't like the idea of the wolves making an easy meal out of them, so I've set traps for them. On our way back down I better check them."

"How did the cats get here?"

Doug led the way down the trail taking a different route back. "I'm guessing boaters. Sometimes people have something they don't want so they drop it off and make it someone else's problem."

"Boy, can I relate to that."

The sun was dropping behind the furthest hill and the sky was purple with something deeper than lavender.

"This is where I've seen the cats."

"Looks like campfires have been made here, too. Yours?" Wynn asked, while kicking some ash in a fire pit.

Doug didn't answer.

Wynn sat on a log and waited for him as he thrashed through the brush finding the traps.

Every now and then Doug would holler about how the food was gone and the cages were still empty. He walked out of the brush carrying a live trap.

Inside was a young orange tabby. It looked frightened as it slammed its body about and growled like a full-grown lioness.

"What a spitfire." She wiggled her fingers through the bars.

Doug yanked it away. "Careful!"

"What are your plans for this wild kitten?" she asked, sliding her hands down into her pockets.

"There's a lady just outside of Kewaunee who runs a feral cat rescue and preserve. It's a wonderful place on acres of land with huge outdoor cages with trees and rocks, and other feral cats. Of course, this one will get its shots, and then be spayed, or neutered first. There it can live out its natural life in relative freedom without harm and without harming."

"Ah, could this lady possibly be your former fiancée?"

A long silence grew. Clearly, he didn't want to answer any personal questions.

She'd have to wait for him to tell her of his own accord.

With the trap in one hand, he started towards the trail that would take them down to the beach. By the time they reached the dinghy, the sun was a sinking tangerine disk in the scarlet heavens, the perfect colors of an eight o'clock sky on a summer evening. As they paddled to the schooner the wolf serenade began.

Wynn stepped up. Doug handed off the packs and the trap to her. She set it all at the keel as he climbed in stern side, taking care of the rubber dinghy. Next, he cranked in their anchor.

Wynn stood in the hull and took pictures of the sky. She couldn't remember being happier in her entire life. She was on the water with life under her feet, and rare plants on an enchanted island. She knelt to talk to the kitten.

"I can't get the boat going."

"Why not?"

"It seems we're out of gas."

"I thought great skippers always looked out for their ships."

"We do…but there isn't much we can do when the line is cut." He wriggled the gas line in the air to show her.

"How did that happen?"

"Sabotage."

"Who would do something like that, and why?" Wynn looked around but saw no one, nor a single vessel.

"One can only guess the pranks kids play when no one is looking." Doug got the jib ready, and then pulled the halyard lines to hoist the sails. "Looks like we're in for a moonlight sail back to Willow Island."

"That sounds quite nice." Wynn settled back into her deck chair. "Anything I can do to help?"

"There's always something to be done on the schooner. I'll have you help with the rudder in a minute. Anyway, there's a beam wind out tonight so we should be back to dock in a little while."

"No hurry."

Wind filled the sails. His tacking left a wide wake. "How's our little traveler doing?" He nodded towards the cage.

"Frightened."

"Here." Doug pulled a towel from the haul. "Wrap this around the cage and it'll give the animal a sense of security."

Wynn wrapped the wire cage in the soft towel and immediately the kitten quieted. "If you don't mind, I'd like to keep it."

"What? You should know that a feral cat can't be tamed, not even a young one."

"I want to try. With it being so young, I might have a chance. It just seems so lonely and afraid. Maybe I can get it to trust me."

"Let's get the kitten checked out, vaccinated, and fixed. If Clara says it's healthy, then you can try taming it. If you find it's too much to handle, just admit it, Clara will gladly take it off your hands."

"So your ex's name is Clara."

"How did you figure that out? Nevermind." He smiled. "Want to help steer?"

"Sure!"

"This is known as the rudder," he explained as he allowed her to take over the steering device. "Let me show you how to tack." He worked the rudder back and forth and the ship easily sliced through the black waters. The moon's reflection wobbled directly in front of their craft as if it was the road home. Dozens of waves, perfectly aligned and shaped, moved past them.

Between Doug and the end of the schooner, the space was so narrow, that her cheek now and again rested on the surface of his shoulder. She kept pulling away, but if she was to be comfortable, the position couldn't be helped.

"Today was nice. I feel like I got a sense of who you are," Doug said with an air of satisfaction.

"I think it was the island."

Doug got up to work the rigging on the mainsheet.

Roxie was wrong about Doug. He had a deep commitment as the islands' unofficial guardian and caretaker, perhaps because his family had owned them at one time. His knowledge and understanding of her research, and the desire to show her more of what he loved was enlightening. She suddenly realized she might be a little bit in love with more than the sea.

The sails began to flap as they slowed considerably.

"What did I do?"

"It takes a while to get the hang of this," he told her, taking the rudder back into his own hands.

The closer they sailed to Willow Island, the clearer

the sounds that crackled over the water.

This was the most settled and peaceful she had felt since coming to the island.

Doug hadn't gnawed on a straw since this morning. Perhaps he was being healed, too.

She felt silly suspecting Roxie of something sinister concerning family information. Wynn decided get back to studying plant life—not human motives. Somehow coming home again had gotten her off kilter. Today had been the best day; good medicine to shake off the mantle of sadness about her father that Willow Island evoked.

Set free on the sea and island exploring had been the perfect medicine. It was time to look ahead, not back. There was plenty of work on her project. She might include getting to know Doug better, too.

"Look ahead, starboard." Doug pointed "What do you see?"

"Is that beam from a lighthouse?"

"It certainly is. But not just any lighthouse. My lighthouse."

"That is so very cool. So, you live in a lighthouse?"

"That I do. Still renovating. Want to see it sometime?"

"I really would like that."

"I'd really like to show you."

She was happy. She'd often felt challenged or content, but simple joy eluded her. She had found a place here in the beauty of untouched raw nature.

Wynn checked on the kitten to find she had calmed. As Wynn sat down something sharp poked her on the wooden seat. She pried it out. It was a brooch, a cameo.

Agatha's?

16

An old man was selling sweet corn from a pickup truck. He sat on the tailgate, tapping his shoes together as he read a newspaper.

Seagulls fluttered over the crescent shaped beach as sunbathers relaxed on sand as white as granulated sugar. In the water, a couple paddling a kayak had trouble. Giving up, they got out and swam towards shore, laughing as they pushed the kayak in front of them.

Not surprised to find several other cars already there, Wynn parked at the beachfront in front of a "NO DIGGING FOR JOESPH REED" sign in the shape of a shovel. In the back pocket of her jeans was her to-do list. Wedged in-between emailing the first part of her report to her professor and finding a new area of the island to explore for flora, was a visit to a particular beachside shop; Sheri's, in fact. Perhaps the shopkeeper would have something left of her dad's store inventories. It was a long shot, but it was worth asking.

A large sign printed in black, "Sandy Beach Treasures," hung near the building's roof peak. Wynn walked into a painted shop. The pungent scent of sandalwood offset local artist paintings, ranging from modern to abstract, displayed at the front of the shop. The room's low ceilings, salmon colored walls, and light linoleum floors were the perfect backdrop for the abundant cornucopia of doo-dads that crammed every inch of each shelf.

On the far wall was a clock, a black cat whose swaying tail ticked the seconds of the day.

Wynn stood still, suddenly remembering a morning like this one, but spent in her mother's kitchen. A memory buoyed with faraway laughter.

ॐॐ

"When a gyrocompass is properly mounted it will always point to true north. This clock will keep me turning the latchkey in the shop door on time."

They had an ordinary life, defined by ordinary moments, which made it exquisite. She had been wrapped up in it, held in it, kept safe there. Dislocated from her past she now floated emotionally out to sea— drifting with the waves while waiting for a rescuer who would put together all the pieces of her life so she could move forward into her future.

ॐॐ

"Wynn, is that you?" Sheri waved from behind the counter. "I wondered when you'd get around to coming."

"I've been busy, but here I am."

"I know why you've really come."

"Oh?"

"You've heard the news."

"News?" Wynn braced for yet another dead, or missing, husband.

"You haven't heard? Oh, good, I get to tell you. The authorities believe the body in Boone's casket

might be none other than Joseph Reed in the flesh—
what was left, at least!"

"Now that I think about the condition of the body,
that sounds about right. The hot sand and cold winter
snow would have served as mummification agents to
help preserve him. I guess it's time for the man to have
a Christian burial. Too bad Anna is deceased, but he
sure has enough relatives on the island to see to it."

"That would most likely be Owl."

Wynn picked up a bejeweled seashell. "Interesting
item."

"Isn't it? I thought it could use some bling around
here to help balance the ambiance of the shop."

Wynn returned the encrusted shell to the shelf. A
remnant of glitter remained on her fingers.

Sheri moved the item to a lower shelf. "This is
where it belongs."

"Has the corpse been identified as that of Joseph
Reed?"

"I guess all the signs about no digging will have to
be taken down if it is. Owl is having DNA analysis
performed on him on the mainland and they're taking
mouth swabs from all of his living relatives. Listen to
this." Sheri moved closer. "Doug Reed is the only one
who refused to partake in the testing. He thinks it's
silly. Know what I call that? Suspicious."

"Taking swabs of all the family members is
overkill. It only takes one blood relative to link a
family. Has Aunt Roxie been told?"

"She's the one who is spreading the news!"

"That's odd. She never said a word about it to me,
and we had morning tea together, too."

"Speaking of Roxie, let me take you on a
memorabilia trip. I'll show you where she and your

mother signed their names when they were in high school." She indicated the graffitied wall.

"Why do you allow people to do this?"

"Because it's fun."

It made the already bohemian atmosphere stranger.

"You're joking with me, aren't you?" Sheri shoved aside a rack containing colorful shirts of palm trees and sunny beaches. Then she tapped the wall with a finger. "Look right here."

"Roxie and Ruth, best friends and sisters forever!"

Wynn starred at the handwriting, so similar the same hand could have written the words.

"I was years behind them in school and I only really got to know Roxie when she started the Bible study. I never knew your mom. Sorry."

"My mom and Aunt Roxie had a falling out. Did Roxie ever tell you what it was about?"

"From what I know, they have always been close and remain so to this very day." She looked puzzled.

Perhaps her dad's signature was somewhere. "Where's my dad's signature?"

Sheri's bright and friendly attitude soured.

"He never signed the wall because he never stepped foot into my dad's shop, leastwise while I was here. His place was just a tiny spot back then, cards don't take up much space. That's probably why the realty company knocked it down and built bigger." Sheri's voice was quick and fearful.

Wynn, although curious about Sheri's attitude, continued along the walls, reading the names until she came to a freshly painted area that was about four inches square. "What happened here? Did someone write a rude comment?"

"Well, look at that. I never noticed."

Sheri was aware of where everything belonged in the shop, down to a blingy shell placed on the wrong shelf. Certainly she was aware of the painted area on the wall.

"Wynn, let me show you a famous signature. It's over there." Sheri led the way to another area.

"On the opposite wall."

"Yes. A television star used to vacation here once a year. I also have other movie and TV star signatures but I will make you hunt for those. It'll be more fun that way."

After politely commenting on the signature, she spent the next few minutes wandering the shop.

"Here." Sheri pulled the cap off a fat marker and handed it to her. "It's time to sign your name."

"I'd rather not."

"You must!"

Wynn gave in and found a spot on the wall between a Betty and a Bob. With great flourish she drew branches of a willow tree, threading it through the names around it. She finished with the words, Wynn in the Willows. Wynn blinked tears, embarrassed to be struggling with her emotions. "You mentioned having bought my dad's shop inventory. Is there a chance some of that stock remains?"

"I sold those greeting cards for just one season, but quickly found I did so much better with post cards. As you can see, I have very limited space. I can't remember what I did with them. Let me have a look up in the crawl space sometime and I'll let you know if I stored them up there, but off hand, I'd say they got tossed. Sorry."

Roxie couldn't remember where the newspaper

clippings were of her dad, and now, Sheri couldn't remember if any of her dad's items remained. Most definitely there was some secret between her aunt and Sheri. The news served to make Wynn more determined to find out what was being hidden. "If you do find them, I will gladly pay you for them," she said in a controlled voice.

"Nonsense you can just have them. But as I said, don't get your hopes up."

"I'll try not to. Thanks for showing me around your cute shop!" Wynn waved goodbye.

The drone of a single engine airplane made her glance up. The sound of waves crashed against the seawall as Wynn headed to her vehicle. She stared at the shovel shaped signpost. The season was short here and each day mattered. Yet, conflict between the personal and professional raged. She had planned to spend her time foraging through remote island vestiges, but now she looked at the water as she considered another alternative.

She pulled her backpack onto her lap and drank some water. Wynn glanced at her watch—9:30. With a couple of deft moves, she pulled her hair into a ponytail, and then turned in the direction of the Ferry's whistle.

The choice for the day was made.

17

Wynn pulled out Roxie's bank key. She'd go to Egg Harbor to unlock some family secrets. She took a parking spot close to the pier where the ferry was now docking. Within minutes, she was seated on the forward bow. The sun filtered down through the top observation deck. Below, the vehicles were secured for the journey across the bay.

White cliffs hugged the shoreline on the north side as glistening blue water ran along the shore. Memories were encapsulated there. The source of her grant was, too.

Depending upon what information she gleaned, by the time she took the evening Ferry back, she just might be the owner of a whole new set of problems to solve, or have all the answers she desperately needed.

She stared at the passing Willow Island landscape; houses, storefronts, beach, and harbor.

"Wynn."

"Doug, I didn't expect to see you." Her heart tugged at the sight of him.

He held up a small trap, which had a water bottle attached to the wire. The kitten was safely tucked into a soft towel. A face of fluff peered out. Whiskers stirred.

"Oh my gosh, but you are so adorable!" she cooed to the kitten. "What a darling face."

The gray kitten stuck its nose out a bit further.

"Look at that. I think he knows he belongs to me."

"You know all that from a nose twitch?" Doug seemed amused. "And how do you know he is a he? I can't get close enough to look."

"I just think so."

"Then it must be so!" Doug laughed and sat next to her.

"And just where are you taking my kitten?" Wynn snatched the trap and set it on her lap. She placed her hand flat against the wire. The kitten stretched to sniff her hand.

"I'm taking him to the rescue center."

"Ah, Clara's. I remember."

"Since you're on your way to the mainland, why don't you come along?" He flashed a killer grin.

"How soon can I take the kitten home?" she asked, without answering his invitation.

"You can ask Clara about that and about taming a feral kitten. She has lots of good tips." Doug looked at Wynn. "But she just might change your mind about raising a feral cat."

"No, there will be no mind changing. I want him." She steadied her apprehensions about meeting Clara. Besides, she was curious about Doug's past.

"Great. My truck is on the deck below. Unless…"

"Unless, what?"

"How inconsiderate of me. You're going to the mainland. I'm sure you have your day mapped out."

"I do. But my plans shouldn't take too long." If her plans were changing, she was glad it had to do with spending time with Doug. "If you don't mind waiting, maybe we can meet somewhere, like say, in thirty minutes after we dock? Unless you're in a hurry?" Wynn couldn't go another day without opening that bank box, but the allure of Doug and the kitten was strong.

"Tell you what. There's a café in the middle of town right on Main. I'll have a cup of coffee there while I wait for you. Do you mind giving me your cell phone number just in case we get our signals crossed or something happens?"

Once the ferry landed, she sat beside Doug in his truck as they drove out.

"I'll meet you right here in thirty minutes."

"Thirty minutes sharp."

The bank was right across the street.

Nerves made her usually calm hands shake. Would someone keep her from Roxie's box of information? What would her aunt do? Ban her from returning? Kick her out of her life? Wynn had suspicions that Roxie was somehow involved in the choices her parents made. Why else would Roxie have paid Wynn's college tuition and give her a rent free tree house for the summer? And she couldn't forget the car that now had her name on its title.

Wynn felt like a criminal as she glanced in all directions before crossing the marble floor. A uniformed guard stood alongside a young bank employee seated at a desk.

"May I help you?"

Wynn noted the circular doorway which led to a room filled with rows of safety deposit boxes. Her heart beat faster. She was within feet of the one belonging to Roxie.

"Ahhhh, yes. I need to get into a safety deposit box." Purposefully she left out the word 'my'. Snooping was bad enough, but lying would be over the top.

The clerk led her into the deposit box room and rummaged in a file drawer. "May I see your ID?" She held out her hand.

Wynn handed it over.

"Oh, Ms. Baxter, I see your name is on this card, but you've never signed it. Please sign it now." The clerk noted her surprise. "Did your aunt not send you one of our signature cards to sign?"

"Is that what it was?" Wynn remembered no such card, but she wasn't saying so now. "I left it at home."

"Well, you can sign it now, right here." The clerk pointed. "Then you have to sign the log-in card, too. And date it so we have a record of who got into the box."

Wynn swallowed. Anyone coming after would know she got into the box. Oh, well. She needed to know, and Roxie meant her to have access at some point or her name wouldn't be here. She signed.

The lock and door opened easily. She slid the box from its slot and placed it on a table.

Wanting to view the contents privately, Wynn went to a small cubicle and shut the door. The box was full of photographs. Wynn was disappointed. She wanted more, a surprising secret revealed. At first, she wondered why these photos couldn't reside safely in one of the albums on Roxie's cottage shelf. However, the answer came as she began to poke through them, the settings and images evoking chills that ran down her body.

All of them were of Wynn at various ages. There was a picture of her with Grammy grocery shopping. She remembered the red coat she wore that winter. It smelled good. The material was soft against her cheek. Another picture was with Uncle Dill at the park. He always pushed her really high on the swings. Another was of her holding onto the railing as she stepped down to get off a school bus.

Ah, there she was holding the blue ribbon for winning the science fair with her project of testing the concentration and effect of minerals and PH in soil and water samples. When they got home that day, there was another card from her mother. Wynn had turned twelve the previous month.

Most of the pictures were taken by a person most likely seated in a vehicle, or someone passing by, or sitting in the back of a room. Wynn was frozen in time, still images of her entire life, ranging from her first year with Grammy, through high school, and college and even her master's degree.

Wynn chewed the inside of her cheek. She took out her camera and spread the pictures out. She'd take her own photos. When she finished, she gathered the photos together.

At the bottom of the box was butcher paper neatly creased into sharp folds. She unfolded it and guessitmated it to be at least ten feet long. It was a timeline. Words were written on it.

Steve, dead. Accident. My fault.

The words made Wynn's heart drop. She sat trying to calm herself. My fault. My fault. It couldn't have been murder or Roxie would have been arrested. Accident. It said. What kind? Blinking back tears, Wynn pulled herself up and tried to steady her wobbly legs. She read down the list.

Ruth and Wynn leave for Steve's parents. Wynn first grade. Won award for reading the most books in her class.

From there it continued on through each year,

including her high school graduation, college graduation, graduate degree, and then abruptly ended after she won the grant.

How odd it began at her dad's death and not Wynn's birth. Her eyes ran with tears as she wondered what made Roxie keep such an odd assortment in a safe deposit box. Her cell phone rang.

"Are you OK?" Doug asked. "We need to get to Clara's if we want to get back in time to make the last ferry of the day."

"I'm so sorry. I got a bit side tracked. Can I make one more stop first? I promise it'll be quick." Her voice was a thin thread.

"Sure. Where?"

"The police department. I want to get a copy of Boone's accident report."

"What for?"

"To read the facts about his death. There's so much gossip and innuendo surrounding the disappearance of his corpse. I want to start with the unbiased information and work my way through the scenario to some reasonable conclusion."

"OK. Are you sure you are OK, cause you sound kind of funny."

"Of course I'm OK. Why wouldn't I be?"

"I'll meet you at the bank."

"I'll be quick." Wynn dumped the pictures back into the box, but slid the timeline into her backpack, and then slipped the strap over her shoulder. The wind had picked up by the time she walked back outside. Clouds were moving in. The sky seemed lower.

She had to find out how her dad died, help find Boone's body so Jackie could have the funeral with closure, and finish her grant. Then what? Only God knew. Why was she thinking about God so much lately?

Doug was waiting for her, truck revved up.

Wynn hopped into his truck and placed the trapped kitten on her lap.

"I see there's a straw in your mouth again."

"Yep. I'm now down to one a day. Pretty soon I won't need them at all."

"Too bad there isn't a straw patch you could wear." She teased.

"Yea, it's hard to kick the habit when they keep putting them in your drinks." He held up an empty foam cup.

"Now just where is your girlfriend's place again?"

"Ex-fiancé."

"I stand corrected." She smiled at the feral kitten. "Where is your ex's feral cat preserve?"

"Kewaunee."

18

Little spits of rain started coming down.

The kitten had turned restless.

Doug pulled off the road and onto a small gravel path. "Almost there," he said. There was no mistaking the joy on his face, a sense of anticipation.

Suddenly she felt a rush of concern—what had she been thinking, coming here to meet Clara? Doug was the first guy in Wynn's entire life that ever held her interest. She hoped he wasn't still harboring old feelings. Broken hearts didn't always heal. Did he want to reconnect? The concern hurt.

The sky was a solid gray. It reminded her of the middle of the ocean without the sound. They faced a sprawling field of grass and large kennels with trees and boulders and small ponds. This definitely was a haven.

A woman approached the truck.

Doug left the keys in the ignition, as he rapidly stepped out onto the grass. He held his arms wide. "Hey, Clara."

"Hey yourself, Doug."

Wynn couldn't hide her surprise as she got out of the truck.

Clara was in her early forties, at least ten years older than Doug, with short brown hair. She was dressed in jeans with a practical blouse. Her boots were splattered with mud. She smiled, a clear open expression on her face. Clara was attractive without trying

Wynn couldn't help but smile back, for the woman was totally at home among the trees and the rich soil, much like Wynn was home in the water and forest.

"What did you bring for me this time, Doug?" Clara's eyebrows rose as she removed her glasses and looked into the cage. "What a pretty gray kitten."

"A feral." There was a smile in his voice.

"Ah, one of the offspring from the cats you trap on your island, I suppose?" she said with a lift of her shoulders before turning to Wynn. "Hi there, I'm Clara."

"Wynn." She held out her hand.

Clara set her glasses at the top of her head and took the cage from Wynn. She turned the cage about to stare at the tiny creature. "Poor little baby. You are scared, aren't you? And also a bit malnourished. Tell you what; I'll put the kitten into isolation until I get a chance to look it over later today. What's its name?"

Doug turned to Wynn.

"Sailor."

"Sailor?"

"I wanted to connect him to where he was found. He might have been dumped at the Federal Reserve by people who might have sailed there."

"Well, Sailor is a good name for this little guy. I like it. Apparently this kitten belongs to you?"

"I'm hoping to bring him home with me."

"Well, it won't be today. I need to run some blood work, and vaccinate first. Perhaps Sailor will be ready for you in a few days."

"I'll be back then."

"I haven't been to Willow Island in a while and I'd

enjoy the trip back. Let me bring Sailor and get him settled in at your place, Wynn."

"That's very thoughtful Clara, thanks."

"And Doug, maybe we can have lunch?"

"I'd like that."

"Come on, let me show you the place, Wynn. Doug, you might be interested in seeing the changes."

After the tour of the grounds, Wynn hugged Clara goodbye and headed to the truck. She sat in the cab trying not to hear their conversation. Then she watched as Doug walked towards the truck.

Clara hung back closer to the house.

They gave a final wave to one another before Doug climbed in and shut the door. After starting the motor, they headed down the gravel drive.

"I like Clara."

"Everyone likes Clara. She is a smart, all around good woman."

"I agree with that assessment."

"But you're smarter. Sweeter." He reached over to squeeze her hand and released it.

"Sweeter?" She chuckled, turning to face the window so he wouldn't catch the blush on her cheeks. "Thanks for thinking so."

"Are you getting shy on me now?"

Her legs were drawn up on the seat as she leaned her forehead against the window. She looked up at the tumbling sky filled with rain and closed her eyes. The space behind her eyelids began to spin.

"What are you thinking, Wynn? You seem so far away." His soft voice floated in her direction.

She thought of the pictures at the bank, now captured on her camera, and the timeline of her life etched out on a carefully folded sheet of paper. She wondered if she should share this with Doug. Things seemed clearer when she said them out loud to him. But maybe she didn't want Doug to know all her secrets. "Have you ever felt like everyone has been invited to a party, but you?"

"All the time." He reached over and took her hand. "Tell me. What is this all about?"

"I was at the bank earlier today while you waited for me. I wanted to check the family safe deposit box."

"I'd like to hear if you'd like to talk."

"OK, remember you asked. If you get bored, or at any point feel it's too much information, just tell me."

"Deal!"

"The first time I thought about returning to the island, I was in sixth grade. You see, my uncles and I came across an article about endangered island species. It raised questions about extinction. I needed to know more. I began thinking about Aunt Roxie living on the island filled with vegetation that I wanted to see. Because she was such a distant memory, I also wanted to connect with her again."

"So why now? Why return now? Why not sooner rather than later?"

"Because I wrote a grant and submitted it. I got it. That's why now."

"And in the mix of your return, you end up with a police report about a missing corpse, and soon will be the owner of a feral cat."

"Uh-huh. That, and much more." Wynn watched the trees go by in a blur. Her mind returned to the day she left the island after her dad's funeral. That was the image she remembered most; along with the sense of loss that never left. Memories of those days living here with her parents were ones she didn't want to throw away. Maybe if she owned something from the island that she could take away to keep, like the kitten, she'd always feel a part of things—reconnected.

"Keep talking."

"There's talk of a silly island curse."

"Perpetuated by my Aunt Wilda. I can't figure her out."

"Speaking of aunts. I have trouble of my own with Aunt Roxie."

"Trouble with Roxie? Can't be. She's a sweetheart."

That was the second time she had heard Doug speak of her aunt in endearing terms. It was obvious he had no clue how Roxie really felt about him and Wynn wouldn't break the news. "Perhaps. But I think she may have had something to do with my dad's death."

"How so?"

"I overheard her tell the ladies of the bridge club, which is really a Bible study, incognito, to keep some secret from me. That piqued my interest. Next, Roxie claims she can't remember how my dad died. Isn't that strange?"

"She is getting older and it was a while ago."

"How can you forget something like that, no matter how old you get? Then, in the glove compartment of the jeep, which she gave to me, I found a love note written to her from someone by the name of Steve. It just so happens that's my dad's name. I can't help but think this isn't just a coincidence. Perhaps there was a tryst between my aunt and my dad that drove my mom from the island soon after his death?"

"Ask Roxie." He hadn't raised his voice, yet there was an irritation that made Wynn wince. Did he disapprove of what she was saying?

"If she won't talk about my dad's death, she certainly isn't about to talk about a sordid affair. Roxie has a security box that I opened today."

"That explains the trip to the bank." His words were nonjudgmental.

"It was filled with pictures of me as I was growing up. But everyone knows I haven't seen Roxie since I was six. There is even a timeline of my life drawn out on butcher paper. It's very precise. Very detailed, complete with pictures glued onto it. Don't you find that creepy?"

"Not creepy at all. I'd say she loved you very much. And it sounds to me as though someone or something kept you away from her. The other day when you showed me the greeting cards from your mom, you were crying and clearly upset because you felt unloved, unwanted. Seems to me you have found love right here on Willow Island and it's in the form of devotion from afar by Roxie."

"Then why did she take all the photos and hide them from me?"

"I don't know the answer to that one. You'll have to ask Roxie that yourself."

"Do you think I should move out of the Tree House?"

"What I think is that you are over-reacting."

"How can you say that when I've been stalked all my life by my aunt?" She looked at him.

"Stalked is a harsh word. It's overly dramatic with a negative connotation."

"OK, how about "followed"? Maybe that word is more pleasing to the ear since family is involved. She followed me for most of my life."

"Ask yourself why. Why would she do this? To harm you?"

"I-I-I don't know. I don't think so." Wynn wanted to tell Doug about what Roxie had written about causing her dad's accident, but held back.

"I don't know Roxie that well. But I would say she loves you and for some reason wasn't allowed to be a part of your life, so she did the next best thing. She made sure that you were all right. When you love someone, you want contact. You want to be with them as much as possible."

She felt ashamed.

Doug drifted in and out of the lanes. He sped up without warning, and then slowed through the small towns.

"Tell me…"

"Tell you…what...?" He looked at her from the corner of his eye.

"What about Clara? How did you meet and what ended it?" she asked in a rush, her pulse ticking.

"Some things aren't meant to be."

"Evasive, aren't you? I opened up. Now it's your turn."

"OK. You asked. But remember if it becomes too much information just tell me."

Wynn burst out laughing. "Deal."

"I lived in Chicago at the time. My friends said that I was too good at being single."

"What in the world does that mean?"

"It means I was really comfortable being alone. I didn't feel the need for anyone to get close. Finally, I agreed to a string of blind dates. All of them were awful. One time, I was in a pub on Lake View waiting for my most recent meet up while talking to a couple of women. She walked in, took one look at me and announced, 'You are not my type!'" I followed her out onto the street."

"Clara?" Wynn started to relax, even enjoying the conversation.

"Clara. She said I was a player."

"Is she right? Are you a player?" Wynn remembered Roxie saying Doug was a heartbreaker.

"Nah! Somehow I convinced her to give me another chance. We had dinner. Talked about what we wanted out of life. It was then things became clearer to me. I wanted to sell my business and return to Willow Island. I was tired of creating things out of metal and pavement. I wanted to restore and preserve nature. Nothing else mattered. It wasn't long after that, Clara moved to the island to be with me. For a while, we were happy. Making wedding plans, and then she bolted."

"Why?"

"I still don't know."

"So we have another woman keeping secrets."

"We have that in common."

They reached the dock. Afternoon had bled into night.

"We just made it. Last crossing of the day."

Cars lined up for the journey were a block long. The traffic edged forward and halted.

"Do you miss her?"

"Nah." His answer was soft.

Was his answer truthful?

19

The ferry navigated the dark, opaque waters. The roar of the engine reverberated across the sea creating a large foamy wake behind the stern.

Doug and Wynn looked over the police report together. The document raised more questions than it answered.

"This is what I'm getting from the report: Boone, while crossing the street, was hit and killed by a truck. His body was taken to the coroner's office, tagged, covered, and put into a cooler. Supposedly, Jackie was called. She identified the body in person, asking for it to be cremated."

"Odd, isn't it?" Doug leaned over and put his arm lightly around her shoulder.

"What is?"

"No eye witness report. The truck driver was jailed and later released the same day. He has a clear driving record and they feel he wasn't at fault for the accident."

"Does it say anything about Boone's luggage?" Wynn leaned back, enjoying the feel of his arm on her back.

Doug pulled the report from her and flipped through it, checking to see if she had missed anything. "Not a word."

"He just came from overseas. There had to be luggage. What happened to it?"

"Think one of the bystanders took off with it? No. There is no mention of it."

"Or he dropped it off someplace."

Doug looked into Wynn's eyes and smiled.

Her pulse raced.

Doug ran his finger around her lips. "What are you thinking?"

"Something Aunt Roxie told me when I was little."

"And what did Aunt Roxie tell you when you were little?"

"If you can't be pretty, at least be mysterious."

Doug burst out laughing. "But you're pretty and mysterious. So what do I do now?"

"Enjoy." She teased, rubbing her nose against his. Time accelerated when she was with Doug. She wished the day could start all over again. It was hard not to ask when she'd see him again.

As though sensing her mood, Doug lifted her chin and looked into her eyes. "I enjoyed today. We should do it again sometime." His words were comforting, reassuring.

Hope spiked, electrifying her. Wynn shivered and rubbed her bare arms. "I wish I had thought to bring a sweater."

"If I had thought to bring my jacket, I would have already offered it to you." Doug's gaze shifted to the shore. "Hey. What's happening on the island?"

Up ahead, the night sky was filled with flashing emergency vehicle lights.

"I didn't know the island had that many police, or rescue power."

"They don't. I suspect some of those vehicles were powered over by special ferry. I haven't seen anything like this since city kids ran a boat up on shore into a group of people, killing some. Something nasty has happened for that much activity."

Everyone on the ferry had noticed the commotion. Those on deck had moved to the railing, while the rest got out of their vehicles to get a better view.

Two police boats approached on either side of the ferry. One of the officers spoke through a bull horn. "Cut your motors, we're coming on board."

Within moments, the ferry was silently drifting on the waves, as six policemen came over the side of the boat.

Wynn leaned into Doug.

He pulled her tight into his side and pressed his arm around her.

"Who are they looking for?"

Doug shrugged.

Then one of the police officers from the island pointed towards them. "There he is!"

Doug's eyes widened. He took a step back in confusion, pulling Wynn with him, trying to protect her by enveloping her in his arms.

"Look! He's holding her hostage!" someone shouted.

"Help her before she's killed!" another voice hollered.

Three officers lunged towards him.

Wynn was smacked in the face with an elbow as they wrestled, trying to pry her from his hold. One of the officers hooked his leg around one of Doug's, making him release his grip. Then, he twisted Doug straight into a wall, planted his hands above his head and frisked him before placing handcuffs on his wrists. The officer turned him around and made a big show, as Doug remained too bewildered to move.

"What's this all about?" Doug asked.

Bystanders screamed and shouted questions. The turmoil was so loud that Wynn couldn't hear anything and stood helpless, unable to think what could be wrong. Dozens of gazes were on them.

"We've got who we came for," one of the officers said brusquely. "So there's no reason for anyone to feel nervous."

"What did he do? Why is he being taken into custody?"

The questions were ignored as Doug was pulled towards the side of the ferry. He looked back at Wynn in total disbelief.

Wynn was released. She fled to the railing.

Doug was lowered into one of the waiting police boats, which headed back to the mainland.

"Doug! Doug!" she called.

Passengers stood in frozen silence, watching.

An elderly man held out a handkerchief.

Wynn blinked hard at the offering.

"You're bleeding. Are you all right?"

It was then she felt the stabbing pain on her cheek. She accepted the handkerchief and thanked him.

The ferry's engine started again and went towards its destination. Finally the boat slowed, turned and backed into the slip, jerking to a stop.

The passengers ran to their vehicles or gathered at the exit gate.

Wynn pushed ahead, anxious to get off the vessel and back onto land.

Doug's truck was guarded by a police officer. Two others were in the process of impounding the vehicle.

"What is going on?" Wynn cried.

A chorus of voices rose, and above it all she heard

the word, murder. No one would speak with her, however. Wynn ran to her jeep and drove to Aunt Roxie's house, ignoring the speed limits. Pulling into the drive next to the cottage, she spotted the Bible study women's vehicles.

Wynn shot out of her jeep and flung open the back kitchen door.

"Roxie!" Wynn hollered.

"Living room, dear!"

Wynn knew she appeared as a crazed person with her windblown hair, the scratch on her cheek and her clothing in disarray. She noticed the blood on her blouse. Not wanting to alarm anyone, she stopped in the doorway of the unlit hall, unseen.

Roxie set her teacup onto the saucer. "There you are Wynn. We've been looking all over for you. There's some terrible, terrible news. Come in. There is much to tell you."

"Then you know what happened to Doug? That's why you're all here at this time of the evening?"

"Wynn, there's blood on your shirt. And what happened to your face?" Roxie jumped to her feet.

"Compliments of the arresting officers."

"What are you saying?"

"I was with Doug when it happened." Wynn shook with rage.

"You were with Doug?" Roxie's sympathy quickly turned to anger. "Tell me you're kidding."

"I spent the day with Doug on the mainland and was still with him when the police took him off the ferry, in handcuffs."

"Look at the suffering he caused you. Faith, would you please get my first aide box. It's in the kitchen next to the stove."

"Yes."

"No Faith, don't. I'm OK."

"Why did you go to the mainland with that man? I told you never to have anything to do with him!" Roxie balled her hands up into a fist.

"Roxie, I'm no longer a little girl. I make up my own mind what I should and shouldn't do."

"Maybe they bumped into each other." Sheri inserted.

"That's actually true. We met while crossing on the ferry." Wynn wasn't backing down. She'd match Roxie's intensity. "It's not the first time I've been with him."

"How can you speak to me in this way?"

"Doug is a good man. Did you know that he even speaks highly of you, Aunt Roxie? He has no clue that you degrade him at every opportunity." Wynn's hands shook with rage. Her cheek throbbed.

Owl's firm hands touched her shoulders. "What's happened to Doug? Why did the police take him to the mainland?"

"Because they found Boone's body." Roxie said, looking at Owl.

"Oh, no. But what does that have to do with Doug?" Wynn's voice rose with despair.

"The body was on Doug's schooner!" Roxie exclaimed.

"That can't be true!"

"It is." Roxie folded her hands together.

"Then someone else placed his body there. But I don't understand. Boone was hit by a car, right? So why are they arresting Doug?"

"Someone thinks it might be murder."

"What?" Wynn looked around. It was only then

she noticed Jackie wasn't there. "Where's Jackie? Is she OK?"

"Agatha is with her at the morgue, identifying the body," Faith said. "We're all upset with the news, but let's not jump to any conclusions for Jackie's sake, as well as Doug's. Let's also remember that Owl is Doug's aunt and she has concerns of her own. When we are together, this needs to be a place of comfort and peace. No accusations. No division."

"I agree with Faith," Sheri chimed. "This is a highly charged atmosphere and the last thing we need to do is to turn on one another."

"Let's take a deep breath and sit down." Faith patted an armchair for Wynn.

"No more negative talk about anyone. Roxie, do you agree?" Faith asked.

"Agreed." Roxie sat.

"And Wynn, be softer to your aunt."

"Now then, let's do what we are really good at. Praying. Together." Faith held her hand out to Owl. Owl held her hand to Roxie. Roxie held her hand to Wynn. Wynn held her hand to Sheri and Sheri took Faith's.

"Bind us together Lord in one accord, be of one mind. Let all the anger and tension in this room melt in your Presence. May we be a source of hope and comfort to Owl whose nephew has been taken into custody. Lord, may Jackie find peace at this time of her husband's passing. Lord, may Roxie and Wynn hold each other up in prayer and allow for all misunderstandings to be resolved and let the truth come out. Let the truth also come out about who murdered Boone. Be with Doug in his hour of need. And may we have love for on another that passes all understanding."

"Amen." They chorused.

Wynn wondered what truth Faith was referring to.

"There's something you all don't know. Something I haven't told anyone, including Doug." Wynn hesitated.

"What?" Sheri asked. "Would you like to tell us now?"

"I found Agatha's brooch on Doug's schooner a few days ago. You know that one she wears at her throat and is always touching?"

"Where is it now?" Roxie asked.

"It's at the Tree House."

"What are you saying, Wynn?" Owl wanted to know.

"I'm not saying anything. I don't want to accuse someone who might be innocent, as Doug has been."

"So, what? What does Agatha's brooch prove, Wynn?" Roxie asked.

"Anyone and everyone has access to Doug's schooner. I have no idea how that brooch got there, but however it did, whether by Agatha's hand or another's, I found it there."

"OK, let's play the devil's advocate. Let's say Doug is guilty. Sorry, Owl. What would be Doug's motive for killing Boone, anyway?" Faith asked.

The women looked around the room at one another.

"Money?" Sheri asked.

"Doug has all the money he will ever want. Not only did he sell his very lucrative Chicago business, but he inherited a huge sum from his family which he has never touched. Not a dime of it. Besides he's the least materialistic person in the world," Owl said.

"Could he be in love with Jackie? Love triangles are dicey," Roxie said.

"Never. If he loves anyone, it's that woman he was engaged to a while back. What was her name?" Faith looked up trying to remember.

"Clara," Wynn said.

"That's right!"

"What is his motive, then?"

"None."

"That's right, none." Wynn agreed with Owl.

"Well, we will have to wait on evidence, you know. But I agree with Faith that we cannot jump to conclusions. The man is innocent until proven guilty." Sheri surmised. "That's just how things work, even on this island."

"Who could have done away with Boone and stashed his body in the schooner?" Roxie asked.

"And why?" Owl asked.

"Ladies, we have a lot of praying to do." Faith smoothed her skirt.

Roxie went into the kitchen. She returned with a frozen package of peas and handed it to Wynn.

Wynn held it to her face and smiled at her aunt. "Thanks."

The women embraced one another before saying goodnight. Wynn was passed around in the same circle they had prayed in, from hug to hug. She loved these women, and she loved Aunt Roxie, too.

Roxie held Wynn's face in her hands. "Forgive me."

"For what?"

"For all the words I've spoken that have been less than kind."

"Then forgive me as well." Wynn pulled out the

key to the security deposit box and pressed it into Roxie's hand. "Goodnight." She avoided her aunt's gaze. She couldn't bear to see disappointment in them. Wynn walked out to her jeep, expecting her aunt to call her back and read her the riot act. But Roxie didn't.

The porch light went off, as did the kitchen and living room lights.

Wynn started up the engine when she saw the bedroom light go on. At the Tree House, Wynn opened all the windows to the night air. This morning was so filled with promise and it ended filled with blame.

The air was humid and Wynn lay in bed listening to the quiet shifting of the trees moving in harmony with the rhythmic tide from the shore.

"OK, God, it's me again. I think I need to start forgiving some people. It's time. Sometimes, I line up all those I am mad at and just shoot hatred at them. It feels really bad. I don't want to do that anymore. Help me know how that works. I don't want to be angry with Roxie, but she's so hard on everyone. When I heard all the things she said about Doug, it occurred to me that I have been pretty tough on Roxie, on my mom, and You, too. Can You forgive me for that? And exactly how does forgiveness work?"

20

They sat beneath the old McIntosh apple tree on timeworn Adirondack chairs.

Wynn was drenched with perspiration. As she reached for a bottle of water, her gaze connected with Roxie's—but only for a moment. There was so much she desired to discuss, yet she was unsure of how to start the conversation.

Clearly, Roxie was furious with her for prying.

"I know I betrayed your trust. I probably need to move out of the Tree House."

"There's a biology position opening at the local high school. I'd love to see you apply. I have a lot of pull with the school board."

"It's really not necessary."

"They pay good benefits. In a few years, you'll be thirty and its time you realize the joy of good benefits."

"Not sure teaching is my forte."

"Of course it is. It's in your blood and mine. The island is pricy, but you may live here as long as you like, and never pay anything. You're written into my will as sole beneficiary. Someday you will own this place."

Wynn sat dumbfounded over Roxie's offer and her not so veiled hint at something. "I don't deserve your generosity..."

"It's what I always planned. I'm not about to change my mind." Roxie crossed one leg over the other and impatiently swung her leg.

"This is where my apology is supposed to go. I am very sorry, Aunt Roxie—about everything."

"I have been thinking about this all night. Not only have you snooped through my belongings, you also raided my security box. I hope you're satisfied with your findings."

"Stumped. I'm stumped." Wynn glanced at her aunt. "Why all the pictures of me? Why stow them away and not put in an album in your cottage?"

"I didn't want you to get the wrong impression that I was spying on you, or something. "

"But isn't that exactly what you did?"

"I wouldn't call it that. I would call it watching you grow up. Besides, I had to keep my distance because of the court order." Roxie's hand flew up to her mouth.

"Court order?"

Roxie looked towards the sea. "It was your mother's doing."

"What a drastic action to take."

"It was." Her voice hummed against her throat.

"What happened to make my mother resort to a court order?"

"Nothing. Really, nothing." Roxie became more agitated.

"People aren't granted restraining orders for no reason."

"My turn to quiz you. What would you call going through my belongings?"

"Research."

Roxie burst out laughing. "Touché. Thanks for the laugh. I really needed it right now."

"Why didn't you just come back into my life?"

Wynn wanted to know. "Once my mother was gone you had free reign. My uncles wouldn't have objected."

"You don't know that."

"You could have gone to court and gotten things overturned. My mother was no longer there to stop you. I was…abandoned."

"I don't know. Maybe I was afraid you would turn me away. Besides, you had excellent caretakers with your uncles. Another change wouldn't have been good for you."

"What aren't you saying?"

Roxie shook her head.

"You've given me a boatload of excuses ever since I've come back to the island." Wynn closed her eyes. "My life is filled with murky shadows. I need to get at the truth. It's so close, but I just can't see it. I can't find it."

"You're talking about your dad, now, and how he died."

"I called his doctor once. He said it was due to a heart attack, but I have my doubts."

"Your mother is overseas and your dad is gone. Can't we just put the past away once and for all, and build on what we have today?"

"I want to be close with you, but something holds me at bay."

"I thought when you returned, we'd at last be as close as I had always hoped."

"I've disappointed you."

"Disappointed, yes. But not with you. Never with you. Only with the results. We seem to be on opposite ends of issues, just as I always seemed to be with your mother."

"And with Doug."

"The man is a fool."

"We all make mistakes."

"Some more than others." She repeated, "Some more than others."

"Is Doug any worse than anyone else?"

"Definitely."

"I need an example."

"Oh yes, the scientific mind that keeps you from God, requires that theories be proven. Here is your example. He gave up a perfectly lucrative business in Chicago to what? Save trees on some small island when people want to build more houses so they can live here. It's good for economic growth."

"Oh please, let's prefer brick and mortar to trees and wildlife."

Roxie ignored the comment.

"You should get to know him, personally. I have. I think he's a great guy."

"Don't get your heart too set on him. He'll leave you high and dry just as your mom did."

"That was hurtful!" Wynn protested.

"But the truth," Roxie said earnestly. "It's time we both face facts. The past cannot be rewritten."

"I just want the truth."

"OK, here is the truth. Did you know that Doug was once engaged to a perfectly lovely woman? It ended when he had a fling with some air-headed summer girl vacationing with her parents. What a fool he made of himself, too. Imagine a thirty something year old man love-sick over an eighteen-year-old girl. How can he ever be taken seriously again?"

Now she knew why Clara broke it off and left the island. If what Roxie said was true then perhaps the other things she said about Doug were, too. If so, then she had sorely misjudged the man. Wynn wondered if loneliness finally had become so consuming that she'd reach out to anyone who showed her a bit of kindness and attention. Was she really that needy? Perhaps so.

"His entire family has no social graces whatsoever. And rude—you've seen that with Owl when she grabbed your éclair." She rubbed the back of her neck. "Rude. A year ago I was at the fishing dock when he bumped into me, causing me to trip and fall into the water. Did he jump in after me? No, he laughed. Laughed! And just reached down and pulled me back onto the dock. It tore my brand new capris—no apology followed."

Wynn gave a belly laugh. "I am so glad you made it to shore all on your own. I am woman, hear me roar!"

"Go ahead and laugh." Roxie bit back her own smile. "But a true gentleman would have thrown himself into the water to save me! Even if I was in just four feet of water. As far as I'm concerned, it's just another bad mark against his character."

"Do you realize that you're the only person I've heard who says degrading things about Doug? What I've heard is Doug is a wonderful businessman and his nursery business is quite profitable."

"He may be a great businessman, but he's still a lousy gentleman. No real people skills," she said defiantly. "Speaking of the Reed family, I might as well tell you the other news."

"Joseph Reed has been found. I know. Sheri broke the news to me. Why didn't you tell me?"

"Slipped my mind."

"How can a two-century-old solved mystery slip

your mind?"

"Listen to me, you need to know and prepare yourself. Doug is about to go before a really tough magistrate. I know him. S. Thomas Miller is his name, and if there is an inkling of guilt, Doug won't be set free. Just keep your heart safe from disappointment."

"Is that what happened to you? You've had so many disappointments that you've become jaded in measure? It seems like you are the one who needs to be set free." Her voice was edgier than she had intended.

"What are you talking about?"

"You say you have the most wonderful gift of salvation, but you're not happy. You're totally miserable and almost rejoice in other's misfortunes."

"I do not!" Roxie puffed.

"There are prisons without bars, and you are in one."

Roxie began to sniffle and wipe tears from under her eyes.

"Aunt Roxie, have you been criticized harshly during your life?"

"What are you talking about?" Roxie's eyes widened as she stared at her niece.

"You read the Bible all the time. The chapters I've been reading are about forgiveness and mercy. But you don't give those gifts to others. You hold grudges. I've wondered why. It just occurred to me that perhaps someone has been too hard on you, so in turn, you get hard on others to even up the score."

"Now you're being cruel and thankless for all I've done." Roxie's gaze clouded and she crossed her arms.

"Thank you for your generous offer of putting in a good word with the school board and asking me to remain with you on the island. But there will always be something hanging between us. As soon as my grant is complete, I plan on packing up. Under the circumstances I will be leaving the Jeep here."

"You can't be serious."

"I am serious." Wynn stood. "Whatever happened years ago between Mom, Dad, and you affects us to this day."

"But I still have hope for us. Remain through the winter, anyway. This just might be our last chance."

"Roxie, that can't be good for either of us."

"It won't be good for us if you leave. Where will you go?"

"I don't know. But I can't stay here. I've ruined things."

"Your home is here."

"I wanted it to be here. I did. But it's too hard. And—I've betrayed you."

"I don't care. I forgive you. I give you back my trust." Now tears ran down Roxie's face.

"But don't you see, you don't have my trust. I'm so sorry. There are just too many secrets, too many hurtful words have been spoken, and not enough true words have been offered."

An awkward pause followed.

Wynn's face burned with tears.

"Please." Roxie looked forlorn.

Wynn's heart went out to her, but she couldn't offer empty promises. She glanced at her watch again. "Sorry, I have to go and meet someone." Wynn returned to the Tree House where Clara waited with Sailor.

21

Clara's Levis hugged her ample hips. A pretty lace top with see-through sleeves was in keeping with the clean slip-on shoes which had buttons at the toes. Her hair was piled on top of her head in a messy manner, held there by a single clip. Her smile was wide, punctuated with dimples on each side of her mouth. Of course, she expected to have lunch with Doug.

"Hey, Wynn. I've got your little guy here with a clean bill of health." Clara smiled. "What's wrong? You look troubled."

"You haven't heard about Doug?"

"No. I called his cell right before you. No answer. I even drove by his place, but his truck wasn't there. I thought he might be waiting here with you."

"His truck is impounded. Something terrible happened."

"Oh no, what? Tell me." Clara reached for her hand.

"Doug is OK. There was a body found on his schooner, and the police are holding him for questioning."

"When did this happen?" Clara's hand went over her heart.

"While taking the ferry back from your place. Wynn explained what the others had told her. "The police took him right off the boat. He should be arraigned soon. His lawyer says he expects charges should be dropped. But you never know. That's what worries me."

"Poor Doug. Can he have visitors?"

"I'm not sure. Can you stay until the morning? Maybe we can visit him together. I've wanted to see him."

"I have to get back to take care of my cats, so I can't do an overnight. But if I can catch the later ferry over in a few hours, I might have time to stop by the jail."

"Doug can use all the support he can get."

"Come on. Let's get the kitten settled. We can talk about this later. Let's try to calm down so Sailor doesn't pick up on our tension. We want the first introduction to your place to be a positive one."

"No negative vibes." Wynn agreed. "Come on, follow me."

Wynn had placed fresh food and water down for Sailor in the bathroom. A few feet away was the new litter box. Serving as a secure hideaway, Wynn had placed a fuzzy rug for the kitten to curl up in.

"Looks good." Clara glanced about the room. "We'll sit in here for a few minutes while Sailor becomes acclimated to the surroundings." She set the cage on the floor and closed the bathroom door. "Because Sailor is still young, he has a chance of being tamed, but I still wouldn't bet on it happening quickly. Show patience, he has had little or no human contact. Allow Sailor to initiate contact with you. He will approach when he is ready."

"How long will that take?"

"It could take weeks or months, if ever." Clara looked a bit sad. "You need patience. Lots of it. When you feed Sailor, sit on the floor with him, like I'm doing now. Try to get him to associate food with you. Also play. Get a soft interactive toy so he will start associating you with fun. When he's ready to be touched, rub his shoulders and the back of his neck. It releases endorphins." Clara slowly opened the door on the cage.

They watched as the kitten stayed huddled at the back.

"You'll do fine. Just take your time." She told Wynn.

"I will. I really appreciate all your help. How much do I owe you?"

"Doug took care of it." Clara looked away. "Poor Doug. I hope the situation resolves itself quickly."

"Me, too."

"He's such an incredible guy. Creative. Don't you love Doug's lighthouse?"

"I've only seen it off the coast."

"He's never taken you there? I can't believe he hasn't shown you the place. He is so proud of where he lives."

"I'd love to see it. Do you think we could drive by today?"

"Sure, come on, let's go for a drive." She closed the door.

The sixty foot lighthouse had been restored. Painted red and trimmed in black horizontal stripes, the foundation was on a small peninsula filled with eddy stones. The cupola lantern room roof had been restored as well as the spiral staircase.

They walked around the base of the building, and Clara tugged on the door. "Darn. Doug usually leaves it unlocked. Weird he didn't this time."

The grass along the shore was bright green. Waves

crashed against the seawall and the spray blew in Wynn's face, making her feel the earth itself would rise up and embrace her. "Maybe he wanted it secure before leaving for the mainland a few days ago. He knew it would be a full day trip to your place and back."

"It never bothered him in the past. We even got into an argument about it once. By the way, I was wondering something."

"What?"

"Are you and Doug serious? Ah, you don't need to answer that. I'm just being nosy, now."

"I don't mind answering. If I were to define our relationship, I would say we're mainly friends, with the hope of something more. At least, that's how I feel."

"It's nice to start out that way; as friends." Clara led the way back to her truck.

"Is that how you two started out?"

"Ah, golly no. It just quickly ran its course."

"I'm not sure what you mean by 'running its course'."

"The flames blew out. Fast. In less than a year."

"What happened?" Wynn recalled Roxie's words. "Was there someone else?"

"No. No one for either of us. We just decided we didn't have enough in common, we were too far apart with how we viewed life."

"I heard that there was a crush on some young woman."

"Who told you that? Oh wait; there was a rumor once before we split. It was when he bought the schooner. He bought it from a man on the mainland. I think he had a daughter who had a crush on Doug. But he wasn't interested. She did start nasty rumors, though. Is that what you're talking about?"

"Might be. I heard that rumor just today."

"These island people need to stop the gossip. Listen, I didn't leave because of anything Doug did or didn't do. I left because I wanted to be on my own. I am a pretty self-sufficient gal and I hate anyone being in my business, or in my space. But in my opinion, Doug needs someone to share a space with. You might be the one for him."

Wynn felt a blush rising on her cheeks.

"Come on, I'll take you back to your place. I'll check on Sailor one more time before heading back."

At the Tree House, they hugged goodbye.

Wynn promised to stay in touch with Clara about Doug's situation.

As Clara backed out she called out the window. "If he needs me, I will come in a moment's notice. I'll let him know that about you, too."

22

Roxie had influence.

Wynn thought it might be worth a try for Roxie to use that with the judge on Doug's case. Wynn called, but there was no answer at her aunt's house. There was a possibility Roxie was avoiding her.

Wynn opened the bathroom door carefully to prevent Sailor from flying out, and just as quick, she shut it again as she stepped inside.

Sailor preferred to be invisible, pressed against the wall that was nearly the same color as him.

She held out a pungent treat of tuna that made his whiskers stir. Wynn placed a small piece in front of him.

Sailor moved forward, and then took the food.

Wynn left another piece of tuna, but this time he snatched the food before returning to the wall.

"How I would love to touch you, but I better wait." Wynn undressed and filled the bathtub with chamomile bath salts. The moment her body sank into the water, she nearly moaned in relief. The tension in her shoulders began to ebb.

Unfortunately, the water did nothing to relax her brain. She kept thinking about Doug. If the police found more evidence pointing to his guilt, he'd certainly be sitting in jail until trial. It seemed impossible for Doug to hurt another human, considering how protective he was of her on the island, but did she really know him enough to make that assumption? Was he planning to dump Boone overboard where he would never be found? If so, why did he wait?

What would be the motive? Could the so-called 'priceless' ring, that hardly a soul had ever viewed, be the motive for murder?

And Roxie was adamant about his untrustworthiness.

Wynn rung out a washcloth and folded it in half to lie across her forehead as she dipped further into the bath.

The body was found on Doug's schooner. Surely, the police would realize it was placed there after the fact. Boone had died weeks ago, and Doug had taken her out on the schooner since then. Which raised another question: where had the body been kept in the meantime? The questions raised by the Bible study ladies kept circling.

"Meow."

She opened her eyes to the kitten sitting on top of the closed toilet lid staring at her. "Progress." She whispered.

After her bath, Wynn shut the door so the kitten would feel safe. Before she fell into bed, she tried Roxie again, but just as before, no one answered. Next, she called Owl to see if Doug had been charged or released, but Owl's answering machine picked up. Wynn left a message.

A paw poked from beneath the closed bathroom door. She knelt down to touch the soft, furry pad, and then two paws appeared. Wynn quickly touched one again, enjoying the warm softness of its coat before the kitten jerked it away.

How nice it would be to sleep with the kitten. But it had to be on her terms. She opened the door and returned to bed, turning off lamps along the way.

By the light of the moon, she was able to keep track of the kitten's movements. He disappeared into the shadow of the room. Quiet followed.

Wynn lay still, hoping the kitten would jump up on the bed and find a comfortable sleeping spot, but nothing happened.

Wynn slept fitfully. Hours later when she opened her eyes, the first thing she saw was the kitten sitting near her face.

"Hi there, Sweetie." Wynn kept her voice low and soft. She held still while the kitten stared. Wynn lifted one shoulder off the bed. "I can't wait to hold you." She moved her fingers slightly which sent the kitten skidding across the floor and back into the bathroom.

Wynn got breakfast for Sailor. "Yes, it's me feeding you. Make that brain imprint please." Then she made toast and chugged a glass of milk while scanning her recent notes.

The TV news pulled her attention. News reporters from as far away as Florida had ferried over to get the latest. There were TV crews and dozens of curious citizens standing outside the one room police station. A barricade had been set up to keep everyone at bay. If Wynn hadn't been so concerned about Doug, she might have found the scene rather amusing. Even the island curse was mentioned.

The next few days Wynn became absorbed in her work, cataloging specimens, writing up notes, taking breaks to eat, sleep and play with Sailor. She could do nothing to help Doug, except wait for whatever was to come.

On a clear afternoon as she ate a sandwich the decorative container caught her eye. Marilyn and Jackie were both looking for the ruby ring. What if it was inside the container? Wynn grabbed a sharp knife from the drawer and worked at the lock, Sailor sniffing at her toes.

At last it popped. She pulled off the lock and tugged at the lid, but it was jammed. She snatched a bottle opener from the utensil drawer. The lid gave way and clattered to the floor sending Sailor back to the bathroom.

She removed the old cotton. An instrument with miniature gears, roller, and a crank was in there. Wynn turned the little crank and music played in light tones.

It was the song her mother always sang. The song she had lost the words to, 'true till death.' A warm happy feeling suffused as some of the words came to her "I put my dreams in down by the water. That's where I'll find him."

Her cell buzzed. Wynn looked at the number and snatched up the phone. "Doug, where are you?"

"Wynn, could you meet me at the lighthouse tomorrow morning?"

She agreed, filled with curiosity. The next morning, she raced out of the Tree House and down the lane.

He drank strong coffee, she drank tea. They sat on the ledge of the cupola lantern roof room of the lighthouse. He had fabulous views out of every window but the view from the top was the most amazing. She looked out at blue sky that curved into the spinning motion of the waves. It was mesmerizing.

"Do you think heaven is like this?"

"Blue water? Tea? Coffee?"

"No, silly." She nudged him. "Perfect."

"Heaven is perfect, but I'm not so sure you can compare it to the sea. Water can be very dangerous—looks calm and inviting on the surface, but once you get in it, the pull can take you places you don't want to go. More than one person has lost their life to it. It's good to be here with you."

"How are you?"

"Fine."

"No, that answer was too automatic." She picked up his hand. "I want to know how you really are."

"It was tough, but it's going to be tougher with everyone wondering if I really killed Boone, and if I didn't, why his body was found on my schooner."

"Do you have any answers?"

"No clue and cannot think of one person on this island who would do harm to another, especially not to Boone. He was a mild mannered, honest businessman. Likeable guy."

Every morning before she got out of bed and each night before she fell asleep, she prayed for Doug. It was a secret between herself and God.

"Do you think God hears all our prayers?"

"Of course. No doubt about it."

"That's good, then." She studied his face. The fixed set of his lips. The robust line of shoulders. The gaze of a man who knew what he was about. Deep gray eyes that had an air of secrecy. Even though tired, he looked handsomely roughed to Wynn; he was freshly showered with a smile that ruined her.

She leaned forward. The small space between them sparked.

He ran his fingers through his short hair and expelled a pent up breath, as though he felt the same electricity.

"Doug, I want to make your day."

"Sounds interesting." He moved closer until their hips touched. "Give it a whirl."

"I think this whole mystery has to do with the missing ruby ring."

"Are you referring to the ring that once belonged to my family?"

"There are paintings at the Inn by Anna Reed which shows her wearing it."

A gleam came into Doug's eyes. The satisfaction on his face made Wynn smile. Something slow and tender in her chest unfurled.

"I found out there are more of Anna's pictures in an art gallery in Greenbay."

"We should go look at them." Doug pronounced. "You and me."

"We should."

"When will this take place?" he asked.

"After the funeral we'll ride over there to look at them."

23

Wynn hit the gravel at the side of the road, inhaling sharply at the chilly sting of the night air. Then she was off and running while thinking about Doug and the unexpected connection she felt with him.

She'd been focused since she was a child on saving plant and animal life, especially the endangered species. It became her mission.

Doug listened to what she had to say; comforted her, shared the love of the sea, had a common goal of protecting the environment—and now, perhaps he needed her. They needed each other.

Was love blooming? Only time would tell.

She ran for a long time, with the lake air cool and fresh against her cheeks. Finally, she stood along the rocky coastal cliffs taking in the panoramic view and fully understanding why people wanted to live here; why Roxie never left. Wynn looked down the shore and noticed Roxie's lights were still on so she headed in that direction.

The Bible study women were clustered around Roxie's TV set, eating their dessert of the week, fresh key lime pie. They were listening to the latest about Douglas Reed's release from custody. As Wynn walked into the room, Roxie gave a small nod of greeting.

Wynn opened her mouth to give Jackie her condolences, but was quickly shushed and handed a piece of pie.

When the segment was over, the women turned away from the TV.

"I thought you met in the mornings." Wynn took a bite of pie.

"It was an impromptu meeting." Roxie smoothed her skirt. "I tried calling you, dear."

"I don't run with my cell."

"It was so impromptu that I was ready for bed when the call came." Owl patted her hair, still wound in pink foam rollers. Her frame was covered by a dark muumuu with a yellow-paisley print.

"I'm so thankful I have Boone's body to bury." Jackie's gaze flickered around the room.

"Owl, I've spent the day with Doug and am relieved he's doing well and feeling positive about his situation. And Jackie, I'm here for you if you, too, if you need anything."

"Thanks, but I don't think I will need anything from you, or from Doug, for that matter." Jackie snipped.

"What are you implying?" Wynn looked at Jackie as all the other women studied their feet.

"You just made it perfectly clear that you feel Doug is innocent. I am not pointing the finger at him, but he hasn't been cleared, either. Until this matter is straightened out, I won't be having either of you to my home. Surely you and Roxie, and the rest of the women here understand my feelings. Right?"

The women uncomfortably shifted in their chairs.

"I do understand and thank you for being so clear and forthright on the matter." Wynn set her pie down.

"My nephew is going through a very hard time right now. I'm thankful for the support of Wynn." Owl covered her eyes and her shoulders convulsed.

"Ladies! We must remember that everyone here is affected by what happened and no one more than Jackie." Faith smiled sadly. "And Owl."

"Thank you Faith. Instead of holding a flesh and blood human being responsible, some want to hold the island curse responsible." Jackie rolled her eyes. "Imagine."

"About time the island curse gets some publicity again now that Joseph Reed was found." Sheri's spoon left a swipe of meringue on her nose. "I'm thinking about ordering a toy mummy in a basket for the shop."

"So it was Joseph's body?" Wynn asked.

"Yes, they know it's a Reed relative, and the age of the mummy indicates it's him." Sheri replied.

"Mummy...sounds a bit like Halloween." Faith mused.

"Agreed, but I may be able to parlay it into a hot selling item."

"You have a real gift for that." Owl concurred.

"Does anyone know who placed Joseph Reed's body in that coffin trying to pass him off as Boone?" Wynn looked from face to face.

"It just shows that someone was trying to cover up a murder, so perhaps it was an accident?" Faith murmured.

"Where has Joseph Reed's body been all this time?" Roxie asked.

"Perhaps this can be termed as another island mystery." Sheri seemed most pleased.

"It seems to me the cases are totally linked: Boone's death, Joseph Reed's body placed in the coffin, and the stranger who was cremated."

"And here I thought you were a scientist, Wynn, but I see now you are really a detective!" Jackie looked ready for a full blown snit.

"Are there witnesses, Jackie, or are you going on blind accusation, like the police?" Wynn flinched.

"Wynn!" Faith cut her off primly.

"Doug's an environmentalist. But a murderer?—could he be a murderer?" Sheri asked to no one in particular. "I can't see it."

"Me, either." Wynn's voice dropped. "Thanks Sheri."

"Owl, are you having a funeral for your ancestor?" Roxie asked.

"Oh, my, yes. He's what has made this island famous over the years. I refer to it as 'hosting' the funeral. I am imagining a big island festival. I'm thinking parade. However, it's only polite that Boone have his funeral first." Owl stabbed the air with her fork before scooping another piece of pie.

"Maybe the festival should be put off until Doug is cleared."

"Wynn, it's been fun having you here on the island this summer," Jackie answered coolly, "but please remember, you are not one of us, you are just passing through."

"Halleluiah, Jesus! Keep us together Lord. Keep us together Lord, in love!" Faith began to sing.

"I don't think those are the exact words, Faith." Owl pointed out.

"What is your point exactly, Faith?" Jackie arched a brow.

"Jackie, we all understand this is a very difficult time for you, but please, let's be civil to one another."

"I'll try." There were dark circles under her eyes. Jackie frowned, and then stood. "I think it's time for me to head home. I don't want to leave Agatha alone for long. Thank you, everyone, for the delicious refreshments."

"Take a piece of pie to Agatha." Roxie got up and moved the last piece onto a china plate. She covered it with a linen napkin and handed it to her friend.

"That's very thoughtful of you, Roxie. Thanks. And I'm sure Agatha will want to thank you the next time she sees you."

Wynn remained seated as the other women took turns hugging Jackie goodbye. At the doorway, Jackie turned and looked across the room. "Goodnight to you, Wynn."

"Sleep well, Jackie."

All gazes were on the door as Jackie walked through it.

"Well, that was certainly uncomfortable." Sheri sat back down.

"Anyone can be a murderer if the circumstances are right. Or, leastwise, cause a death, since we're not really sure a murder has occurred." Roxie glanced about the room.

"I hope you didn't invite me over here tonight just to try to get incriminating information out of me about Doug." Owl snatched a piece of flaky crust from Wynn's discarded plate and swirled it around in the lime meringue. "And if you are insinuating my nephew caused Boone's death you better think again, Roxie."

"I'm not insinuating a thing! Why is everyone so touchy tonight?"

"It's because everyone seems to have a dog in this fight." Sheri tugged her braid.

Again Faith hummed. She held out her hand to Wynn.

"It's so hard because we all want to keep peace and Jackie wants justice." Sheri added before chiming in with Faith's tune.

"We all want justice, most of all Doug." Wynn accepted Faith's hand.

"That's the spirit, Wynn!" Faith sweetly smiled and went back to singing. "Everyone join me!"

"These times try us all especially our friendship. I believe we are to hold strong onto each other and our faith at this time." Sheri reached for Roxie's hand. "We shouldn't be judges of this matter."

"Is there anything new about the case?" Wynn took Owl's hand.

"Nothing. So far, Doug is the only suspect in what may or may not be a murder." Owl sighed.

Everyone swayed side to side as the women continued humming.

"Have they determined cause of death?" Wynn raised her voice.

"No, as Jackie said, they are still waiting on lab results." Owl sounded out of breath.

"Slow down on all the questions, Wynn, will you?" Roxie said as she swayed in time to their humming. "Keep us together, Lord!"

Several minutes of singing passed, and then the women dropped their hands.

Faith stopped humming.

Wynn was thankful for the silence. She pressed for information. "Have they gone over the schooner for fingerprints?"

"They found nothing, not even Doug's. Can you imagine?" Faith added.

"Then someone must have wiped it clean. Mine should have shown up. I'm telling you, someone else put that body on the schooner, and then wiped it down. This proves it."

Roxie looked totally enrapt hearing this information. Her gaze went from Wynn's to Sheri's to Faith's to Owl's. Then she said quietly, "We are a family of faith here, would you agree?"

Everyone nodded their heads, except for Wynn, who still considered herself a person of science.

"Wynn said words here tonight that have made me rethink some things. As a Christian, I've been harsh and judgmental and I hope God, and all of you, will forgive me. I honestly don't know who killed Boone. Maybe it was even an accident. However, I've made a decision. I want to help find out what happened to Boone, no matter where it leads us." Roxie looked at Wynn. "You do want to find out what happened to Boone, right?" She asked Wynn.

"Yes, I do."

"Even if Doug's guilty of something."

Wynn's stomach pitched. "Even then."

"Then we will all help. Each of us can do a part in the research, and then meet back to discuss our findings. Wynn can help organize us because she is a scientist." Owl stated excitedly.

"And scientists are detectives, too." Sheri smiled. "But I'm game too, how about you, Faith, and Roxie?"

"You know I am."

"Me too, but where do we start?" Faith took a notebook from her purse and posed her pen on the paper.

"First, we need to get a copy of the coroner's report and the lab results. I have a copy of the police report. Between the two maybe we can establish a timeline," Wynn said.

"I really do think Wynn is a detective!" Owl gushed.

"The man who was struck by the truck on the mainland, his body has been cremated. Sadly, we may never find out who he was and what part, if any, he plays in this mystery. It's important to interview all the witnesses. The only identification he had on him was Boone's wallet. How did that happen??"

"Perhaps he pickpocketed Boone."

"Maybe he's our killer!" Owl squeaked. "That means our killer got killed."

"If so, then how did Boone get from the mainland to the island without anyone noticing?" Roxie asked.

"Good point, but let's not overlook this idea, or any idea, so write it down, Faith," Wynn suggested. "We need to make a list of suspects."

"You should try the computers, too," Sheri said. "I'm more of a snow globe person than a computer person, but I've watched cop shows and they have the ability to trace almost anything these days."

"They took Doug's history so I'm sure they have Boone's, too." Owl patted her curlers.

Faith went back to her paper and read: "Wynn already has the police report."

"For our next meeting, I'll make notations and copies for everyone. If anything on it raises more questions, I'll attempt to find the answers." Wynn and Roxie exchanged glances. "Let's work together on our assignments, Aunt Roxie."

"Good teamwork. Roxie, you and Wynn can also trace Boone's whereabouts from the time his plane landed at Greenbay. Owl, talk to Doug's lawyer directly to find out the kind of evidence the police have on him. Sheri, you keep an ear out for island gossip about any murder or unexplained death."

"I wonder how, if Boone was murdered, what happened? A gun shot? Strangulation? A knife wound?" Sheri leaned forward.

"A heart attack?" Wynn interjected.

"Then why was his body hidden on a schooner?" Sheri asked. "No, the cause of death is something much more dramatic."

"The biggest problem will be getting the coroner and lab results." Wynn said.

"Why?"

"The public isn't privy to that information."

"I'll see what I can do to help, and bring the refreshments for the next meeting," Faith said.

"Will they be made by Chef Frank?" Owl asked.

"Of course!"

"Going back to fingerprints, Faith, how do you know the police didn't find fingerprints on the schooner?" Wynn asked.

"I know because I'm showing homes to Frank and he served lunch to the police officers just yesterday."

"Frank is looking to buy on the mainland?" Roxie was curious.

"As a matter of fact, he's hoping to find something he can afford on the island," Faith answered.

"Hasn't that been his dream all along?" Sheri smiled.

"Yes, it has been."

"What part of the island is Frank looking for a house?" Roxie asked.

"He wants a lot to build on." Faith explained.

"But lots and consent for new builds are nearly impossible to get anymore," Sheri added.

Faith shrugged. "I tried telling him that, but he is

bound and determined to find something, and is certain he can get the authorization."

"Maybe he feels this way because he has the inside track with owning the Inn. Island officials are quick to accommodate business owners. Wouldn't that be marvelous?" Owl was excited.

"Tell Frank to come by and see me. I have an acre at the back of my property I might consider selling to him." Roxie got a smug look in her eyes.

"I can't wait to tell Frank the news. I think I'll head over to the inn right now. Thanks Roxie."

Then like a dam breaking, the others got up and followed Faith out of the cottage.

Wynn hung back to speak with her aunt. "You're not so sure about Doug's guilt anymore, are you?"

Roxie answered. "No."

"Why not?"

"Too many variables."

"Ha, you are sounding like me now."

"We have more in common than you think." Roxie pulled a loose strand of hair behind Wynn's ear.

"Murdered people have families who care about them, too. Just like these women. I need to remember that before I speak."

"May the Lord fill your mouth with blessing."

"Amen to that." Wynn kissed her aunt goodnight. Outside she found Owl waiting for her. They walked up the drive towards the Tree House.

"Would you look at the stars through the trees tonight. So many of them." Wynn admired.

"Don't they look like pin pricks on black paper!"

"On this kind of night, I sit out on my porch among the tree tops, just listening to the waves crash against the shore. I used to only feel part of the land

and trees and sea and sky, but lately, since I've come to the island, I'm starting to feel connected to people more and more."

"Are you referring to Doug?"

"Yes, but not only him. Also to the ladies of the Bible study." Wynn squeezed her hand.

"And we all love you, too, dear."

"Well, maybe, but certainly not true of Jackie." Wynn looked at her with troubled eyes.

"As my mother used to say, 'This too shall pass.' Just wait for her to come around. Rest assured it will happen."

"The other day, I woke up to lovely words swirling around in my mind. It's like a song you hear, but can't quite get out of your head. Poetic, yet somehow sad. That's where I'll find him."

"I'd like to hear it."

"OK—it's short." Wynn cleared her throat. "'I put my dreams in down by the water'."

"Nice. You should write an entire poem centered on that romantic thought."

"I'm not a writer. What do you suppose it means?"

"Something important was somehow lost."

"I certainly have a lot to pick from."

"Whatever you lost, I hope you find it."

In the distance, Wynn caught a flicker of light as though the moon glanced at itself in the water. She kept staring at the sky, hoping to catch it happening again, but a large bird took flight and broke her concentration. "How are you holding up, Owl?"

"I have my good moments and bad. Ever since Doug's parents died, my husband and I have been close to Doug. He's a good man and I say that because it's the truth, not because he's my nephew."

"He is a good man. You know a lot of island folklore. One is about you."

Owl seemed to get a kick out of this and bent over laughing. "Island curses, and now folklore."

"Walking is good exercise, but why do you walk at night instead of the day? It'd be a lot safer."

"Let me ask you this, why do you think I walk at night?"

"To get everyone talking?" Wynn giggled.

"No mystery. No folklore. Just prayer time. I walk and pray, walk and pray. No one stops me to disturb my thoughts."

"Really? Every night?"

"Every night for the last forty years except during blizzards."

"What do you say to God while out walking around?"

"I ask that people will be drawn to Jesus. I pray for protection, for good health. I praise God for His blessings. Whatever comes to mind. When I am particularly troubled like now, I can walk and pray till dawn. Come along with me sometime."

"Then we'd both have tongues wagging. I'm so pleased the women of the Bible study are involving themselves to get to the truth about Boone's murder, if it is murder. And…"

"And what?" Owl lifted the lid off a trash can and began raking through the contents. She held up an old shirt. "This just might fit my husband. Go on, honey, I'm listening."

"What are you doing?" Wynn asked in horror.

Owl laughed. "Finding good stuff that others have no need for."

Wynn looked around for the others. She didn't see

anyone, but for good measure, she moved closer to Owl. "Are you good at keeping secrets?"

"That I am."

"Good. Two big things are bothering me. First, I found Agatha's brooch on the schooner the other night when Doug and I were coming back from the island preserve. It was lodged under the seat like it was purposefully left."

"What was Agatha doing on Doug's schooner? Do you suppose she had something to do with Boone's body showing up there? It might make sense."

Wynn shrugged. "It could have been planted. Ah, there I go again, being a detective."

"Don't pay attention to Jackie's words. Where is the brooch now?"

"My place. I had no idea a body was about to turn up, so I took it to give back to her. Dumb of me. I think this could be termed as contaminating a crime scene. If only I had left it, it might have turned the investigation in a different direction." Wynn shook her head impatiently. "What this investigation lacks is focus."

"You mentioned there was something else you wanted to say?"

"Where do you suppose the real ruby ring is? The one Boone was supposed to take to his grave."

"Wish I knew. A lot of people would love to get their hands on it—possibly even a private collector."

"Really?" Wynn felt taken back. "What's so special about it?"

"It was given by the Queen of England, the sickly Anne Stuart, centuries ago to one of her lovers. He left England soon after her marriage and came to America with it, where he lost it in a poker game to one of my distant Reed relatives for land. From that time it was passed on down to the first born Reed son every generation."

"It should be in your family. How did Boone end up with it?"

"His great-granddaddy won it in another poker game from my great-great granddaddy. Obviously, Jackie doesn't know the history of the ring, either, and I sure don't want her to find out. Now it's your turn for secret keeping. It could be the very thing that hangs Doug."

24

"Wynn, perhaps you and Doug shouldn't attend the funeral." Roxie stood beneath the shade of an oak.

"Aunt Roxie—please, not again. I thought we resolved this last night. Isn't it important for us to be with her, especially at this time?"

"I don't mean to hurt anyone's feelings. Jackie is my priority right now. She's still in a bit of shock. Bible study last night was, well, rather intense. Since she's doubtful of Doug's innocence and your support of that, it might be wise not to be present."

Wynn looped her arm through Doug's, displaying a united front. "I've done nothing wrong—and neither has Doug. These should be the times that draw us together; not tear us apart."

"I think Roxie is right, Wynn. We'll leave." Doug nudged her. "We can do something special for her once this is cleared up. Nice seeing you again, Roxie."

"Doug. You, too."

"Doug you have to decide what is right for you. If you feel Jackie would be more comfortable with you not in attendance, then you shouldn't come in with me. But, I am going inside the church. I want her to know I'm standing with her at this hard time, just as I stand with you."

"Thanks for that. But I'll catch ya later." He wore a grim expression as he kissed her forehead and walked back to his truck.

Tears glistened and Wynn prayed the sting of hurt would wash away. The prayer came so naturally and quickly, that it took only moments to realize she had actually spoken to God. The thought sent goose bumps over her skin. She shivered.

Roxie had already entered the church without her. It hurt her heart to think perhaps her aunt might be ashamed to be seen with her. Head down, Wynn slowly walked up the old stone steps.

Roxie stood in the foyer, waiting for her. "We're separated on some issues, but when it really matters, we are here for one another. We need one another."

"We do."

"Wait a minute, what do you have all over you? Is that cat hair?" Roxie began to pick at her clothes.

"I'll explain later."

The amount of flowers seemed to be heavier and more splendid than Boone's first funeral. Jackie stood at the front by the open casket. Jackie's face opened into a warm smile and she held out her hands. "Roxie. Wynn."

"I think she's forgiven me," Wynn murmured.

Roxie gave her niece a small nudge. "It appears so. You go first. You and Jackie have a bit of making up to do. This might be the right time."

Jackie looked exhausted.

Jackie and Wynn embraced; holding one another for a long minute. Then Jackie gradually pulled back. "Thank you for coming. I needed you today."

"I want to be here for you, particularly today. I'm sorry for our words at Bible study. Please forgive my insensitivity."

"Of course I forgive you. We forgive each other. And now you're here. True sisters in Christ." Jackie squeezed her hand. "We don't always have to agree, but we do have to forgive. I don't know what I would do without you and Roxie and the women of the Bible study. Still, I feel I'm falling apart."

"I'll help keep you from doing that."

"You will. I just don't want to lose my mind." She rubbed her forehead.

"Have you arranged for grief counseling?" Wynn asked gently.

"Marilyn couldn't get to her therapist fast enough."

"I'm not talking about Marilyn. I meant for you, and maybe Agatha." She looked at the young woman seated in the front row, fingering the place along the neckline where the brooch used to be. Wynn's eyes glinted with moisture. She brushed it away with the tips of her fingers. "Dang eyeliner. Did I smear it?"

"No, you are as lovely as ever."

Jackie looked towards the casket. "Boone really loved me. You don't know that because you never saw us together, but we were crazy about one another from the very first moment. Except for his business trips, we were inseparable. We laughed together over his silly jokes. He was so patient with me, so caring. Our life together was like one big holiday. I had so much hope after the first funeral that Boone would turn up safe and alive. I prayed it would happen that way."

"You sound as though God let you down."

Jackie held a handkerchief to her mouth and whispered into it, "Yes, I do. There is no good reason for this senseless death. He was young and strong. Our years together were snatched from us."

"I understand how you feel. And it made me hard on the inside. I'm cynical that prayers are actually answered. I look at you and Roxie and the other women and admire your faith. You all have this confidence and trust that everything will be OK, no matter what happens. It keeps you alive and filled with hope. It fills you with courage. You can get through today. And the next day, and the one after that. Boone left his love with you. I keep thinking back to the day I went with you to your accountant's and what you said to me."

"What was that?"

"You said, 'Even if God doesn't help me, or never answers another prayer of mine, He has already done everything for me.' That is a powerful statement of faith. Think about the time you've had with Boone and how enriched you are for having had him. Most people never experience that."

Jackie looked deep into Wynn's eyes. "To have had Boone for even a little while is better than never having had him. Thank you for reminding me of my blessings. And you brought my words back to help heal. How blessed I am to have you standing here with me when I needed you the very most."

"Boone is a part of everyone who knew him and that way, he will be kept with us. Sometime, I want to hear about how you met and how he proposed. I want to hear about your first argument."

"I'd love to tell you."

Roxie walked up to them.

"You have a very special niece."

"I know I do."

"And Wynn, now I have you, too." She pressed Wynn against her.

Roxie wrapped her arms around them both. Wynn looked at Agatha and held out her hand. "Come

Agatha." Agatha crossed the floor to join them.

"There's a confession I made to God and its time you both hear it, too. My pain has been so unbearable, so stinging over Boone's death that I wanted someone to pay. I haven't sought justice, but vengeance. Doug was the one the police zeroed in on. So I did, too. I wanted him dead. Then last night, as I prayed, I thought about mercy and forgiveness. And I wondered if he really is innocent. I want to know the truth."

Wynn smiled at her aunt. She understood at that moment God was at work sparked by prayer.

"I believe it was God. Now I am not saying Doug is innocent, but I am open to finding the truth. The pain will always be here." She put her hand over her heart and swallowed hard. "It never will go away. Right now, I just want to find out what happened to Boone. I want that person brought to justice if Boone was murdered. I owe my husband that."

They fell silent. The seconds ticked off.

Wynn looked to Roxie for approval. "Should I tell Jackie and Agatha?"

"Not here, not now." Roxie looked stern.

"Well, you'll have to tell us now." Agatha insisted.

Wynn narrowed her eyes. "By the way, Agatha, I've been meaning to ask you something. What happened to your brooch?"

"What?" Her voice quaked.

"The brooch is always right there." Wynn pointed at the spot.

"I must have dropped it on the way into church."

"Really?" Wynn now focused on Agatha.

"I better go look for it."

"Oh look, Marilyn is here. I better show her to her seat since the ushers aren't here yet. Excuse me ladies."

Jackie hurried to the back.

Agatha quickly followed.

"That was close!" Roxie snapped. "Your timing is off, dear. Now isn't the time to talk about our Bible Task Force. Save it for later."

The women took a seat together.

Wynn was relieved Jackie didn't think of introducing her to this corpse.

The church filled with mourners. She thought of Jackie and how to help with her loss. At the front of the church was large statue of a robed Jesus with his hands held out. Behind Him a lighted cross added to the serenity. The organ music was soft and not sad, but hopeful.

Wynn silently prayed. "I need hope, Lord. Fill me with words of joy and hope that I may pass them along to others who are hurting." A warm glow spread out until she felt tingly. It made her weep.

Then the tune from the box began to play. The tune she remembered well, but whose words she couldn't completely remember. "True till death," Wynn mouthed. Roxie opened her black beaded clutch and pulled out tissues for Wynn.

Wynn dabbed her face. "What is the name of the song that just played?"

"Faith of Our Fathers." Roxie opened the hymnal to the page and handed her the book.

Faith of our fathers, living still,
In spite of dungeon, fire and sword;
O how our hearts beat high with joy
Whenever we hear that glorious Word!
Faith of our fathers, holy faith!
We will be true to thee till death.

Faith of our fathers, we will strive
To win all nations unto Thee;
And through the truth that comes from God,
We all shall then be truly free.
Faith of our fathers, holy faith!
We will be true to thee till death.
Faith of our fathers, we will love
Both friend and foe in all our strife;
And preach Thee, too, as love knows how
By kindly words and virtuous life.
Faith of our fathers, holy faith!
We will be true to thee till death...

Wynn had been given these words just when she needed them most. No matter how imperfect her family had been, how imperfect she had become, they all had one element in common; faith.

The words that once fully comforted her as a child now comforted her as an adult. A peace swelled over her and she knew no matter how things turned out, everything would be all right. Once Grammy and Gramps passed, she stopped thinking about God. Neither uncle ever brought the subject up, not even on special Christian holidays like Christmas and Easter.

After the funeral, the Bible study women met together for lunch at Jackie's.

Wynn was full of happiness which made her want to weep more—a feeling she was totally confused over. "I'm sorry." She kept dabbing at her face with a linen napkin. "I can't seem to stop crying."

"Are you thinking about your parents, dear?" Roxie asked. "Sometimes funerals remind us of losing our loved ones."

"No, it's not that. It's just that..." Wynn looked to

the horizon. "One of the songs we sang this morning at the funeral stirred me. Even though I'm crying, I feel so happy. Ridiculous, I know."

"Not ridiculous at all," Owl said. "I've been praying for you on my nightly walks, ever since you came to the island."

"You have? You prayed for me?" Wynn asked. "What did you pray about?"

"Yes, I prayed for you, sweet girl. I prayed that you would find peace and know that you are very loved."

The women looked at one another.

"Sounds like you've had a spiritual awakening." Jackie batted back her own tears.

"Me? A spiritual awakening? Really?" Wynn wanted faith. She wanted hope. But did she want God? How would He change her? Would He ask things of her she wasn't able to give? It would be a commitment, not something that was rubbed on her like perfume only to disappear at the end of a day. She wanted it to be real. She was stuck on the fence between faith and fiction.

"Give it time," Roxie said. "Enjoy the touch you felt this morning. Don't try to frame it in scientific terms."

The remark caught Wynn off guard. She fell silent, her lips thinning, her eyes shining. "Thank you."

"Where's Marilyn?" Sheri asked. "Didn't she want to join us for lunch?"

"No, Mother wanted to get back to the mainland. She said the island creeps her out now," Agatha informed.

"Interesting. I'd like to speak with Marilyn next time she comes to visit," Wynn said.

"What about?" Jackie pressed.

"Well…I'll tell you about it another time. Not important, I assure you." Wynn promised.

"I want to apologize to everyone for my behavior last night," Jackie said.

"Jackie, there's no need. We understand." Faith patted her hand. "Don't we, ladies?"

"Anything interesting happen after I left?" Jackie dropped the napkin onto her lap.

All the women fell silent.

"What? Something did happen, tell me." Jackie looked from face to face, stopping at Wynn.

"We've formed a task force." Wynn confessed.

"A task force?"

"Yes," Roxie plunged right in. "Each lady is taking an interesting aspect of Boone's case to acquire additional facts and information."

"Except for me," Sheri butted in. "I'm gathering island gossip and unsubstantiated rumors."

"We'll meet in a few days at Roxie's and discuss our findings," Faith said.

"May I be part of this little group of yours?" Jackie asked.

Roxie immediately nodded her head. "Please don't feel hurt we didn't initially include you. We all know you've been busy mourning Boone."

"I want to be a part of this group." Jackie looked around at all of them.

"Of course you are. The most important part, in fact, but I don't think you should be gathering information. You can help us fit it together."

"You are considering other leads than just Doug?"

"I think it'd be wise to do so. You never want to narrow research." Wynn was troubled. "Thank goodness Boone wasn't cremated. Blood work may give us some answers."

"If you want that, you will have to rely on me to procure since I'm the closest relative," Jackie said. "I can get a copy of the coroner's report, too."

"I never thought of that," Faith said.

"Me, either." Wynn confessed.

"See? You do need my help with this little investigation of yours."

"Will this bother you, Jackie?" Roxie asked.

"This will help me. I need to help."

"Jackie, I want you to know, that if Doug did murder Boone, I want him to be held accountable for it," Wynn stated. "One of the questions I have yet to answer is, was Boone a preselected victim, or was it some sort of an accident, and then covered up?"

"I think we need to get all the facts in order to determine that."

Since she had arrived to the funeral earlier in the day with Doug, Roxie gave Wynn a ride home.

"I'm going to change my clothes and feed my yard birds. Want to come in for a bit? I have some nice snacks in my fridge if you are still hungry."

"No, but thank you for the offer." Wynn decided to take a drive and clear her thoughts.

With Roxie's cottage in the car's rearview mirror, she had an unexpected memory. Her parents left her with Aunt Roxie for a few days. Wynn couldn't remember what the occasion was for her parents to be gone, but she didn't feel saddened by their departure. She knew it was temporary and her aunt would take wonderful care of her.

Roxie lived far enough from town that there were no children around to play with.

"Play with Jesus. Talk to Jesus," Roxie told her after they baked cookies together. "He's always around and would love to hear from you."

At Christmas, they left cookies with milk out for Santa, but this was the only time she saw Roxie doing it for Jesus, making two places at the porch table. It occurred to Wynn that it was a wonderful way to show a child He was reachable, to speak in terms of her understanding at that time in her life. Jesus would listen to what she had to say at anytime, at any place. That day it was cookies. Tomorrow it would be scraped knees. Later on, it might be a scraped heart.

How odd she recalled things just like that, when for so long she could hardly remember living on the island. These memories were like a gift. If it hadn't been for Roxie's generosity, she wouldn't even be here right now. She had to make everything right. She headed back to the Tree House.

Wynn walked straight down to her aunt's cottage. The back door was already open. Quietly she padded through the cottage.

Roxie was on her knees in front of the couch her hands folded together. "Oh God, can't you make this all go away?" Roxie wept.

Wynn had always thought of this woman as strong, not in need of anything. "Aunt Roxie?" Wynn touched her shoulder.

Roxie's hair was in disarray, her face covered in sorrow. Her cheeks were pale and her eyes bruised from crying.

"I know, I should have knocked, or called. I am sorry I disturbed you." Wynn felt something catch in her throat. "Are you OK?"

"Yes, yes, yes. I'm really fine." Roxie gripped

Wynn's hand as she pulled up.

"Did you say something about a snack a little while ago?"

"I surely did!" Roxie's countenance changed as she bustled about. She cut brownies and poured milk, placing the snack in front of Wynn on a linen napkin. "I was thinking; why don't we go into Egg Harbor tomorrow and do our part of the investigation together?"

"Sounds good. I'll drive."

"OK. Pick me up by seven so we can make the eight a.m. ferry."

Wynn took a bite of brownie, filling her mouth with the chocolaty, creamy delight. "Oh, these are worth every pound I will gain."

"These are even better than Chef Frank's, if you can believe it."

"I most certainly believe it. Nothing is better than these." Wynn took another square. "Are you really selling a piece of your property to him to build a house?"

"I'm considering it. My closest neighbors are still quite far from me and it'd be nice to have someone near, since you aren't sticking around much longer."

Wynn felt shamed and began to shred the second brownie. "I'm sorry things didn't turn out the way you hoped."

"No one is sorrier than I. But I understand that you must live your own life. "

"Some good things have happened by coming here."

"I'd like to hear them, because right now I feel I have failed you in many ways."

"You have never failed me. Not ever. Except…"

"By not telling you about your dad's death?"

"Right. I consider it the most important part."

"You may not believe this, but I try very hard not meddle, although I like to warn you when I see impending disaster. I thought if I allowed you to rediscover things on your own that the memories would come faster and be honest ones, without me planting anything in your brain. If you had just enough information, it would keep you here. I was wrong. I know now you have to watch out for yourself. Decide what is best for you."

"Like I always have done."

"Yes, like you always have done. But I have loved you all these years." Roxie's voice broke.

"I know that, now." Wynn swallowed hard. "At first, I didn't understand. But I've since realized that love comes in many forms and can make a person do crazy things. Aunt Roxie? I want you to know that I love you, too."

Roxie reached across the table and took her niece's hands. "I'm here whenever you need me."

"You've always been there for me. My uncles couldn't have afforded my college, but you paid in full each year. I always counted on that—on you. I missed home and you so much even though I had only lived here for six years. Much of it I cannot remember. It's been covered over with time, like when leaves cover the ground—the earth is right there under my feet, but I just can't see it."

"Wynn, the answers you seek are right under your nose waiting to be discovered."

Wynn's Tree House was dark when she got home. She hadn't turned on outside lights before she left, and now her tiny place was hard to see nestled in the woods. She fumbled with her keys.

She stood still in the closed doorway as Sailor greeted her with rubs around her ankles. This was his first initiated contract with her, and it was best to not push things by picking him up.

She opened all the windows allowing the cool night breeze to sweep in. The words of faith the Bible women spoke to her about spiritual awakening, with Roxie's parting words, enveloped her.

Deep in contemplation, she walked into the kitchen area and opened the fridge. Raking through the items, she noted she was the proud owner of a quart of green tea, vegetables, and two pounds of Tillamook cheese.

Sailor swirled around her feet like smoke. She took down a can of cat food and emptied it into a dish for the kitten.

Wynn went out on her deck, careful to close the door, not wanting the kitten to escape. The moon was in its waning phase, and it was hard to see the tops of the oaks and pines against the dark night. The chilly air covered her arms and legs with goose bumps and she hugged her middle as she looked towards the sea.

In circles she walked, asking God to reveal Himself to her in some stunning manner so she would be certain it was He and not some silly fluke, nor a misplaced emotion.

Drawn here by memories of her dad's death, what kept her here was something different; Boone's death.

"A preselected victim. A death of unknown origin. An unidentified man who was cremated. A missing heirloom ring. This might turn out to be the biggest island mystery ever." Wynn suddenly felt very determined to solve the puzzles.

25

Suzi wore a pink rose bud stuck into her waitress nametag, and when Roxie asked her about the day she witnessed the man plowed by a truck, her eyes got big. "Oh, my, how horrible it was! I still see it happening even in my dreams—which are actually very bad nightmares. There are dark circles under my eyes, see? Can't sleep."

"Do you need to sit?" Roxie slid down the booth.

"Thanks, but I'll be fine." Suzi focused on her job. "Can't sit with customers. Not allowed. We have delicious honey ginger tea today, if you'd care for some. It's new."

"Certainly, we'll each have a cup."Wynn said, after Roxie nodded.

Suzi returned with two steaming white mugs and set them down.

"In the police report, you are listed as a witness."

"You must be from the insurance company." She stuck a pencil behind her left ear. "How can I help?"

"Tell us what you remember, dear." Roxie smiled in a motherly fashion. "It's very important."

"I was on my way to work that afternoon and was about to cross the street just outside the coffee shop here, when I saw someone stagger—most likely drunk—out into the street. Poor Mr. Ottoman tried to brake, but it was no use. It was a horrid sight. But Mr. Ottoman was not at fault. The guy stepped right out in front of him."

"Mr. Ottoman—he was the driver of the truck?" Wynn asked as Suzi refilled Roxie's cup.

"Yes. I know him. He's a trucker from Egg Harbor. On the road most of the time."

Wynn quickly scanned the police report wondering why the truck driver's name was left out. She reached into her purse and withdrew a pen to scribble the name in the margin. "Do you know Mr. Ottoman's address?"

"Let me write it down for you." Suzi wrote it on a lunch ticket, tore it off the pad and handed it to Wynn.

"Wow, you have it memorized. You don't happen to know everyone's address in town, do you?" Wynn laughed.

"No, of course not. In high school, I dated Mr. Ottoman's son. That's how I remembered it."

"Makes sense. So, he was going the speed limit?"

"Yes, he was, but a man with too much booze in his gut is no match for a two ton truck, even if its load is empty. By the way, he's on a month truck run so he's not home."

"Oh, OK." Wynn was disappointed they'd not be able to speak with the driver today.

"Do you suppose the man could have been pushed into traffic?" Roxie sipped her cup.

"If so, I didn't see it. I only noticed him when he stepped off the curb and out into traffic. Several cars swerved."

"Why did you say the man was drunk?" Roxie asked.

"He had to be drinking, because when he got hit the bottle in the bag he was carrying broke all over the street." She shrugged her shoulders. "Whisky, I think."

"Do you happen to know the name of the man who was killed?" Wynn asked.

"Doesn't it say in the police report?"

"Says 'unknown'."

"Well, I know about everyone in town. Lived here all my life. I didn't know the man. He was dirty and his clothes raggedy. From time to time, we get hitch hikers and train riders. In other words, the homeless, in town." She looked over her shoulder, back at the kitchen. She clucked her tongue. "Listen, I better take your order before my boss gets after me. What would you two like to eat?"

The women ordered salads.

Not wanting to be overheard, Wynn leaned across the table towards Roxie. "I don't understand why the truckers name wasn't in the report when almost a half dozen witnesses are named, with their addresses."

"Was that body ever identified?"

"No, because someone showed up, mistakenly identified it as Boone, and said to cremate."

"Maybe it wasn't done so mistakenly." Roxie's voice gained an edge.

"What do you mean?"

"What happens when someone pushes you from behind?"

"Huh?"

"Stand up."

"What?" Wynn was confused.

"Come on. Stand." Roxie got to her feet.

Roxie took her by the shoulders and spun her around. Then she pushed her. Wynn fell forward a few yards.

"Point made. You stagger when pushed." Wynn sat back down.

"So the supposed 'drunken' man may not have been drunk after all. Just taking an opened bottle of whisky home to drink?"

"Correct," Roxie said. "Mark that down on your paper there. We have to go through all our suppositions when we get with the ladies."

"He might have been pushed. Someone thought he was Boone. Someone knew who the homeless man was and wanted him hurt so he was pushed. How did Boone's wallet get into his pocket? Why did they want him dead? Murder or accident? I think we are building a mystery around this nameless, homeless man."

"Whether someone wanted him or Boone dead, that's how he ended up. Anyone who knows Boone would know it wasn't him. Boone doesn't touch alcohol and he is always clean and impeccably dressed," Roxie said. "What do you think the motive is for killing Boone?"

"I can't say for sure, but I feel the ruby ring is a strong contender."

"The ruby ring? Jackie and Boone's ruby ring?" Then our list of names grows longer. Doug, Marilyn, Agatha, Frank, perhaps even Jackie. Even though it pains me to say that."

"The first I heard of it was at the first funeral."

"Me, as well."

"It seems as though word is spreading." Wynn took a sip of tea. If Boone's body hadn't shown up, I'd say he was still alive some place."

"I keep thinking about the man who was killed and his family. I find it rather sad that they will most likely never know their loved one is gone. Or be able to bury him." Roxie leaned on her arm. "I wonder where his ashes are now."

"Maybe we can make that the next priority of the Bible ladies; find out who this man was. Locate his family and his ashes."

"Oh Wynn! Does that mean you're planning to stay on the island? You're taking the Biology job at the high school, after all, aren't you?" Roxie was elated.

"I haven't applied," she replied, but inwardly thrilled that Roxie still wanted her to be here.

Witness number one, two, three, and four on the list didn't have any additional information. "I thought eye witnesses were called that because they actually saw something," groused Wynn, feeling frustrated as they pulled up to witness number five's place, which was more of a waterside shack.

"Well, perhaps this Conrad Bellaire will be of more help."

The women introduced themselves to the weathered fisherman. They sat on his deck overlooking the water.

"I remember a very beautiful sight there on the street that day."

"A beautiful sight?" Wynn asked. "I don't understand. A man was killed. Surely it was an alarming sight; a horrifying sight; anything but a beautiful sight."

"Calm down, Missy. Let me explain." Conrad had a curious look on his face, as if many things had become magically clear since that day. "Yes, it was an alarming sight, but then compassion entered the scene when a woman ran out of the crowd and knelt beside him right on the street. She knelt and prayed right beside him. Right out in the open. Touched me deeply the caring she displayed."

"Did this woman know him?" Roxie asked.

"Perhaps so, ma'am. Maybe they both were Catholics and knew one another from church. Maybe not, what do I know?"

"Why do you think they were Catholic and not some other denomination?"

"I don't know. Not for sure. But the Catholic Church has an Empty Bowl Program where they feed the indigent. I got the impression that he just might be homeless from his disheveled appearance. But her appearance was something to behold." He gave a cat whistle.

"What did this woman look like?"

"Beautiful, like an angel of mercy." He nodded wistfully, staring down the rocky shore. "I thought perhaps she was a nurse tending to his injuries."

"Would you describe her for us?" Wynn posed her pen to take notes.

"Let me see." Now he looked up at the clouds. "As I recall it, she had on a summery dress without a blouse on underneath. You know the kind where the arms are bare and shoulders show. The straps held up the whole dress—I think you ladies refer to it as a sundress. It was green as I recall. She was skinny. And her shoes came off when she ran towards him."

Wynn paged through the police report hoping a pair of woman's shoes would turn up. She nearly shouted for joy when she saw it on the list of objects found at the scene. Size 8 ½ green, slip-on shoes with a daisy accent made by Curio's of Davenport. She circled it and showed Roxie.

"What color hair did she have?"

"Dark, maybe black, done up real nice and neat at the top of her head."

"If you saw a picture of her would you be able to

recognize her again?" Wynn asked.

"I wish. I didn't see her face."

"How old would you say she was?" Wynn pressed.

"Can't say. Couldn't have been a teenager, though, because they are wearing it messy these days. Seems to be a style with them."

They thanked him and returned to Wynn's car. "Do any of our female witnesses fit this description?"

"I don't think so. Only one of the women had dark hair and she wasn't skinny. There's just one more left on the list to speak with, right?"

"Yes, just one. An Alice Godfrey. "

Alice was a petite, stooped woman with gray hair and fine lines around her eyes and lips. "I had just come from helping out at church when I saw the accident."

"It wouldn't have been the Catholic Church, would it?"

"Why yes, indeed it was."

"Did you ever see him before, on the street or at church?"

"Never." She looked from Roxie to Wynn.

"How close were you to the scene?"

"Practically front row. Right next to him. That scene has shaken me to my soul. Turns out I needed some psychological counseling to clear my head of the jitters that have been with me since that day."

"How are you doing?" Roxie leaned over and squeezed her hand.

"Recovering. Who was the man who was killed?" Alice asked. "I want to light candles for him. God surely knows his name, but I would feel better saying a Rosary for him if I had a name to go with my prayers."

"We don't know."

"Surely the police know." Alice insisted.

"No, they don't," Wynn answered.

"That's because his identification was stolen." Alice was adamant.

"Stolen? What do you mean?"

"Seconds after the man was hit, a woman in the crowd ran up and knelt beside him."

"Oh, you are talking about the woman who prayed for him. Perhaps you know who she was?"

"No, I don't. But she didn't just pray for him. She stole his wallet! That's what she did. Pray for him, my foot. That's what she pretended to be doing."

"What?" Wynn and Roxie said it at the same time.

"She tried making a show of praying for him. I watched her closely. First, she reached into her purse and then into his pocket and back into her purse. I saw her put something in it."

"Could she have been a nurse?" Wynn asked.

"Nurse, my foot. It would be the first time I ever saw a nurse pickpocket someone."

"Do you know this woman?"

"I've never seen her."

"Could you identify her if you saw her again?"

"I'm not really sure. It all happened so quickly. I am so sorry." Alice rose from her chair.

"May we pray with you before we leave?" Wynn asked, trying not to react to the surprised look on her aunt's face.

"Yes, let's." Alice took their hands.

It was getting towards sunset by the time they stepped back outside. A jasmine vine grew on the porch railing and a dead tree stood in the front yard. Shadows of bare branches curled like empty hands across the yard and fence.

"Next we go to Marilyn's." Roxie was decisive.

"Are you kidding? Marilyn's? But why? I know she's on our list of suspects, but she isn't about to give up any kind of information. And it's getting late." Wynn looked at the screen of her cell phone. She wanted to talk to Doug about today.

"Remember, the Bible study women are doing a covert operation, which means no one outside the group can even be aware of this. And we are only disclosing the facts with our suspicions at the next meeting of the Bridge Over Troubled Waters Bible Study. No sense in getting the police upset with us, or anyone's hopes up. It's just between us women, OK?"

"Of course. It's our little secret for now."

"And don't worry. We can stay overnight in Egg Harbor if we miss the last ferry. After trips, Boone always saw his mother before he took the ferry home. Only this time Marilyn insists she didn't see Boone, which seems out of character."

"Might be true. He may have been killed before he saw her. That certainly would have interfered with a visit. I'm sure the time of death is in the coroner's report."

"The report only Jackie can get her hands on. Let's not count on Marilyn's truthfulness. Come on. We won't stay long. I can only take her in small doses, but I am working on tolerance and patience so this will be good practice for me. Still, if Boone didn't see Marilyn, I wonder where his luggage is. Maybe he was killed for something he brought back from Nepal."

"Write that one down."

By now, Wynn's thoughts were raw. She felt both weary and wired. Knowing they were about to visit

Marilyn made her even more unsettled.

The neighborhood was a residential mix of houses, townhomes, and condos.

Wynn parked on the street and they set out on foot. But, first, they ducked into an ice cream shop and ordered chocolate sundaes, gathering their sugar nerve to see Marilyn. Finally, they were at the large oak paneled door of the two story house.

Roxie put on her game face.

Wynn did, too.

But what greeted them was not expected. A rattled looking Marilyn, with mussed hair and no makeup, opened the door. Her khakis and pink colored blouse maintained a certain rumpled air that spoke of sleepless nights, and perhaps, a secret that was tearing at her. She blinked in surprise. "I didn't expect to see you two here. Ah, please come in. Let's, ah, sit in the living room?"

They followed her into the other room where two white chenille couches flanked a stone fireplace. Above it was an oil painting of Marilyn, Boone, and Agatha in a gilded frame.

"You'll have to excuse my appearance. I'm on anxiety medication." Marilyn sat beside Wynn, making Wynn's heart bump so hard she wondered if she was about to have a heart attack.

Wynn couldn't forget the cruelty Marilyn displayed towards Jackie on the day of Boone's first funeral.

"May I offer you both something to eat? I was just cutting Wisconsin cheese to have with grapes for my evening snack."

"No, thank you. Not hungry."

"Me, either." Roxie's lips barely moved.

"OK, ladies, since you have never visited my home before, I suspect this is not a social call. Is this to do about Agatha? Is she OK? Did something happen to Jackie?"

"No, they are fine. This has to do with Boone."

"Boone?" Her eyes immediately flooded with tears.

"Did you see him the day he arrived from Nepal?'

"Absolutely not! I already told the police that, many times. He always comes here first before returning to Willow Island. I was expecting him, as always. When he didn't show up, I thought perhaps he missed his plane, or Jackie insisted that he come right home. It was early the following day when Jackie called with the terrible news." Marilyn sobbed.

Wynn almost fell for the information until she happened to glance at the entry door that had a dry cleaners bag caught in it. "Marilyn, I am feeling hungry. Grapes and cheese sound so good to me, after all."

Marilyn stopped sobbing and her innate hostess duty kicked in. Being needed seemed to bring the tears to an end. Within seconds, she could be heard in the kitchen taking down plates and setting them on the counter.

Wynn jumped to her feet and opened the closet door. A receipt was still stapled to the top. "Roxie look," Wynn whispered, reading the receipt. "This silk suit was dry cleaned the same day Boone came back from overseas."

"Silk? I told you he always dressed impeccably."

"This receipt proves Boone was really here that day. What reason would Marilyn have for lying?"

"I don't know. Let's ask her."

Roxie sat with the receipt in her hand.

Marilyn returned and set the silver tray on the table. "Care for cocktails?"

"No, thanks." Roxie held up the ticket. "What's this?"

Marilyn blanched. Her hands began to shake while her neck turned red.

Wynn knew then she hadn't been truthful. "You did see Boone."

"I have a feeling you know a lot more about that day than you are saying." Roxie stood her ground.

Marilyn sat still, her lips pressed together.

"The day Boone arrived back to Egg Harbor, a man was hit by a truck, and mistakenly identified as Boone."

"Old news. We all know that."

"A number of witnesses described a well put together woman knelt at the man's side. One claimed she stole his wallet."

"I would not steal from someone who was kicked down in his life." Marilyn looked away, and then up at the ceiling. "If you must know, Boone dropped off this suit with me on the day he left, not the day he arrived. I had forgotten all about taking it to the cleaners until the day he was due home."

"You know a lot more about that day than you are saying," Roxie said again.

"I don't need accusations from two busybodies. This isn't work for amateurs. My Boone is dead and you're asking about some receipt. I think it's time for you ladies to leave." Marilyn grabbed the receipt from them, walked to the front door and held it open.

"I guess we should be leaving now. What do you think, Roxie?"

26

The persistent sense of impending doom drew Wynn to press Doug to view Anna Reed's paintings in the Greenbay museum. After perusing the paintings online, Doug agreed that detail can be lost on a computer-generated picture.

They decided to re-familiarize themselves with Anna Reed's paintings displayed in the main lobby of the Willow Inn. The first time she saw them was for pure entertainment with Chef Frank, this time it was a purposeful study.

Just as Wynn lifted her camera to take a shot of the first painting, she stepped back onto someone's foot. It wasn't Doug's; he was at the opposite end of Willow Inn's very small gallery. She turned to apologize.

Chef Frank's beefy face was flushed red. His cheeks were covered with sweat. "I saw you get out of the landscaper's truck and thought I might be of assistance."

"Hi Frank. Nice to see you again." Wynn's heart sank. They had a ferry to catch and she hoped Frank wasn't chatty.

Frank nodded and removed his chef's hat. "We are running wonderful lunch specials today."

"And there's no one who enjoys a lunch special more than me, but today I'm here enjoying paintings, and then I'm off to the mainland."

"Is there more information I can provide you

with?"

"Yes, please." She moved back to the first painting.

The picture was of the front of the Inn during a storm. The colors were dark and grim, not as bright and colorful as the others. Mustering up her memory from Art Appreciation 101, she asked, "Can you explain why Anna painted this one in this manner? In some ways, it doesn't seem in keeping with her style."

"Many think she didn't even paint this one."

"Really? Why is that?"

"Look at the strokes. These are long and wild. Many are curled and thick. If you note the painting right next to this one has lines that are thin, quick, and patient."

Wynn spared a glance at Doug, who had a curious look on his face, as if many things were crossing his mind. "But her husband died in a storm. Wouldn't it naturally denote anguish? And the strokes are more about the storm than a lovely day on her veranda would be."

Frank's gaze followed as Doug sauntered past without a word. "Looks like your ride might be ready to leave."

"He can wait. Is there anything else you can tell me about the other five paintings? Like this next one?" Wynn put her arm through his and walked him to the painting of Anna playing with her children. Her left hand was raised in the air and there, on her finger, was the ruby ring. The sight of it made her heart beat faster. She desperately wanted a close-up shot of it without being conspicuous. "Oh, my throat is very dry. I would love some water. Please."

"How about lemonade? Fresh squeezed with a touch of real raspberry juice."

"Even better."

Frank obviously thought she was flirting with him—she could see it in his eyes. A twinge of guilt fought with her need to look at the painting. Wynn dismissed it, hoping she could apologize later. The moment he disappeared into the kitchen, she studied the ring in the picture.

In the middle was an oval shaped ruby surrounded by what appeared to be emeralds. That descriptive detail had been left out by Jackie—that is if the artist hadn't taken liberty.

Wynn held up her camera, focused, and began snapping shots. Then she hurried down the line of paintings taking multiple shots of each one, glancing back over her shoulder towards the kitchen. With Frank lurking about, she didn't have the luxury of taking her time. Just as she slid her camera into her backpack, Frank returned with a silver tray.

Not only was there a crystal goblet with lemonade the color of raspberries, but there were a half dozen pastry cookies in various shapes and flavors.

"Ah—do you happen to have a to-go-box?" She pointed over her shoulder. "I need to go."

When she climbed back into the truck, she smiled at Doug, balancing the large to-go- box along with two covered cups of raspberry lemonade. "This drink is mine. The one with the red straw is yours."

"Didn't I tell you that I have conquered my intense desire for straws?"

"Just in case you have a relapse, I'm here for you."

"Thanks, and by that expression, I'll bet you have a story to tell." There was a light in his eyes.

"That I do. Treats!" She opened the box lid and held it under his nose. "We have fresh corned beef sandwiches on rye bread along with all kinds of pastries for dessert."

"Chef Frank?"

"Chef Frank."

"I believe he's trying to impress you."

"I'm impressed."

Doug passed over the sandwiches and went right for the chocolate dipped meringue. "Wow!"

"There's a painting on the wall that is accredited to Anna," Wynn helped herself to a wafer-like buttery sugar cookie. "But I'm thinking someone else painted it during the same time period. The fine age lines running through it are the same as in the others. But the strokes and personal expression are all totally off. But, I know very little about art."

"Who could have painted it?"

"No idea."

"In some of the paintings Anna wore the now infamous, and well sought after, ruby ring. And I have pictures!" She scrolled through the pictures to show Doug.

"A little blurry, don't you think?"

"Blurry? Really?" She furrowed her brow swiping through them. "Wait, this one is good. See?"

Doug selected another cookie and nodded his head in agreement.

"Have you ever seen the ring in person?"

Doug considered it for a moment and nodded. "Yep. It's the one in the one un-blurred picture. That's it."

"I didn't know it also had emeralds. No one ever mentioned that fact."

"It has emeralds. It's now been officially mentioned. Anything else?"

"Yes. I was asked out on a date." She lifted a brow.

"Ah, don't tell me. Chef Frank?"

"Chef Frank."

"You going?"

"Nah. My immediate inclination was to turn him down flat and that is exactly what I did."

"Maybe you should reconsider." His face was composed.

Wynn felt a stab of pain. Had his feelings changed? Certainly she hadn't misread him. Or had she? Suddenly her day seemed bleak. A lump formed in her throat. "Ok." She lost her smile and turned to the window. "You want me to go out with him?"

"Well, not in the manner you're inferring. If you take advantage of his offer, it'd be a good time to ask questions about the Inn. Catch him off guard."

"The Inn?" She turned to face him again.

"He knows all the nooks and crannies of the place. The history."

"And that would have to do with the case…how?" Her emotions lifted.

"Just a feeling. I hear he wants to buy it."

"Why not? It's popular—thanks to Frank, the cuisine is nearly a destination in itself. Chefs always want their own restaurant."

"It could be a motive."

Wynn eyed Doug over his comment, thinking the ring could be a motive for him, as well. "Do you think Boone was killed for the ring?"

"I certainly do."

The art gallery was located in the center of town. Doug paid the twenty dollars admittance fee for both of them. They ignored the other exhibits and went straight to find Anna Reed's.

"There must be twenty of her paintings in here."

"With long, lonely winter nights, you need something to fill your time. And remember, her husband was dead."

Wynn playfully punched him in the arm. Then she saw it: A painting of a large, shaped key hole that allowed the lavishly furnished room on the other side to be viewed by the patron. "Wow, look at this neat concept."

Doug walked across the room and gazed at it for several minutes. "Hey, I have something to show you now."

Wynn followed Doug to the opposite wall and pointed. "In this painting Anna is wearing the skeleton key hanging from a bracelet around her wrist. One son is looking at what she's pointing to, while the other is fixated on the key. There's a bit of mystery here."

"Interesting. She's pointing to a wallpapered wall."

"Any idea of what it means?"

Wynn leaned in to look more closely at the wallpaper. "It's blue toile of a pasture scene."

"What does it mean?"

"Nothing to us, but to her it could mean everything."

"Would you please step back from the painting?"

They turned to see a jacketed curator standing behind them. "You are way too close to the painting. You must remain behind this line." She pointed to blue masking tape on the floor eighteen inches away from the wall.

"So sorry. Can you tell us anything about Anna Reed's paintings?" Wynn asked.

The curator nodded and explained aspects of each

painting, but added nothing to what they already knew. She also totally missed the skeleton key and the door latch.

After the tour they headed for the parking lot.

"We have a newly missing ring dating back to the 1800s, the found corpse of Joseph Reed—which leads me to ask—"where have you been all this time, Joseph?" Wynn counted off the clues. "We now have Boone's fresh corpse, but who killed him? And why?"

27

For the next several days, Wynn worked feverishly to finish her grant to the University. On the final day, weariness hit her hard. What possessed her to work all day without taking a break? At least her research was complete, but her shoulders and neck had paid the price for her diligence. She'd gone too long with not enough sleep.

The sky was just darkening, but she needed a good run to work the aches out before bed, or there'd be another sleepless night; nights Sailor enjoyed because they'd end up playing on the wooden floor with cat toys and getting to know each other better, which Wynn loved. Lately, either her brain or body kept her awake in the long dark hours from midnight to dawn. Tonight, nothing would hold her back.

She pulled on shorts with a loose t-shirt and sneakers. Then she kissed Sailor at the top of his head, and dragged herself down the steps. The cool air gave her goose bumps.

Just as she passed the mailbox, something caught her eye. The lid was pulled half way down. She peeked inside to see something at the back of the box. The slip of paper was neatly creased into fours. No envelope. She unfurled it. It wasn't written by computer, but by hand in script.

When I turn my boat to shore

When the wind is behind me,
When the day is waning
I think of you
I see your hair on your shoulders
I imagine the softness of your skin
Your throat where it meets your chest
Your quiet voice calls me home
Your eyes light my way.
You are mine, Wynn in the Willows.

Though she had read Doug's words just once, she remembered each one. Did he actually consider her to be his home? She wanted to be. Home. She had been searching for so long. Maybe it wasn't really a location marked by latitude and longitude lines on a map, but a place with another person. Gladly she'd sit in the rocking chair of his arms forever. Feel the sea breeze from his embrace. Know the touch of heaven from his lips.

She held the paper to her heart. The words rolled into her heart, and then poured out into the fresh air once again. She wouldn't, couldn't fight her feelings for him any longer. It was time to go to him.

But first, she had to change her clothes. His poem had made an imprint on her soul; she wanted to make an imprint on his.

She scrambled out of her jogging clothes. After running a hot shower, she blew her hair dry until it dropped below her shoulders in curls. She applied just a bit of blush and eyeliner; a touch of lip stain, and then stepped into a white gauzy dress. She skipped to the car, only wanting to see him—Doug.

Windows down, her dark tendrils whirled in the wind. She swiped them back behind her ears but it did no good. The hem of her dress flew up from time to time, revealing her well-muscled thighs. By the time she parked along the shoreline near the lighthouse, her hair was a wild mess. After smoothing it with a brush, she stood at his door, knocking; breathless, heart pounding like a fist in her chest.

There was his silhouette through the glass.

The door opened and he stood in front of her. His cheeks were rough with a five o'clock shadow. There was an awkward moment while they simply studied one another. He smelled of fresh soap and his hair was still wet from the shower. His pants fit loosely and he didn't wear a belt. His shirt was unbuttoned down the front as though he was just sliding into it when he heard the knock.

Her gaze became locked on his steely gray eyes.

He gave her a pointed look, his gaze questioning. "What, Wynn? What is it?"

She held up the paper. "The poem you wrote to me. It's beautiful. I wish I knew how to put words together like that. Yet, I feel them." The sound came out of her like a flutter and transformed into breathing.

"It's just a poem." Doug's face warmed.

"It's more than a poem. How could you know me in ways I don't even know myself?" Wynn wanted to reach for him, but suddenly she felt shy. "I know it's late. May I come in, anyway?"

He pulled her close.

The rise and fall of his chest against her cheek was reassuring.

Doug lifted her chin and looked down at her lips, his face filled with tenderness.

She was consumed by his touch. Her senses came to life.

He smelled of air and earth and sea. "You feel good." His voice was soft and grainy as he lowered his face. His lashes scraped against her cheek as he kissed her.

There came a restlessness in her nature—a hunger for something she had yet to find. The air became electric with possibilities of what could happen between them. Could this moment of new beginnings and sweetness someday morph into memories? She pushed those thoughts away and floated until the kiss finished, and she pulled away.

Slowly, she walked around the living room, trying to get a sense of how he lived. Worn, brown leather furniture; a couch and two armchairs with a hassock, and a large square coffee table absent of anything other than a large conch shell held the center of the room together. The TV hung above the stone fireplace. There was no overhead lighting, but several lamps were lit, giving the place a warm welcoming glow.

He watched her with a tight, dark look in his eyes.

"Say something," she murmured.

"I'm not sure what you want to hear." His voice remained neutral. "Let's sit."

Wynn sat next to him, settled back and tossed off her sandals, curling her feet enough to nestle against the side of his hip, wishing she had given herself a pedicure. She felt the muscled bands of his arms and legs. This was the first time she had ever been totally alone with a man at his place.

"Tell me why," she whispered sweetly.

"Why? I'm not following."

"The mailbox, the stone, the poem." She held out her hands as though she felt the weight of the gifts in them instead of her heart.

"You deserve to be happy. I want to give that to you." He ran his fingers over her lips.

She wished she had a magic wand to make this moment last forever. "I'm probably not like the other women you've known."

"How do you know?"

"I'm not sophisticated—I feel ill at ease in crowds. I feel natural in the woods. I was raised in my two bachelor uncles' home so I never learned etiquette, or decorating skills. My place consists of presents that nature has given me along the way. I wore clothes from Goodwill; one was a pair of purple jeans, which I hated. But I never knew any other way, so I'm fine with it. However, it didn't go unnoticed by the other kids who made fun of me. I never cared. I only wanted to spend my time discovering things about the woods."

"The forest is a good place to be."

"Oh, another thing." She gave a bounce on the cushions and held her finger against her mouth. "I can't wear high heels. I twist my ankles and fall. So I usually do not wear dresses, except for this one."

"I like that dress on you. But do you really think I care about any of that?"

"Do you?"

"I care about you, Wynn Baxter." He pushed hair from her eyes.

"Why?"

"Because high heels make you fall. Because you'd rather be in the woods than at some event. Because you are comfortable in your own skin." He ran his fingers along her arm. "Now, tell me what I am."

"You're a gentleman, Doug Reed. You know what you want and you go for it, never taking no for an answer."

She desperately wanted another kiss. She was uncertain if she should wait for him, or just go ahead and take it. The decision was made when he reached up with his calloused hand, cupped the back of her neck, and dragged her over to his mouth. She felt warm, strong lips against her own. She wrapped her arms around him.

Suddenly he halted.

Her eyes widened. "What's wrong?"

The phone rang again.

Doug left her side to answer. "Really?" she heard him say. "Why is that?"

He returned.

She curled into his side again, but he immediately pulled back.

"Aunt Wilda said you and Roxie spent time on the mainland talking to people about Boone's accident. Even paid a visit to Marilyn's house."

"True."

"We were together all day yesterday, and yet, not one mention of it. I thought we were finally open with one another. Close. Am I wrong about our feelings? Can't you trust me? Or is there another reason?"

"What other reason could there be?"

"That with talking to people in Egg Harbor, coming here, to my home, is your way of getting me to talk and maybe finding out I'm not as innocent as you claim that I am." He scowled.

"Doug. Please listen. We are open. I'm just not ready to disclose everything my aunt and I discovered. But as far as you and I go, I am honest with my feelings. I care about you. Very much. Believe me."

"I do believe you. What did you find out?"

"I can't say just yet. I hope you understand."

"Listen Wynn, my life is at stake here. I could be re-arrested at any moment. I need to know what you found out." He reached for her hand.

"I can't divulge things to you, not yet. Not until after my next Bible study meeting with the women."

"Sounds to me like you are doing far more than Bible reading."

"That's right, we are. But we are in this together. All of us."

"Not all. Not me. You and I went to Egg Harbor yesterday and we've spent hours looking at and discussing the paintings. I cannot help but feel deceived."

"I'd never do that."

Doug walked across the room. "Jackie is part of that group. Remember, Jackie, the one who wants me arrested as soon as possible?"

"Not so much anymore. Doug, please listen to me. I've been on the outside all my life. Finally, with these women, I feel I have a place. I can't betray them by giving up evidence to you when they've asked me not to until we make sense of it."

"So there's evidence?" Doug folded his arms.

"Maybe that's the wrong word choice."

Doug crossed back to Wynn and took her hands in his. "Wynn, tell me."

She turned away.

"But I'm the one who is in trouble. The accused. Remember?" His voice had an edge.

"I can't forget." She gazed at the floor.

"Then help me out."

"Look, talk to your aunt; she's part of the group. After we reveal all our information at the next meeting, she can tell you everything. I will turn over all the findings to you and your lawyer. But right now, I don't feel it would help you, anyway."

"Let my lawyer be the judge of that."

"I think I should go." Wynn felt her beautiful relationship with Doug was ruined. She started for the door.

"Stop!" Doug snapped the word astonishing loudly in the quiet room.

Wynn froze.

"Please sit down," he said more quietly.

"No." Her hand was on the doorknob and she wasn't letting go.

"Sit down!"

She reached for a kitchen chair by the door and sat, crossing her arms and legs. She looked up at him.

"I'm sorry. I didn't mean to yell at you. Forgive me."

"I forgive you. But, I better get going now."

Doug walked towards her. His hands were trembling. The circles under his eyes were more prominent and his mouth was set in a tight expression.

She wished she could wipe away the dark circles, turn his lips into a smile. She wished she was the kind of person who could go to him and put her arms around him spontaneously. Wynn lowered her gaze, not wanting him to see her tearing eyes.

He knelt in front of her and drew her back to him. He feathered her hair with his fingers and swept the tendrils from her face.

"Again, I'm sorry. I may have over-reacted." He apologized.

"I would never betray you."

"Are you going to be around in the morning?"

Wynn stood and opened the door. 'Call me to come back to you', she thought. 'Call me back, one more time and I will tell you everything.' She felt tears trickle down her cheeks.

Doug remained silent.

She left the lighthouse and went to her car.

The lamplight behind him made his features impossible to make out.

She looked up and counted the stars until the tears dried.

'Call me back.' She looked at the window.

It was empty.

28

Jackie, Owl, Faith, Sheri, Wynn and Roxie assembled on Roxie's front porch for the task force meeting.

No one smiled this morning. Today they had serious matters to discuss. Everyone held their private notebook and a pencil, ready to take notes as packets of information each had gathered about their discoveries was handed out.

Faith served dessert—crème Brulee with a thick seared coating of sugar covering the top.

Wynn shuffled her notes. "Ready?"

Everyone nodded.

"Let's start with updates. Anything current happening with the case that we should be aware of?"

Everyone shook their heads.

"OK, let's move onto evidence. At our last meeting we assigned Faith to speak with Frank about anything else the police may have divulged about the case when he personally served them lunch at the Inn last week. Owl was to talk to Doug's lawyer to find out how tight the case against him was, Jackie you were bringing lab results; I have the police report, and Roxie and I interviewed witnesses together."

"You also spoke to Marilyn." Jackie cut in. "She wasn't happy with that unexpected visit."

"And we have some interesting information on that one." Roxie finished her dessert.

"I can't wait to hear." Jackie clasped her hands together. "I always felt that Marilyn saw Boone on the day he died, but she is adamant that isn't true. What did you discuss with her?"

"We need to go one at a time. Who wants to start?" Wynn asked.

Everyone pointed to Wynn.

"OK. I will begin with the police report." She read what was found at the accident scene focusing on the shoes. "Jackie, here is a picture taken of the shoes. Do you recognize them?"

Jackie narrowed her focus. "Marilyn has a pair just like those."

"Could they actually be Marilyn's?" Faith asked in horror.

"That's what we are trying to find out. If so, it puts her at the crime scene."

Roxie picked up where Wynn left off.

"As you see there is a short list of witnesses and we visited almost every one of them!"

"What did you discover, dear?" Owl wanted to know

"A sweet lady said that someone fitting Marilyn's description took the homeless man's wallet, but Marilyn vehemently denied it. And Wynn spotted the dry cleaners receipt on Boone's suit."

Jackie came up out of her seat. "That proves Boone was with Marilyn! I knew she lied! She is holding something back! I'm calling my lawyer and the police, right now."

"No, wait." Wynn held out her hand towards her. "We aren't finished with all the reports. There will be time for all that once we've all had our turn."

Jackie reluctantly returned to her seat, but sat

jiggling her right foot anxiously.

"Sheri, you are next."

"Well, there was so much gossip and people just plain making things up. I kept up with it and took notes. I, too, have made copies." Sheri handed out the papers. "As you can see, the consensus on the island is that Doug is in love with Jackie, whom he was having an affair with."

"Stop right there!" Jackie was on her feet again. "I most certainly was not!"

"Jackie, please don't take this personally," Wynn pleaded.

"I didn't say you were having an affair with Doug, I just said that is what people are saying."

"I'm as angry as you are, Jackie. I don't understand why people have to make up stories about others," Wynn said. "But it's still good to know what people are suspecting."

Roxie fanned her with a copy of the police report to calm her.

"Please continue Sheri, we want to know everything." Wynn prodded.

"I stuck up for you Jackie, don't worry. You'd never have an affair with Doug, or anyone else, for that matter. There are two camps of thought, actually. I just reported what the first camp believes." Sheri took a sideways glance at her friend, not wanting to repeat it. "The second camp believes Boone somehow hurt himself on the schooner and died quickly. Oh, and a couple from the mainland, which I shall refer to as the third camp, said they thought Boone was Joseph Reed re-incarnated and that is why he suffered a similar death."

"Re-incarnation is totally preposterous!" Roxie

said.

All the women nodded in agreement.

"Similar? It's not similar at all." Jackie protested.

"That's correct," added Owl. "Especially since we don't know how Joseph Reed died, and we may never find that out."

"And that's all I have about gossip and innuendoes. Who's next?"

Owl raised her hand. "I would like to speak next. The lawyer said it looks very bad for Doug."

"What is the motive, then?" Wynn asked.

"They are still digging for one."

"Of course, because there isn't one."

"Careful Wynn. Remain impartial. It's the only way this can work," Roxie pointed out.

"Excuse me." Faith was soft spoken. "I spoke with Frank again to ask about any added information he might have been told by the police. Of course, I didn't tell him about our task force. The police feel it has to have been done by someone familiar with the schooner because they knew about the hiding place. It also had to be someone very strong in order to hoist Boone up onto the deck like that."

Wynn thought about Agatha's brooch and wondered if she may have been an accomplice. Then again, she appeared to be way too small and weak to hoist her brother onboard. Agatha was odd, but Wynn was fairly sure she was not a murderer, if it turned out Boone was murdered.

"Who discovered the hiding place, anyway?" Roxie wanted to know.

"There was a note sent to the police department saying where Boone's body was. The smell by that time was so horrid that he was easily located." Faith continued. "Sorry Jackie, I know that must have been hard for you to hear. The police also discovered that one of the ropes for the jib had been wrapped around him and they suspect he was taken aboard by pulleys."

"That tidbit hasn't come out in the news." Owl said. "I wonder if the police have released this information to the defense and prosecutor. Is that the cause of death? Strangulation by hanging?"

"Jackie, for a time, you received anonymous notes. Have you gotten any recently?" Sheri asked.

"No, I haven't. I guess it's my turn now to share. The cause of death is determined. I have the lab report." Jackie held it up in the air before passing it to Wynn. "I don't understand all this. Perhaps you will."

"I'm certainly not a medical examiner, nor a doctor, but I might be able to interpret some of the terminology and blood results." Wynn scanned the report. "It says here everything was within normal ranges. Wait. There was an extremely high level of retinol in Boone's body which is extremely toxic. That means he also has signs of acute toxicity."

"Which are?"

"Skin turns orange. Loss of hair. Bone pain. Slurred speech. Vomiting. Death." Wynn's voice trailed off.

"How horrible!" Jackie covered her eyes. "But isn't retinol in the eye? How could it be in all his tissues?"

"No, that's retina. Retinol is a form of Vitamin A. And he had a toxic level in his system. Was he taking a lot of vitamins?

"Yes, he believed in them, but certainly never overdosed on them." Jackie answered. "Boone is a precise type of person. I mean, he was."

Everyone paused in a moment of respect for her

reignited grief.

"I think it would be nearly impossible to take this much vitamin A on one's own. I wonder how that much got into his system?" Wynn couldn't come up with the answer.

"Maybe someone tampered with his vitamins." Roxie pulled at the hem of her skirt.

"It says right here that cause of death is Hypervitaminosis A."

"And now I know." Jackie sighed.

"Now we all know," Wynn said.

"I didn't identify Boone's body the first time, and the second time he was identified by tissue samples and dental records. His body was so decomposed that I wasn't allowed to see him until he was 'fixed up'. The first time I received a call from Mr. Hanover with the news that Boone had been struck by a truck in Egg Harbor and was pronounced dead at the scene. He asked if I wanted him to make arrangements for him to be embalmed there and they would have him brought over by special boat. I agreed. It seemed like the right thing to do. Then he was cremated instead, but I never asked for that. But that wasn't Boone's ashes, it was someone else's."

"Let's add Mr. Hanover to the suspect list." Roxie instructed Wynn. She agreed and wrote down his name.

"There's something else very interesting in the coroner's report." Wynn turned the page. "It says minute pieces of antique colored paper were found under Boones fingernails. That is so strange."

"Why would that be there?" Jackie wondered.

"On TV I've seen where DNA of the attacker's skin can be found under the victims nails," Owl offered.

"Evidence under fingernails is very common."

"I just don't see why this paper would be under Boone's fingernails." Jackie looked stressed.

"I keep thinking about the woman who was described by not one, but two witnesses, as kneeling beside the homeless man—possibly rendering aid or robbing him. Wasn't Marilyn a nurse once?" Faith picked up the dessert plates to take to the kitchen.

"I was." Marilyn walked in, followed by Agatha.

The room quieted.

Roxie sprang up and pulled up two dining room chairs for them to sit.

"We were just…"

"I know. It's the task force. Agatha told me about it. That's why I've come." Marilyn looked drained as she leaned over the coffee table and in the center, placed the ruby ring encrusted with emerald jewels. "I had it all along."

Wynn breathed a sigh of relief that Doug hadn't taken it, after all. But she still wondered if anyone connected the missing ring to Boone's death. For now, she would remain silent about her supposition.

"Why didn't you tell anyone?" Jackie snapped.

"It's no one's business but my own. This ring belongs to me." She turned to Jackie. "Not to Boone, certainly not to you."

"But Boone said…"

"I don't care what Boone said. The truth is the truth. It would only belong to Boone after my death. However, I don't want it anymore. It's brought nothing but distress and death." Marilyn starred at the ring.

"Jackie, I guess the ring is yours, then," Roxie said.

"I don't want the ring, either." Jackie shuddered, crossing her arms.

"Then I will put it in my wall safe. You both might very well be fighting over it in another month." Roxie slipped the ring onto her finger and admired it. "Marilyn, tell us about that day; the last time you saw Boone."

"Boone did go to your place first, before taking the ferry, didn't he?" Wynn asked.

Marilyn nodded. "I lied to Wynn and Roxie."

"You mean you lied to the police and everyone else, too." Jackie spat.

"That's right, Jackie. I did see Boone when he returned from Nepal. Just as always, he came to say hello to me first, and bring me a few presents from overseas. A cashmere, hand embroidered shawl, some gold pieces of jewelry are what he gave to me. Everything seemed almost normal, like all the other times, except this time he seemed distraught. He said his business was bankrupt. It was about to be seized by the IRS. He would lose everything. Boone asked for the inheritance from his father. That ring."

Wynn was mesmerized. "Go on."

"I told him he couldn't have it. That it was my ring. Not his inheritance; not yet. We argued. He said he always supported me and Agatha and would continue to do so, but needed the ring to pay off debts or we would all be living off welfare."

"Where is Boone's luggage?" Jackie asked Marilyn. "I want it just as he left it. Nothing removed."

"It's at your house. I left it there before coming here today. Boone changed out of his suit when he arrived, into casual clothes. But everything else is there, just as he left it."

Wynn cleared her throat. "One of the witnesses thought perhaps you were a nurse giving aid. Someone else said they saw you take his wallet. Still, another witness said you put something on him."

"This is so hard." Marilyn took a deep breath. "Boone's suits are always filthy when he returns from his trips. I took it to the cleaners. When I got there, the clerk went through the pockets and found his wallet with his identification. I slipped it into my purse to return it to him."

"And when the homeless man was hit, you saw your chance to trade identities."

"Not at first. Not at first." Marilyn swallowed hard. "I knelt beside the man to check for his pulse. There wasn't any. I reached into his pocket to find an ID. There wasn't any. That's when I thought about Boone's wallet with all of his information. It was a spur of the moment decision. If Boone was pronounced dead, we could collect on his life insurance."

"But Boone wouldn't go along with that," Roxie said.

"That's right. But at that moment on the street, the idea seemed to be the solution to all of our problems."

"How did you propose to hide Boone?"

"No hiding. We'd move some place warm, overseas. But when I returned and told Boone my plan, he was livid. We argued. He left in a rage, leaving his suitcase behind. I thought he was going to the police to get things straightened out concerning the accident. But I swear, I don't know what happened after that."

"We believe you." Jackie crossed the room and hugged her trembling mother-in-law.

"I called the coroner's office about the homeless man. I assumed Boone would be also headed that way to get his wallet back. But when I called, I found out that Boone hadn't come for his wallet, after all. The coroner asked me to come to identify Boone's body. So I did. I asked that he be cremated. Here is Boone's wallet, Jackie."

29

Wynn placed her samples between glass before covering them in layers of bubble wrap, and then double boxing them. Her notes and papers went into a separate container. By the time she was finished loading everything, the entire backseat of the car was filled with her completed grant. She took a deep breath and thanked God for seeing her through it. Before she headed to the post office, she decided to deadbolt the Tree House for the first time.

Too many mysteries seemed to be swirling around the island and she didn't want a nasty surprise to greet her behind a closed, unlocked door when she returned. Now that she had a kitten, she needed to keep him safe, as well as all of the expensive scientific equipment.

Roxie might like to go for a swim in the cove with her once the packages were mailed. Lately, she felt connected to her aunt in new ways. Whatever the truth was about her family, she would forgive. Spending time with the Bible study ladies and in prayer had taught her many things, but the most valuable lesson was mercy. Most of her life had been spent being critical of her mother and aunt. Just recently, she realized she needed to offer forgiveness.

At the turn of the drive she noticed the Bible study ladies' cars. Not wanting to intrude, she headed back towards her own car, feeling wounded. No one had mentioned any meeting today; either Bible study or task force.

All the way into town and even standing in line at the post office, she tried to divert her thoughts from the meeting, and towards her future. By fall she'd leave the island, whether Doug had been exonerated or not, whether the mystery of her dad's death was solved, or not. Perhaps there are things that should be placed into the hands of God. Isn't that what Roxie was always trying to teach her? Wynn twitched a smile in thought.

Dare she stay here and risk disappointment? But wasn't that what living was all about? Hurt and joy? Disappointment and gratification? Her heart kept arguing with her mind.

In truth, she wanted to remain here; get to know Doug better. She desired to live among the vegetation and wildlife, be a part of those lovely Bible study women, and most of all, regard Roxie as a mother she never had.

She managed to find her way into a community of women who were smart, independent, supportive, and enjoyed one another's company without ever competing against each other. They were the oasis she had needed all her life.

Wynn stopped for an ice cream cone and decided to head to the cove alone to enjoy the sun and the waves—right along with the rest of the day. Nearly there, the car suddenly listed to the side. She slowed. Wynn pulled over, and hopped out to examine the car. There it was—a very flat, right rear tire.

Wynn pulled out her cell, but there weren't bars. She popped the trunk and looked in. OK, she could do this. She hadn't changed a tired since high school. She found rocks to stick under the rear tires to keep the car from rolling, and then set out the reflective warning. She pulled up the flap trunk's covering and unscrewed the wing nut releasing the tire. Wynn returned to the trunk to get the jack and the lug nut wrench.

A brown paper sack fluttered in the wheel well. Wynn opened it expecting to find tire changing instructions.

The temperature around her filled with humidity. The world seemed to stand still, nothing moved; not a fly, not a leaf, not a rabbit's tail—certainly not a cloud—for a split second there was only silence ringing loudly in her ears.

The heartbreak that had hidden for a lifetime suddenly revealed itself as the horrifying truth. It made her stand frozen in time—all due to the blue and white model speed boat she held in her hand. A light switch came on in the dark room of repressed memory and now she could see clearly as if the frames of a movie sped by.

る○ふ

It had taken them months to paint, put together, seal, and attach the water proof electrical motor. Wynn turned it over in her hand and flipped the switch. A weak roar began that gradually became louder and louder. She ran the fingers of her right hand through her hair because she had a death grasp on the boat with the other hand.

Six-year-old Wynn drank orange juice. They were in the kitchen, an airy, art filled room lit by the morning sun which filtered through glass doors opening onto a tiny porch.

Dad was staring at her with that marvelous smile

that always made his lips seem crooked. The very same smile she had seen on her own lips in the pictures Roxie had hidden from her.

She looked down at her hand—no longer the hand of her adult self—but of her six-year-old self holding the boat. "Dad, please let's go to the lake today."

"No," her mother contradicted. "It's way too choppy. Your boat will be lost in the waves. You may have to wait until spring, now."

Wynn furrowed her brow. "No. I want to go now."

"How about if we try the tub, pumpkin?" Dad was eager to appease her.

"Can we please put it in the lake?" Wynn begged again. "I want to see it go fast!"

After a moment of hesitation, he capitulated. "I guess it'd be OK, but just along the shore." Dad went for their coats. "Come on, Ruth!"

"This is what spoils her, Steve, you always giving in to her—just like Roxie."

The back door creaked open. "Did someone say my name?"

"Aunt Roxie you're here! Yay! Now you can come, too!" Wynn hopped on one foot, and then on the other.

"And just where are we going?"

"To put this in the lake!" Wynn held out the boat.

"Sounds like fun."

"Not fun. Too cold." Ruth adamantly shook her head.

A frown covered Roxie's face. "Your mom is right. It is cold out there."

"Who's cold? I'm not cold," Dad said.

"Who's cold? I'm not cold," said Wynn.

"Who's cold? I'm not cold," said Roxie.

"OK, OK. I see I am outnumbered." Mom laughed, pulling on her jacket and bringing the hood down over her head. "But just the shallow end. Agreed?"

"Agreed!"

"Agreed!"

"Agreed!"

They walked through piles of blowing, colored leaves with Wynn in the lead. When they reached the shoreline, Dad let Wynn turn on the motor, and set the toy boat into the water. It gurgled at first, and then whizzed twenty feet along before getting hung up on old lake weed.

"I want to take it out there where other boats go." Wynn pointed to the horizon.

"No."

"Take my inboard." Roxie held out the keys tethered to a cork bobber.

"Roxie, you aren't helping." Ruth glared. "We are going home now, Wynn."

"Wynn, your mother is right; this is as far as we go with this. Now you have to wait until spring." Dad pulled the zipper up on his coat.

"Ruth, you and Steve go on home. My boat hasn't been put up for winter, yet. I'll take Wynn up the shore to my place and we'll go out for a just a few minutes."

"Oh yes, please, please, please." Wynn placed her hands together as she turned to her dad with plea-filled eyes.

"Well, if someone goes out, it will be me in the boat with Wynn." Dad was insistent. "I'm the captain and Wynn is my First Mate!"

Overjoyed, Wynn clapped. There was the odor of water over stones and the musk of decayed fall leaves, a wild, fragrant sensation filled the air.

"Come on!" Dad led the way. It seemed to grow colder by the minute since there were only a few hours of daylight left, but Wynn felt icy hands and toes were well worth it. By the look on her dad's and Roxie's face, they felt the very same. She couldn't see her mother's face, but she felt tension.

They stood on Roxie's dock together. Dad's voice was soft, explaining in uncomplicated terms what they were about to do with the toy boat. Wynn nodded her head, pretending she understood, wanting so to please her dad.

Dad removed the tarp from the inboard and reached towards the pier to help Wynn into the boat. He strapped a life jacket on her.

Ruth reluctantly hopped into the boat.

"Come on Roxie, you're next." Dad held out his arms to her.

Roxie hung back. "I think this is a mommy—daddy—Wynn event. I'll watch from here. Everyone needs a cheerleader. I will be yours."

Dad's face caved. He nodded, and then untied the boat from the slip.

Mom started the boat and she slowly drove through the choppy water as an occasional cascade of lake water rained over them.

Wynn remained portside, close to her dad, while Mom kept her eyes locked on the sea before her.

"This is far enough from shore!" Dad called, cupping his hands around his mouth and shouting.

Mom slowed more and cut the motor.

Dad leaned over the side and placed the toy boat in the water, aiming it towards shore. There it went, dipping in and out of the waves.

They clapped and shouted "Hurrah!" Suddenly it

disappeared from sight.

"We need to go in, Steve! It's freezing and we are all soaked to the bone!" Ruth called. More words were said between them.

Wynn rubbed her forehead and tried to remember them.

Her mother started the boat again; then turned and aimed for shore. That's when they caught sight of the toy boat again, seemingly out of gas and at the mercy of the water bouncing it about. Mom got as close as she could without running it over, but it seemed as though the waves took the big boat in one direction and the toy boat in another.

"Get closer Ruth! I can almost reach it."

Wynn pictured the extension of his arm, his wide hand, and the long fingers reaching towards it, a few inches too short. Then he leaned out even further, his waist over the side of the boat. Now he hung precariously above the water. Just as his fingers touched the tip of the toy, a large wave pushed the big boat sideways causing him lose balance and drop overboard, landing in the water at the same time his head hit against the boat.

Blood painted so many swirls and twirls in the water. His unconscious form drifted down, down, down until Wynn could no longer see him.

Wynn screamed and opened her hand. The toy boat dropped to the road and cracked. She knew why no one wanted to tell her the truth about her dad's death. No one wanted to tell a six-year-old she killed her dad.

30

"Hello? Are you all right?" a man in a convertible stopped. "Can I fix that flat for you?"

"What? Yes, please." Wynn felt disoriented. When the new tire was on, she offered money which he waved off.

Wynn started up the car and found a place in the road to turn around. She drove too fast towards home, expecting to be stopped at any moment, but what police golf cart would try to chase her down?

Wynn staggered into the cottage reaching for the back of an empty armchair in the living room where she collapsed. Flinging her head and arms down over her knees, she sobbed.

Roxie knelt in front of her. "Are you all right? Wynn, tell me what happened."

"I remember now." Wynn looked up with a tear streaked face.

"Remember what?" Roxie asked with trepidation.

"I killed my dad. It's my fault. He took me out on the water when the weather was too bad; mom warned us, saying we shouldn't go. But I kept insisting. No wonder you wouldn't tell me." Wynn moved to the floor to be closer to her aunt and wrapped her arms around her, needing her more than ever.

Roxie rocked Wynn in her arms. "You didn't kill him, honey. But I wanted you to remember for so long and now I wish you hadn't."

Wynn pulled back, choking on her tears, gasping for air and looking at her aunt. "I needed to know. I just have to find a way to live with it now."

"You will find a way through this. We both will." Roxie pushed Wynn to arm's length. "Wynn, look at me. You did not cause your dad's death—you witnessed his death, and then blocked it out of your memory for many years. A lot of things happened, or didn't happen that day, that contributed to it. You were just a little girl wanting to see your boat run in the water. I was an adult and knew better. Much better."

"Don't blame yourself. Roxie, please forgive me. When I tell you about something, you will never forgive me."

"I'd forgive you anything."

"Not for this. Ever since I came to the island I thought you and Dad had an affair. Ridiculous. Don't you see how wicked I am?"

Roxie's eyes widened. She got to her feet and walked to the windows which overlooked the lake. "No. Not totally ridiculous."

Wynn stopped sobbing. She got up from the floor and moved to the armchair. "You and my dad had an affair? Did Mom know?"

Roxie turned from the window to face her niece.

"Please tell me, it's time for family secrets to come out." Wynn sighed heavily. "For a while this summer I even thought you were my mother."

"If only. If only." Roxie sat on the footstool in front of her and ran her hand around Wynn's face. "But I will tell you everything. It is time."

"Good." She breathed out.

"Remember our talk the other day when I said all

the clues are in front of you?"

"Like this one?" Wynn pulled the cracked boat from her backpack and set in between them.

"So that's how the memories came back. Yes, I put that in the wheel well." Roxie held Wynn's hands. "It was important that you find the facts of your life—to remember them on your own. I didn't want to taint your memories."

"But there are still gaps. Things I never knew. Things I need to know. What was your relationship like with my mom? Sheri said you two got along really well."

"Not true, but don't blame Sheri for the misinformation. She doesn't know. The truth is your mother and I never got along. Our mother, your Grammy, used to say that we fought one another even in her womb.

"As toddlers we knocked one another off our feet. In elementary school there was fierce competition about who had the best grades, winning the most awards, being teacher's pet, who our parents loved best. During high school there was less competition, thank goodness, because we started to change and become individuals. Ruth was a cheerleader, I played in the band. I began waitressing to save for college; while your mom chased boys and browsed catalogues for dish patterns. I wanted a career and she wanted marriage." Roxie laughed with the memory. "Then I met someone the summer before college. Steve Baxter."

"Dad," Wynn said with a voice filled with love.

"Yes, your dad. The first look at him and I was smitten. Forever smitten. He was the love of my life."

"Is he still the love of your life?" Wynn asked.

"It's been so long Wynn, I just don't know, but

probably."

"Maybe Dad is the reason why you never married?"

"I never married because I never met anyone who measured up." Roxie dabbed at the tears in her eyes with her fingers. "Here come the tears, even after all these years."

"It's OK to cry. Tell me more about the triangle; You, Dad, and Mom."

"What an appropriate name for us. Steve knew my dream was to be a teacher. He also knew that would put me around a lot of new men. So, to keep me faithful, he gave me a promise ring before I went off to college. Here I was semi-engaged when it was Ruth who wanted marriage. But Steve changed my thinking about so much. About everything. We had so much fun when we were together. We talked far into the night. Oh, how that man made me laugh!" Roxie seemed wistful. "I came home every chance I could to be with him. He loved the island and wanted us to settle here. I didn't mind. Just being with him was an adventure."

"So what happened? How did Mom get involved?"

"I was gone a lot, as one is when at college. Steve became lonely. I had my books for comfort. Steve had your mom. It started with visiting your Grammy and Gramps, and of course, Ruth was always there. As a result of both being lonely, they began doing things together—as friends many times do. And feelings between them budded, and then grew. I spotted it right away when I came home for Christmas during my junior year. I was heartbroken. Soon after I went back to school, Steve called to say that he loved Ruth and asked for me to release him from his promise to me. I returned the ring. The pain was searing."

"How long did they date before they married?"

"About six months. It was a lovely wedding. I was the maid of honor."

"That must have been brutal on you." Wynn squeezed her aunt's hands, offering comfort.

"Yes. And in some peculiar way, Doug reminds me of your dad."

"Doug?" Wynn found this strange. "You loved Dad, but he reminds you of Doug, whom you dislike."

"It finally occurred to me that the reason I distrust Doug so much is because he reminds me of your dad who left me for your mother—not once, but twice. The staggering hurt I still feel to this day, at times, thinking of what might have been. I loved him so much. I don't want unrequited love for you."

"Tell me more about my parents."

"Ruth and Steve were married that summer, under the maples in our parent's field. Our parents gave their home to them as a wedding gift, and then returned to live on the farm on the mainland."

"That doesn't seem quite fair to you."

"Oh, I was given this cottage as my inheritance." Roxie explained. "There were problems between your parents from the start, but I didn't spot it for months. I must admit I was very wicked because I was pleased about it. After all my sister had snatched the man I loved right out from under my nose and now she was paying the price. Marry in haste, repent in leisure.

"I did my best to keep my pleasure in check. I knew my feelings were wrong; sinful, but I couldn't help myself. I wanted to be married to your dad. I wanted to have children with him. That desire never stopped. The following summer I tried to stay away. Instead of coming home, I worked on the mainland so I wouldn't see Steve, or your mom. What was wrong they had to fix. And to this day, I still feel as though I was the right choice for Steve—well, if it wasn't for you."

"You said you were hurt by Dad twice."

"Yes, when I was hired as an elementary school teacher here on the island, his attention slowly returned to me. Your mother didn't go away physically like I had done when I went to college, but she became remote. Chilly. Icy. That pulled your dad and me even closer. He was lonely in his marriage. I was lonely in my singleness. We were the ones who had that first connection.

"While your mother was lost in her world, he turned back to me. I think he gradually fell in love with me all over again. He said your mother and he had very little in common. We even talked of being together. Excuse me for saying too much, Wynn. This has got to hurt you—but this happened all before you were born."

"Knowing the truth helps heal me. How did Dad end it with you?"

"One day, your dad and I met at our secret place in one of the coves. He told me he decided to stay with Ruth—end of discussion. So, for the second time, I fell apart."

"I'm sorry."

"You are sweet to say that, dear. But I am the one who is sorry. The day your dad died, your mom didn't want to go to the beach, but your dad and I insisted. We had the control over going or not going—not you—not your mother—and together we overruled. It had been many years since your dad and I had been alone together. But I was still trying to prove to him that I was the better choice for him. When we were at the beach I brought up the idea of taking my boat out because I was trying to demonstrate that I was the fun aunt, the better choice to be your mom. I stood on shore, watching you all go out into the lake.

"The waves were terrible—just as your mom had said. Instead of staying, I decided to go back to the house and make hot chocolate for everyone. I had just gotten to the house when I heard sirens. You and your mom were on a boat flailing about in rough seas, while your dad had drowned feet below. I did so many things wrong, selfishly hoping to be with Steve again; wanting you as my daughter. I am a terrible, terrible person." Roxie sobbed into her hands.

Wynn let her cry for a good while as she assimilated the new information. "We were all culpable in some way. Dad didn't wear a life jacket either, did he?"

"No, not that day." Roxie looked into Wynn's eyes. "Don't hate me."

"I don't hate you. I love you."

"I would give anything if that was the truth." Roxie searched her eyes.

Wynn slowly pulled her backpack up on her lap. She unzipped it and reached inside. "I have something I swiped from the bank box." Wynn handed her aunt the timeline. "I'm sorry I took this."

"Thank you." Roxie got to her feet and started to tape the paper to the living room wall, but it was so long it kept tearing.

"Let me help." Side by side the women unfolded the paper a bit at a time and carefully reattached it.

"Later, I'll go to the bank and pick up the pictures that go with this."

"I'll help." Wynn took the tape from her aunt. "Did you ever find out why my dad broke up with you for the second time?"

"Never."

"I do know."

Roxie's mouth slacked.

"There was a letter addressed to you that I found in the car's glove box."

"A letter?" Roxie was surprised. She gulped hard. "From Steve?"

Wynn nodded. "It was signed 'Steve'.

"Oh my….can you tell me what it said?" Roxie seemed anxious, as though everything was pinned on the answer.

"You can read it for yourself." Wynn smiled. She pulled the envelope from her backpack and placed it into Roxie's hand. "When you said the answers I seek are right under my nose, I guess you never looked for your answers under your own nose."

"I feel like I am recovering from the shock of this." She kept blinking back tears as she unfolded the paper a bit at a time. "This is like a time capsule." As she read, a wide smile spread across her face. Then she pressed it to her chest as Wynn had pressed Doug's poem to hers. "Steve probably imagined I would find it someday."

"And you did. Mom was pregnant with me at the time. And time had to wait until I had grown up to come back to you, so I could hand this letter to the recipient."

"You dad loved me. Steve did love me."

"And I am sure that you and Ruth always loved

one another, even though you didn't get along. And now I know Dad loved you both, as you both loved him. And as for me? I was born into this love. I am loved." Wynn's voice broke off for several minutes. "It's a gift. It's a gift I have needed all of my life."

"You are so much like your dad. You've always been fascinated by the croak of a frog, the chirp of a bird, an overhead branch with an unusual twist, the unfiltered sparkle on a hidden marsh. Being with you is like being with your Dad, too."

"Dad. My dad wrote this letter to you about me."

"Yes, and here we are. Finally together."

"I think he's watching over you and me, just as he watches over Mom. This clue was inside of my car, just as faith was inside of me—both were waiting to be discovered. And I've made a conscious decision to accept the Lord who brought me back home to you— where I've belonged all along."

31

"If you aren't busy tonight, I thought, perhaps, we might do something together."

"It just so happens I am not busy tonight. Is there anything you have in mind?" Wynn held the cell to her ear, thinking Doug sounded kind of coy and mysterious.

"There's a drive-in at the end of the peninsula."

"A drive-in on the island? That's so old school and it sounds wonderful. What's playing?" Already she was wishing she had more time so she could buy something special to wear.

"The best movie ever made; a killer view complete with sounds of the sea."

"Now I know what you mean. You are right. There's nothing better." She wound hair tendrils around her fingers.

"The moon will be out by then and dancing on the waves. There's no one else I'd rather see it with."

"I'd like to see that with you, too."

"We might as well join the moon and water, and dance together."

"I'd like that."

A short silence fell between them filled with light and longing and anticipation. She welcomed each emotion. Tilting her head back she looked at the reddening sky 'sailors delight'. Her pulse was rapid and she tried to remember the last time she felt like this, realizing with a start, this was the first time that joy and hope made her heart race.

"Well—see you about nine."

"See you at nine."

Maybe this is a dress kind of a night. Wynn laughed, feeling girlishly giddy. She opened her wardrobe closet and saw nothing but jeans, pullover shirts and plenty of sweatshirts. There was one funeral dress. No good. And there was the white gauzy, peasant dress. That's what she'd wear. She held it up and stood in front of the full length mirror trying to imagine dancing in the moonlight with Doug. And then she thought about Roxie and her mom, Ruth, and her dad Steve. How all three loved one another, but in the end, lost each other. Yet, she still had Roxie. She would hold onto Roxie.

After showering, blow drying, make-uping, powdering, and brushing, she put the dress on and stood again in the front of the mirror. She had to admit that she didn't look so bad. Perfume was considered, but then just as quickly dismissed for it was a lightning rod for bugs. She decided to go to Roxie's for her opinion. As she passed the mailbox, she noticed it slightly ajar.

She looked inside and there was the unique skeleton key. It seemed to be identical to the key Anna Reed wore in the museum painting. Her hands began trembling. Suddenly a sickening feeling enveloped her. "Are you toying with me, Doug?"

She slipped the key into her pocket as she walked down to the cottage. The door was locked. Roxie never locked her home. Worried, Wynn walked all the way around the cottage peering into windows to see if anything appeared amiss. The place was just as tidy as ever. Next she tried her cell phone. It went right to voice mail. "Roxie, I found an old skeleton key in my mailbox. It's too long to go into, but I think there is a door at the Willow Inn that this just might fit. Meet me there? I don't want to look around alone."

First she'd lock her Tree House. She'd miss Doug before he arrived. She hated herself for standing him up, but she felt rattled. Doubts were creeping back about his innocence. How could she care so much about him and have reservations about his virtue?

As she ran up the steps, she began considering that Doug wouldn't have put something as obvious as this key in the mailbox even if he was the killer. And if he was innocent, wouldn't he want them to go together to find the lock where the key fit? After all, why kill her? Maybe he thought she had the ring? Would Owl have told him that Roxie had it? Chills ran up her arms. Maybe she should go to the police with what she knew and give them the key and Agatha's brooch. Where was that brooch, anyway? She dug through a dresser drawer, found it, and slipped it into her purse.

By now, it was heavy dusk and shadows were long in the room. She needed to go now if she was to avoid Doug. In all politeness she should leave a note. Sailor lay on the bed near the desk. "Hi, sweetie." She tried to pet him, but he jumped under the bed. "Well, phooey on you, little man."

As she took pen in hand, there were sounds coming up the steps. "Doug? Roxie is that you?" Wynn peered down the corridor and saw a figure dressed in black coming right towards her.

"Who are you? Stop right there." She slammed the door and decided to run to the porch for her escape. She could shimmy down a tree. Only she had waited a moment too long to figure her route. Just as she reached the middle of the room, a pair of gloved hands wrapped around her neck.

Trying to fight him off, she twirled about and her legs got tangled up with her attacker's, making her fall to the floor—he fell on her. The crack of her head on the wood floor radiated through her skull. Her vision went blurry.

A dark figure loomed above. Over his face was a stocking cap with the eyes cut out. Without a word, he slung her over his shoulder and carried her down the flight of stairs, rolling her into the back of some kind of SUV, before covering her face with a mask with a sickening sweet smell.

When she awoke, she was in a small room with peeling blue toile wallpaper. She tried to focus and take brief inventory. There was a single unmade bed. An old scuffed dresser. But what fascinated her was the glass coffin lined in velvet that was now decayed and torn.

Beneath the rocker was a long cylindrical object: a red straw. Fear set off anger and panic, igniting like sparklers on the 4th of July.

Doug just happened to be on the same ferry taking Sailor to Clara's on the same day she was going to the bank. A good cover story to keep tabs on her and get information. He even encouraged her to accept Frank's date invitation. Days later, when he took her to the museum he called her attention to the key. Perhaps the same key was placed in the mailbox just hours ago when he planned to take her to a view of the sea; a killer view, he told her.

Why her? For ransom? Roxie had the ring in her wall safe. So now she was about to be disposed of just like Boone. But how did he get all that vitamin A in his system?

The room looked like the one in the paintings, but the furnishings were all very different.

It was so hot that she felt the room had to be near the roof line of the attic. Slowly she moved her hand towards the red straw and pushed it down into the pocket of her skirt.

"I need a hypothesis." She tried to get her mind off her weak stomach. Scientific reasoning made her think more clearly.

The giant man looked down on her.

"Who are you?" she barely moaned. Despite every muscle in her body hurting she managed to push herself up into a sitting position.

The giant didn't respond.

"You killed Boone. Why?"

Still no response.

"Who is working with you? Certainly, you aren't doing this alone."

"Why not?" His voice was gruff, yet familiar.

"You tell me." She shrugged. "How'd you get Boone to the island without help? How'd you lift him up on the boat without help? How did you kill him? And why?" With each question she rose until she was standing. There was such a burning desire to hurt this person and she took several steps forward. She tried to kick him in the thigh, but it was like kicking a boulder. He grabbed her foot and lifted it high, causing her to lose her balance. She fell back on the floor. This wasn't Doug. This man was way too large. But she did get a whiff of something. Vanilla?

"Frank?" she puffed out the word before thrusting her body forward. "Polar bear!"

"What?" the giant shook his head.

"You took me on a tour of the Inn. There was polar bear meat in your locker. Polar bear's liver has high levels of vitamin A which can poison. You killed Boone! It's you, Frank! You look pretty warm in that mask. Might as well take it off, now that I know who you are." She spotted her backpack on the floor a few yards from Frank's feet. Suddenly she remembered the brooch with the nice, sharp clasp.

The giant removed his wool mask, and then his cap and jacket. He sat down. "How'd you know?" Frank said looking defeated.

"You're a chef and chefs smell like food. Today I would say you are making pastries. I smell vanilla with a bit of almond." Wynn sat down on the floor hoping he would consider it a submissive position while moving her hand towards the zipper on her backpack. She groped around on the inside until she felt the brooch. She kept the piece of jewelry on the inside of her hand.

"I really didn't want to hurt you. I didn't want to hurt Boone, either."

"I believe you, Frank." She moved a little closer to him. "Tell me about it."

"He was coming back to the island on the five o'clock ferry. We were supposed to buy the Willow Inn together. Said that he had a piece of valuable jewelry to make it happen. First, he needed to get it from his mother. But when I saw him, he said he had changed his mind. He wanted the Inn for himself only."

"You met him at the ferry."

"That's right. I thought we'd take the ferry back and we could set a date for closing. Discuss the new menu."

"That must have been hard on you to see it

suddenly fall apart." Wynn tried to appear sympathetic as she got even closer.

"It was. I told everyone I was buying the Inn. Clearly I was about to look very stupid to the islanders. I cannot stand people going back on their word." He sniffled. "Boone was so cold-hearted. He said he needed to think about himself and his future."

"I can't stand people who go back on their word, either. Poor Frank." Wynn shook her head sadly. Now she was by his shoe. She figured she could get one good stab in, and then head for the door. "So, what's going to happen to me?"

"Pretty soon Roxie O'Malley will be getting the first ransom notice for you. I want the ring."

"You and Doug murdered Boone, and then hid him on Doug's schooner to later drop at sea. But who sent the note to the police? And the threatening notes to Jackie? Doug? Or was it Agatha? Were they in on this with you?"

"What makes you think either one of those jokers helped me? I'm smarter than they."

Wynn sat up straighter with a jolt. "They didn't have anything to do with Boone's death?"

"Not at all. It was all me." Frank seemed quite proud. "I fed the polar bear liver to Boone and locked him in this room. It's pretty sound proof. He was way too sick to make a noise, anyway. He lay right there in that bed clawing at the wallpaper, until he passed. Late at night, I took him to the schooner and hid him. I also wrote the notes. All of them; to the police, to Jackie. For good measure I put Agatha's pin thingie she always wears on Doug's ship."

"You mean, this pin?" Wynn jumped up and lunged at Frank, stabbing him in the groin where the clasp went in three inches.

Frank started screaming.

Voices came from the hallway. Someone started pounding on the wall and was trying to get in the door. Wynn did her best to unlock the door but it wouldn't budge.

In one loud scream, Frank pulled the brooch from his groin and hit Wynn with a giant right hook. She fell flat on her back and he hung above. He booted her several times, before the door was kicked in.

༒

Wynn lay on her side on the duvet in her aunt's porch. Her knuckles were still so swollen that she could hardly hold the tea cup without pain. She had a bandage wrapped around her chest and cuts and bruises all over her body. Surgical tape covered four stitches on her forehead. Her right foot was in a brace.

"You look like you've been in a bad accident." Doug laughed a little.

"What's so funny about that?"

"You won. The idiot tried to kill you, but you won, and he's behind bars."

"It surely would have evolved into another island mystery, 'whatever happened to Wynn Baxter?' I'm sure Sheri is disappointed."

"That's right. Your mummified body could have turned up in another three hundred years."

"Just think of all the knick-knacks that could be sold between now and then," Roxie said, carrying in a tray of lemonade and butter cookies fresh from the oven.

Doug bent forward and put his hand on Wynn's

face. "I was so scared when I heard someone had put that skeleton key in your mailbox and you were on your way to the Inn without me."

"But you saved me."

"Come with me. I want to show you something."

Precariously Wynn stood. It hurt, but she would do anything for Doug.

"Lean on me," he assured her.

"Where are you taking me?" she asked.

He helped her through the cottage to the outside. "My truck is right here." Carefully he lifted her onto the seat. He drove and stopped just before the turn of her Tree House. "This is where you get out."

"Get out? Aren't you heartless?" She chided him as he pulled her into his side tighter and kissed her forehead.

"It's something you have to see on foot."

"As in my twisted foot?"

He laughed, picked her up and carried her. As they turned the corner, she caught sight of the most gorgeous lilies in every color, she had ever seen. Tears enveloped her eyes.

"Doug? You did this?"

He set her on a bench and removed his cap. Apologetically he said, "I know they aren't Calypso orchids, but they sure are pretty."

"Pretty? They are the most beautiful flowers I have ever seen. I see the colors of sunset in those, and look, the colors of sunrise over there, and I also see the moon, but where is the sea?"

"The colors of the sea are in your eyes, Wynn, and try as the hybridist may, they can never duplicate the beauty of those."

She looked at Doug and wondered how her

dreams could be coming true. The wind blew her hair and flooded her with thoughts of the possible. "The lilies look like the sky in the ground."

"I was hoping you'd stay at least one winter to see them again in the spring."

Bees began introducing themselves to the treasured soft petals. "Look, they are already pollinating."

"It's the end of the season for them, but they will be back again next spring with new friends. Your garden will be fuller with every summer."

Her gaze slid away as she nodded.

"Have I lost you? What are you thinking?"

"After all these months, I'm grateful to be here right now. And I'm thinking about Joseph Reed interred in that room for all this time, while people have dug and dug for him."

"I wonder if we will ever know why Anna Reed never told anyone she had found his body?"

"Well, I already know."

"Tell me." He played with her hair.

"Anna wanted to keep him all to herself where no one else would ever find him. Yet, she wanted someone to eventually find the room and perhaps put him in his final resting place beside her in the cemetery. That's why she had the key as a bracelet and painted 'Looking Through the Key Hole."

"So that is the name to that piece."

"That's the name. Ah, just look at this garden you have given to me."

His hand squeezed hers as she looked at the myriad of colors surrounding them. She laughed, and then covered her mouth. "I can't get over that you did this for me."

He knelt in front of her. "Yes. For you." Then he moved next to her as the lilies glowed all around them, the background music of the sea singing. His face was turned towards her and she could see his gray eyes in the drops of filtered sunshine through the leaves.

32

The women of the Bridge Over Troubled Waters Bible study had come to order. After reading scriptures and praying together, Faith served box cookies from the grocery store. "Sorry, ladies, but it seems my brother will be in prison for a long, long time. This is the best I could do for dessert, since I don't bake or cook."

"Faith, we are so sorry about Frank," Jackie stared at her friend.

"It's I who am sorry, Jackie. I never thought Frank had it in him to murder. I considered making this my last Bible study meeting."

"Why, Faith?" Wynn asked.

"Because of Frank." Faith held back her tears.

"Nonsense! We all love you, don't we ladies?" Sheri asked.

All the women bobbed their heads.

"You are one of us," Roxie said.

"And these are wonderful cookies too, Faith!" Owl murmured. "I am sure I can get used to them."

"We are here for you, Faith, just as everyone was here for me when Boone passed." Jackie smoothed her hair.

"Will you be staying with Jackie, Agatha?" Wynn asked.

"Yes, I am. Mother is busy doing court assigned charity work because she lied to the police and obstructed justice, and did a mess of other things, like stealing wallets. She's just lucky, I mean blessed, that she didn't get prison time," Agatha explained.

"Wynn, will you be staying on the island and be part of us, too?" Owl asked.

"I haven't made up my mind yet."

"Oh please do, Wynn," Faith begged.

"Well since my best friend asked, I just might."

"I am sure you want to learn the details of Boone's death," Jackie said. "I'm ready now to tell them. Boone's business was going bankrupt. He never told me his problems. Never confided in me. Yes, that hurts me, now. I thought we were so close."

"But you were close," Roxie insisted.

"Not really. He knew his mother had the ring which would take us out of debt, plus allow him to buy the Willow Inn. Frank somehow thought they were buying it together. Frank met Boone at the dock where he was told they were not going into business and his mother refused to give him the ring."

"Why did Frank write the ransom notes to you, Jackie, and not to Marilyn?" Wynn asked.

"Location, location, location," Faith answered for her. "Jackie lived right here, whereas Marilyn was on the mainland. It was less conspicuous."

"Frank fed Boone polar bear liver, which is poisonous, as we know, thanks to Wynn. He ate such a huge amount that he quickly died. Then he hauled the body to Doug's schooner to hide in order to point the finger at him. Oh by the way, here is your brooch, Agatha." Wynn raked through her backpack. "I found it on Doug's schooner."

"I have no idea how it got there, but it fell off my blouse, sometime. Maybe Frank found it."

"He did tell me that it was planted on the schooner."

"I hear Frank held you in the room where Boone died, Wynn. It must have been terrible for you." Faith tore open another package of cookies and handed them out, three at a time.

"Well, it wasn't easy." Wynn admitted. "That room also had a glass coffin in it."

"I heard that!" Owl gasped. "The story now is Anna did find her husband and put him in the coffin in that room so she could visit him. He was there all this time, until Frank took him down to the ocean."

"And I feel so bad that Wynn got hurt because I had the ring," Roxie said.

"But I'm all right now, Aunt Roxie. No more worries."

"Wynn, I have something for you." Sheri timidly approached the two women with an envelope. "Wynn, I know you were looking for old greeting cards and I did look for them, but they were all gone. Sorry, I think your mom cleaned the place of them when she left—but what's in here is just as good—maybe better. I found them in the attic of the store; old postcards of the town and the Sea Walk from twenty to thirty years ago. I thought you'd like to see it how it was back when you lived here."

"Thank you so much, Sheri." Wynn studied each postcard before moving onto the next. "You are right, these are better."

"And here is how your dad's shop once looked." Sheri pointed to a particular colorized postcard.

Owl walked up to Wynn with a paper bag in her hand. "When I told you that I walk the island at night and I pray,. that's the truth, but not the entire truth."

"I knew it!" Roxie clapped her hands once.

"I especially prayed for you, Wynn, because you didn't know the Lord, so that needed special prayer attention. However, I also pick up trash from the tourists and while I pick up trash, I might as well go through the garbage. You wouldn't believe all the valuable things I've pulled out to keep. Your mom knew of this little habit of mine. She asked me to dispose of the boxes she filled with your dad's belongings to give to the charity shop. Of course, old habits die hard. She said I could go through them and take what I wanted. So I did. Until that time the best item I ever found was a pair of brand new shoes my size. But that day I found the best thing of all. It's something your dad wore all the time. It reminded me of him so I kept it. Now it goes to you."

Wynn accepted the bag from Owl and pulled out the same sweater she had begged her mom to keep. Wynn held it up to her face and cried into it.

The women sat silently and allowed Wynn this moment.

Finally she looked up. "You will never know how much it means to me." Wynn slid her arms through the sleeves and buttoned the front.

"Last week we planned this little party for you and what we were going to give to you," Roxie explained. "I felt so badly when I saw you come towards the cottage, and then turn away back up the drive. I feared you would think we left you out."

"We would never leave you out," Faith said.

"I see that now."

"I bought you a cake from the bakery this morning." Roxie went to the kitchen and rolled out her tea cart. In the center of the chocolate cake with white buttercream frosting were the words 'Congrats Wynn!'

"Not that Faith's offerings of bagged cookies weren't delightful; I wanted something very special for you. We are celebrating the completion of your grant."

"Thank you."

"Before we cut the cake, I have a happy note I wish to address with you ladies." Jackie clasped her hands together. "It's been a hard summer on us all, starting with Wynn's and Roxie's rocky relationship, which seems to have smoothed out nicely. Boone's death, God rest his soul. Things became more complicated when Doug was arrested for the murder. Then there's Marilyn and Agatha—need I say more on that subject? Thankfully, Doug was innocent, but it only hurt another family, especially Faith, to learn it was Frank who murdered my husband. All of us here in this room were affected in some awful manner. But now, with the Lord's help, we are moving forward, still bonded together in friendship and love."

"Please Faith, don't make us sing again," Sheri whispered a soft prayer.

"And now the season of fall is soon to be upon us. I finally have some happy news. In the last few weeks I discovered that life is a series of journeys; not just one long one. When I married Boone twenty years ago, I thought that was it for me. I would be his wife forever. That we would grow old together. It wasn't to be. And now my feet are on a new path. I have a new destiny. God is not done with me, and my future certainly isn't over. In fact, it's just beginning. With Boone's insurance money, I bought the Inn. I am the new owner of the Willow Inn!"

33

"The sea is the same sea, but it's me who has changed." Wynn ran her hands through her hair, marveling at how much had changed in such a short summer. She was a stronger woman, a dutiful friend. She began to fall for Doug. She had learned how to make her own happiness.

Jackie was in her thoughts a lot these days. A woman who had been dependent on her husband now roared forth with strength since Boone's death, deciding Willow Inn was her next journey.

Wynn knew the time was here for her to make up her mind about the Biology position at the local high school. If she left, she knew she'd be back someday. If she stayed, Roxie insisted she and Sailor move into the main cottage for the winter due to the fact there wasn't any heat in the Tree House.

The following week, Wynn boxed her belongings, not sure how long most of it would be in storage. She was tired and her back hurt, but she was satisfied with her life. Wynn shut down her computer and stretched. The tin container with the music box caught her eye. She took it out and again listened to Faith of Our Fathers. Maybe she'd ask Roxie about it. Since she found it in her car, perhaps there was a new memory just waiting to spring out.

Wynn loaded her car once again with boxes, but this time they contained her clothes and equipment.

Sailor was coaxed into a carrier to ride next to her in the passenger seat. By that evening, she had settled into her new place enough to feel comfortable.

Wynn leaned against the pillows reading her Bible. If the Bible ladies had taught her anything it was about forgiveness and new beginnings. And tomorrow would be her new beginnings. Meanwhile, Sailor was somewhere under the bed still unsure of both Wynn—and Roxie's cottage.

There was a knock on her bedroom door. "Come in!"

Roxie walked into the room, handing Wynn a wrapped gift, and then sat on the slipper chair. Before Wynn could get the wrapping off, Sailor sprang up into Roxie's lap and curled up.

Wynn's mouth dropped open. "He never has curled into me or let me pet him!"

"He likes me. What can I say?" Roxie stroked his head and ears with a smug look on her face.

Wynn lifted the lid. Inside was a faded blue jean school bag with appliquéd A, B, Cs and 1, 2 ,3s and smiling children, a schoolhouse and a bright sun. It made her cringe.

"I used that to carry my papers when I taught elementary school." Roxie gushed. "And now it's yours to carry your sophomore class papers in."

"How nice." Wynn mustered up her best fake smile. "Thank you. I shall think of you each time I carry it. I have a question for you before I turn out the light."

"All right."

Wynn picked up the small music box and turned it on. "I found this in a tin in my jeep weeks ago. Do you happen to know anything about it?"

"I might." Roxie stood and placed Sailor on the coverlet. He jumped off and slid under the bed again. In a minute Roxie returned with a wooden box.

"I remember seeing that on your dresser." Wynn pushed up in bed.

Roxie placed the small music box inside the larger wooden box. Then she wound it up. Faith of Our Fathers played. Wynn's eyes grew large. "Why was it removed?"

"Because I wanted you to remember what it was like between us. I wanted you to listen to the tune, the words, and regain your childhood faith." Roxie laid it on the nightstand. "It's yours, now. It's done its job." Roxie kissed her goodnight.

Wynn turned out the light.

☜☞

Wynn walked down the hall with a new purse she wasn't so sure she liked in one hand, and the school bag in the other.

In the kitchen, Wynn heard the familiar singing voice, soft and melodious, although older now and filled with cracks. Roxie was singing 'Faith of Our Fathers'.

A sense of the past returned—a dizzying flash of uncontrollable memories. Wynn remembered everything perfectly. Aunt Roxie's eyes, her voice when she sang. It hadn't been Ruth who sang to her whenever she needed comforting, it had been Aunt Roxie.

Wynn had it all wrong; it was mixed-up in the mind of a child. It was Roxie's tenderness that stayed with her and kept her all those years, calling her back until she returned.

"Wow, you really look nice in that suit." Roxie tugged at Wynn's sleeves and pulled the material up at the shoulders.

"I feel odd."

"You only look odd because you are showing that you feel odd. Loosen up!"

"It's a skirt. I have on a skirt and nylons."

"Yes and you look lovely. Sit. Eat your breakfast. I want to take a picture of you for the timeline!"

Wynn stood against the wall and smiled.

"Now, it's time for a new picture!" Roxie held up her camera.

"You need to update your cell phone to one with a camera and get a printer."

"Never you mind. Stand still, because I am taking the picture right now." Roxie smiled proudly, and then taped it to the wall where it said, First Day of School. "I may have missed the first day of your going to school growing up, but I shall never miss another."

Wynn closed the back door and went out to the car. On the seat next to her, Wynn placed her teacher's book bag. Inside she had her lesson plans for the week and a sack lunch. Jittery with nerves, she prayed for wisdom.

At the end of this very long, nerve-racking day, she'd meet Doug on the beach for dinner. They'd roast hot dogs over an open flame, and follow that up with s'mores – the gooey graham cracker, marshmallow and chocolate treat of campfires far and wide. If the rain held off, they'd watch the sky and hope for shooting stars. Before going home, she'd tell him about her first day as the new Biology teacher at Willow High School, if he was interested. She was in love with the sea, but she was also in love with him.

Doug was in love with her, too. He'd told her so, and though they'd not made plans yet, a wedding was on the horizon.

The sun was barely up and the grass still wet and polished with dew. Wynn drove along the curve of the drive that passed through the orchard where the air was heavy with the scent of apples from the trees that dotted Aunt Roxie's property. The morning glory vine that covered the fence had died away from the first frost. At the crest of the drive, she braked for the little fox that ran across the road ahead.

And with that, summer had slipped away.

Made in the USA
Middletown, DE
06 December 2021